MARK MANNOCK

DEATH COMES EASY

The LACHLAN BYRN Thrillers (2)

For my brother, Nigel

Contents

Acknowledgement

My heartfelt thanks and love to Sarah, Anisha and Jack for your love, tolerance and support. Lachlan, your counsel and wisdom has always been appreciated.

Chapter 1

It made no sense, none at all.

Byrn looked around. The terminal was flooded with humanity, a loosely framed chaos of people arriving and departing, the joy of reunions and the tears of goodbyes.

But the assassin really didn't give a shit. To him, Beijing Capital International Airport was like all the others. An over-designed pompous statement of bureaucratic posturing. The sea of people surrounding Byrn meant nothing to him. He had no relationship with any of them; they held no purpose in his life.

Or so he'd thought.

Every fiber of Lachlan Byrn's being told him he was being watched. Although unable to identify the asset observing him, the assassin remained convinced. Byrn's intuition was as finely tuned as the state-of-the-art weaponry waiting for him at his next destination.

He knew he was right, but it still didn't make any sense.

So Byrn had managed to catch somebody's attention. Why?

It was a moot point. Byrn shrugged his shoulders and pressed forward toward the exit of the long terminal building. He would establish the identity of his stalker soon enough, just as they would discover the ramifications of their pursuit.

Byrn increased his pace, weaving in and out of the surrounding people. A hundred yards along the polished walkway, he stepped abruptly to the side, entering a small shop that sold tee shirts, hats, and other tourist paraphernalia. He held no interest in the vendor's merchandise, but he did pay attention to the large mirror attached to a support pillar near the front of the store. He'd noted it fifty yards ago, figuring that it meant he wouldn't need to make the too obvious about-face that would alert his tail of their potential discovery. The assassin's hand grazed shirts on a rack, while his eyes remained locked on the mirror.

He saw nothing. No one increasing their clip, no one scanning the crowd with panicked urgency. Everything seemed as it should. Byrn allowed himself a small grin. At least now he'd established it was likely his pursuer maintained some level of professionalism. That limited the field.

A couple of minutes later, Byrn stepped out of the shop and rejoined the crowd on the concourse. He considered the option of retracing his steps to catch out someone doing the same, but that would tip his hand. Better to keep his pursuer in the dark. Byrn continued toward the exit, this time at a slower, more leisurely pace. Matching the crowd.

In his mind, the assassin contemplated the possibilities. It was unlikely that his pursuer was regular airport security. They could easily have stopped 'Mr. Smith' as he'd been processed through customs. But Byrn had noted no hesitation or nervousness in the Chinese Customs agent as his documents were inspected. As per Byrn's normal procedure, Mr. Smith's passport had been ripped up and flushed down the first toilet he'd encountered after clearing customs. With his new passport secure in his jacket pocket, along with other appropriate identification papers, Byrn's short but productive relationship with Mr. Smith was over.

Byrn considered a second possibility far more likely. His former handler, Zhen Su, could have agents watching entry points for a Caucasian man of his description. That, however, would soak up resources. As a high-level operative within the Chinese security services, Zhen would have access to those resources. On the other hand, his former handler had recently botched an important job for his masters. Accordingly, his influence may not be as potent as it once was.

Byrn was acutely aware of the job Zhen had blown. The task was to eliminate an active assassin as part of an attempt to disavow a Chinese-sponsored operation in Estonia. The original mission had been to assassinate the president of the Russian Federation, Vadim Aleyev. It was a wild dream, an unlikely fantasy with little chance of success. Yet it had succeeded. Aleyev was dead. Lachlan Byrn didn't need the papers to tell him it was so, because Byrn had been the one who had killed him. He was also the operative Zhen foolishly attempted to destroy.

The assassin almost reached the end of the vast space. The exit doors were in sight when a muted cry from behind caught his attention. Naturally, he turned around, quickly scanning the crowd before focusing on the noise's source.

"Get your hands off me."

She was tall, slender, with long dark hair. Her deep, almost black eyes seemed on fire as she addressed her accoster, a shorter man in an airport security uniform.

"You have no right…"

The woman's voice, though restrained, was intense.

A circle formed in the crowd as people looked on.

"Madam, I need to see inside your bag, please."

"Why?"

The officer sighed.

"The owner of the jewelry franchise you just left reported you as loitering about his shop. He believes you may have taken a piece or pieces of his merchandise."

"I most certainly did not."

The woman appeared distracted as she glanced around the concourse, only partially focused on the officer.

"A simple inspection of your belongings will resolve the situation one way or another, madam."

The woman looked frustrated, but quickly acquiesced to the officer's demand and opened her bag.

Nothing more than a distraction, Byrn swung around and resumed walking. He didn't give the woman any further consideration… until he did.

As the automatic doors to the terminal parted before him, a thought occurred to him. The woman seemed sincere in her protests of innocence. So why did the shopkeeper suspect she was loitering with intent rather than browsing? In a busy airport environment, staff would be skilled in discerning the difference. She may have been loitering, but perhaps without intent. At least not with the intent of robbing the store.

Hmm. Interesting.

The assassin sensed his lips tighten as he passed through the terminal exit.

While he would be cautious, his focus was elsewhere. He'd arrived here to work.

If Zhen Su had sent someone to watch him, that meant the Chinese handler was worried. Probably a smart call.

Because Lachlan Byrn had come to Beijing to kill him.

Chapter 2

As Byrn sat in the rear seat of the taxi heading down the Capital Airport Expressway, he felt his chest tighten. The sensation didn't surprise him. The assassin tried to distract himself by focusing on the calmness of the tall trees adjacent to the road, then the majesty of the growing city skyline looming in the distance. The attempt at distraction failed, as anticipated.

"Duōjiǔ?" How long? Byrn asked the driver.

The man raised an eyebrow before responding.

"About twenty minutes, sir."

A Beijing cabbie who spoke English. Handy.

Byrn nodded, sat back in his seat, and stared ahead. He could sense the darkness rising in him, pressing down on him like a ghost in the night. Involuntarily, he shivered.

Naturally, the assassin hadn't expected otherwise. Returning to this place. The years he'd spent held captive by Chinese Intelligence, the damp dark cells, the anguish, and, of course, the torture. It occurred to Byrn that torture was a retrospective word. A term you used when reflecting on a situation.

In the moment, it was simply survival.

And Lachlan Byrn had survived.

In the end, Byrn did a deal with the devil to get out. He'd traded his 'special skills' to reclaim his freedom. But it wasn't really freedom at all. Not while his Chinese masters were controlling him, pulling the strings, manipulating. While almost anything was better than being imprisoned in those soul-destroying conditions, Byrn was always going to respond poorly to control and exploitation.

And that's exactly what had happened.

Finally, he reached a reluctant understanding with the Chinese authorities. That was, until the unforgettable face of Zhen Su, the Chinese operative in charge of Byrn's file, reappeared in Greece with a last assignment. The promise had been an unconditional end to their relationship. A final and everlasting liberation for Byrn.

It transpired that Zhen and Byrn had held a contrasting interpretation of the arrangement. Zhen's idea of true freedom involved death. Byrn's death. The assassin chuckled to himself. Of course, Zhen was correct. Ultimately, death was the only real freedom from this world.

Byrn detected the cold numbness in his body gradually being replaced by a warm, rippling sensation. He knew what it was immediately. To Byrn, the anticipation of an impending kill was a physical experience. It was as close to joy as Lachlan Byrn ever experienced, and he sensed it throughout his entire being. Byrn understood that the structure of his own psychology was complex. How many humans could identify the physical transition as they journeyed from the depths of deep depression to the intense excitement of anticipating the act of murder?

Perhaps only a serial killer.

Another slight widening of the lips, not quite a smile.

Byrn couldn't wait to set Zhen free.

"We're here, sir."

Byrn barely noticed the taxi drawing to a halt.

As he pushed open the door, grabbed his small backpack and stepped outside, the façade of the Beijing Central Railway Station towered above him. In Byrn's eyes, the blend of classic Chinese roof structures soaring high above the contemporary functionality of the lower levels seemed to symbolize the struggles of the country's modern inhabitants.

The assassin paid the driver, his heels clicking on the pavement as he strode toward the facility's main doors. The internal battle for his soul would have to wait. Lachlan Byrn was an expert at discarding emotion. Compartmentalizing. He had a job to do.

The first step involved emulating the four million other tourists who visit the People's Republic of China's capital every year.

Within minutes, Byrn had immersed himself into the throng of people.

Unnoticed.

Unnoticeable.

Chapter 3

REGAN DIA

He was good. Exceptionally good. Yet she'd expected no less.

Every moment spent researching him had contributed to the picture of a dark but frighteningly efficient killer with a cryptic personality type bordering on psychopathic. However, Regan Dia developed her own slant on the man.

Enigmatic.

He presented as a puzzle to be solved. In reality, to Dia's employer, he appeared as a problem with the possibility of evolving into a solution. From her concealed location behind a newsstand, Dia closely monitored as Lachlan Byrn paced himself and his movements so carefully that she needed to concentrate hard to maintain sight of him. He moved like a wiry cat, his slender physique unrestricted. She knew there may be better positions in some of the surrounding shops, but after the fiasco at the airport, Dia felt compelled to improve her 'browsing while surveilling' technique.

The incident had the potential to cost her dearly. Her employer didn't tolerate mistakes.

Dia slipped a hairband off her wrist and manipulated her long dark hair into a tight ponytail while she observed Byrn perform two loops of the station's main concourse. It was clear that he was cautious. Systematically cautious. She figured that he was aware of the precise location he had to go, but would only proceed once he was convinced he was not being watched.

Dia withdrew further behind the stand.

Despite all the research and the resources placed at her disposal, Dia couldn't truly be one hundred percent certain of the facts that she'd managed to dredge up about the man. She wasn't even sure that Lachlan Byrn was his real name. There were rumors. Many rumors. A kill here, a disappearance there. The latest one was the most absurd. Could this man really be responsible for the death of the Russian president?

Sure thing. And maybe Elvis was still alive.

Dia held no doubt that her employer possessed more information about this killer than had been disclosed to her. She was also smart enough not to push it.

Byrn reached the midpoint of the third lap when he suddenly veered to the right. Dia checked his purposeful body language before scrutinizing the path ahead of him.

Then she looked back at his position.

He was gone. Disappeared.

Shit.

Dia possessed a skill set and background that more than enabled her to handle the situation. She had two choices. Stay put and wait until he resurfaced, if he resurfaced, or push ahead trying to follow. She decided to push ahead. The decision risked greater exposure, but she figured Byrn would exit the facility elsewhere if she tried to sit it out.

It was the smart move, but it failed.

Sixty minutes and way too many steps later, Regan Dia

realized she lost her target.

She'd been outwitted and there would be hell to pay.

Chapter 4

LACHLAN BYRN

It was a straightforward maneuver.

Byrn made an effort to appear as if he was going to the back of the concourse area when he spied what he'd been searching for. A group of businessmen talking in earnest, moving forward in a small but tight-knit pack. The assassin stepped quickly to their right-hand side before inserting himself into their midst. As he did so, he crouched slightly. Of course, the men were surprised, but as Byrn expected, they were too polite to react. Almost like the Secret Service guarding a VIP, the huddle progressed up the elevator. Upon reaching the top, Byrn stayed with the men until they neared a corridor on the right, then hurriedly left them.

Experience had taught the assassin that eliminating movement was the most effective way to avoid detection. That became his purpose. He slipped through multiple corridors before reaching a signed door.

'Zhǐ Gòng Zhíyuán Shǐyòng'

Staff Only. Byrn pulled a small, pointed tool from his pocket and shifted it around in the lock. A few seconds later, he turned the handle and eased the door open. A few minutes after that, he sat ensconced in a cubicle of the male staff toilets.

He waited there for an hour, aware that patience is not only a virtue for a professional assassin but also an essential skill.

Eventually Byrn made his way back to the central concourse. He stood in the shadows now lining his previous escape corridor, for another twenty minutes. No one appeared on the hunt. Satisfied that the concourse had fulfilled its purpose as a filter for unwelcome eyes, Byrn strode across its length and out into the forecourt. The assassin immediately swung left and into one of the luggage offices. This had always been his destination.

Byrn checked that the staff were well occupied with other travelers before striding purposefully down between the rows of blue lockers. Finding the number he sought, he inserted the code that had been sent to him and the locker door unlatched itself. Byrn glanced around to ensure his privacy before opening the door halfway.

Everything appeared as it should. The locker was just big enough to hold the rectangular flexible zipped case that would contain the rifle, along with three smaller cases. One would conceal an array of assets for hand-to-hand combat, including two hunting knives. The second, of similar size, would hold an array of explosive devices. Inside the third, slightly smaller case, would be the three pistols Byrn had requested.

The assassin unzipped each case just enough to confirm its contents before shutting but not locking the door. After confirming his privacy one more time, he then took two steps down the narrow corridor and opened another locker with a different code, sent to him by an alternate source. Byrn opened the door slightly and glanced inside. The space was totally empty.

Satisfied, Byrn then transferred the contents of the first locker into the second, erasing any trail to him or link with the supplier of the weaponry. The caution was warranted, particularly considering the vast connections of his target.

Byrn closed the initial locker before reaching back into the second and again unzipping the smallest case. His fingers easily found one of the pistol's handles, along with several boxed rounds of ammunition. He checked the pistol was fully loaded, as requested, before slipping the gun and ammunition into his jacket pockets. He then shut and locked the door.

The assassin confidently exited the luggage office and made his way back to the forecourt. As he walked, he ran his fingers over the gun in his pocket. Like greeting an old friend. Byrn was all too familiar with the QSZ-92 recoil operated, locked breech pistol. They were standard issue in Chinese intelligence ranks and he had used them many times when working for his Chinese handlers.

Briefly, Byrn pondered how Zhen would feel if he knew he was about to face the wrong end of such a weapon's barrel.

With the station forecourt well behind him, Byrn followed the crosswalk over *E Zhenjiang Hu Tong* northward, creating more space between himself and the weapon stash before picking up another cab. He had to be absolutely sure he wasn't being followed.

Halfway across the road, the assassin found the certainty he sought.

As the sun moved out from behind a cloud, the small

park on the far side of the street that had been bathed in shadow suddenly brightened. A large man in dark pants and an equally dark softshell jacket quickly retreated into the diminishing shade. The assassin wasn't alarmed by that alone, but the man's scrutiny of the crossing and the clear bulge in his jacket did the trick.

Byrn immediately assumed he was one of Zhen's men. It therefore made sense that there would be an operative behind him as well.

If so, the situation required a quick resolution, but on Byrn's terms.

A second later, that option disappeared.

"Please keep walking across the road, Mr. Byrn. I suspect you've noted my partner's presence. A man with your renowned skills of observation would not have missed that opportunity. Sadly, for you, that means we're going to have to bring the timeline forward on our little operation. By the way, Zhen Su sends his regards."

Byrn quickly looked back. Another faceless man in dark clothes smiled at him. He had a brown leather satchel over his shoulder, his right hand thrust deeply inside. Byrn held no illusions about what would have been in the man's hand.

"Okay, you've had your look. Now keep walking and swing left when you hit the sidewalk, please."

The man was professional enough to keep a safe distance behind Byrn. Besides, the man in the park, now openly observing them, had his right hand shoved into his jacket.

Byrn reached the sidewalk and turned left.

As he did, the man in the park fell into step with his colleague. Byrn noted that it was a phone rather than a gun that he'd retrieved from his coat. That probably meant bad news.

Communication.

Reinforcements.

"Four blocks ahead, you will find a small laneway to the right. Please proceed down that lane," said the first man. "Incidentally, if you have a weapon, don't bother reaching for it. I'm certainly not naïve enough to get in close proximity to a man like you to perform a search, but I am an astute reader of body language. You try a move and I'll know it before your fingers touch your firearm."

Byrn remained silent. Thinking. The assassin was well aware of Zhen's personal hit squad. He knew of several occasions when they had eliminated people who had stood between Zhen and his goals. Without a doubt, the men following him were members of that squad.

The assassin was sure that if he walked into that alley, he wouldn't be walking out. Conversely, given their connections, they could shoot him dead on the spot. Even on the main street with countless witnesses, they could blame his demise away with carefully constructed false pretexts.

Byrn was pissed. He wasn't afraid to die. He almost welcomed the thought. But he was pissed about dying in some dark laneway at the hands of the very people he'd fought so hard to escape. It was doubly frustrating that he'd go down before taking out Zhen.

An intolerable frustration.

Lachlan Byrn had a unique capacity to become completely calm when enraged. He traded emotion for calculation in a split second.

With each step forward, the assassin examined his options. The cupboard looked quite bare. There may be a chance, however, that the second thug's phone call could present the opportunity Byrn needed. Byrn wasn't a betting man. His world was one of engineered violence and control. But when circumstances prevailed and spontaneity was the only option, he could play the game.

Byrn noted the laneway approaching. The men behind him quickened their step in anticipation. It seemed a shame they were in such a hurry to die.

The assassin refined his calculations.

Six yards to go.

Byrn sped up his pace slightly, turning the corner a second before his assailants expected.

The laneway was about two hundred yards long.

Perfect.

At the far end of the lane stood two more men in dark clothes. This time in suits. Lachlan Byrn smiled and waved at them. He noted the momentary look of confusion on their faces. In the same moment, the assassin bolted forward toward them.

Byrn sensed the operatives behind him react. There would be a moment's hesitation. It would take each of them a few seconds to access their weapons and bring them to bear. Phone man would need to retrieve his from his jacket, the first man would want his gun free to aim accurately rather than fire blindly from his satchel.

Byrn counted to three as he belted forward. The men ahead of him had their guns out. Given they were in the heart of the city, each of the operatives had attached some form of suppressor to their weapon. That may affect their accuracy. It made no difference to Byrn.

Four, five…

Byrn glanced back, positioning himself between the men on his right at both ends of the laneway.

On cue, the men fired just as Byrn hit the hard ground.

Hoping the agents would shoot each other was too much. That only happened in movies. While there was a slightly better chance that one, or perhaps even both, may be wounded, it was the distraction that Byrn was counting on.

As he hit the concrete, Byrn retrieved his QSZ-92 and fired on the man at the distant end of the alley. Ignoring the result, he spun and took his opposite number at the end nearest him out.

That left only the first two. The left-hand-side men.

Phone man clutched his shoulder, blood oozing through his fingers.

Good, he'd keep.

At the far end, the remaining operative perched on one knee, raising his weapon.

He never got to fire it. Byrn flicked himself around with lightning speed and placed a round into the center of the man's forehead.

Satisfying.

Byrn rolled onto his back, raising his arms for the next shot, when brickwork splintered above his head.

Radio man had balls.

Then he didn't, because that's where Byrn shot him.

Byrn surveyed the scene. Three of his attackers were motionless. No longer of this world. The fourth, the man with the satchel, softly moaned and squirmed.

Good. Byrn liked to send messages, and he needed a messenger. He'd let him live.

Byrn knew it would be only seconds before the laneway

was flooded with police. Zhen's operatives may have had silencers, but he didn't.

The assassin climbed to his feet, breathing hard.

Having confirmed his victims' condition, he observed a small exit appearing behind the fallen men at the alley's end. He bolted toward it.

Before fleeing, the assassin glanced backward one final time. A figure briefly appeared, silhouetted against the sun at the far laneway entrance.

Tall.

Long hair.

Slender.

Female.

Damn it.

As Byrn broke onto the next main road, turned east, and continued at a brisk walk, he considered the circumstances.

Maybe Zhen didn't have enough manpower to cover the whole city and had just got lucky, or perhaps there was something else. Everyone in Byrn's chain of support was a tried-and-true professional with too much to lose by talking. Anyway, most suppliers he dealt with didn't even know who he was. They preferred it that way, as did he. On the other hand, Chinese intelligence operatives could be extremely persuasive. Byrn, more than anyone, appreciated that.

As he marched forward, Byrn reached the conclusion that somebody had given him up. But there was more to this. Byrn could just sense it.

And the figure at the end of the laneway.

What the hell was going on there?

Chapter 5

Dia jerked her head away. She didn't think she'd been seen. She didn't think he'd seen her.

She stood with her back to the wall, her heart pounding.

What the hell was that, anyway?

How was it even possible?

After she'd walked away from the train station, Dia had changed her mind and doubled back. She figured she'd rather spend the rest of the day checking out the station than explaining to her boss that she'd lost the target.

Avoidance.

Surprisingly, she'd caught Byrn leaving the luggage office and heading across the road. She then noted the man coming up behind the assassin on the crossing. His body language, including the hand stuffed into the satchel, painted a reasonably clear picture of what was going down. When the large guy from the park stepped in beside him and began speaking on his phone, Dia's suspicions were confirmed.

When Dia saw the entourage turn down the alleyway, she suspected things would not end favorably for Byrn. A minute later, when she craned her head around the corner for a better look and noted the two men at the farthest point of the laneway, Dia knew for certain what was about to happen.

Five men entered the alley, only four would return. Lachlan Byrn was as good as dead.

No one could change that.

What she then witnessed was remarkable. Byrn's skill level was incredibly impressive. The speed and accuracy he employed in taking down his kidnappers was, in her view, unmatched. She actually found herself losing her breath as the tension escalated.

Astounding.

Never one to retreat in fear, Regan Dia waited two minutes before re-entering the laneway and following Byrn's trail. She had no illusions that if the assassin caught her tagging him, it wouldn't go well for her.

Chapter 6

LACHLAN BYRN

This operation was going to shit before it even started.

Byrn worked in the shadows. His work required stealth and secrecy. His livelihood depended on it. Not that he cared much, but his life depended on it, too.

Byrn knew the smart course of action would be to hightail it out of China. On any other job, that's exactly what he would do. But this mission was different. It was personal.

Byrn normally engineered his kills with precision. He was the one who made the rules and compelled others to play his way. Since setting foot in Beijing, his movements had been reactionary. Almost everything he did was in response to someone else's actions.

That was about to change.

In fact, it was changing already. Byrn had now sent a clear message to Zhen Su. 'You've underestimated me.' He held no doubt that his former Chinese handler would react. It was now up to Byrn to anticipate Zhen's reaction. After years of working for him, he had a fair idea how the man operated. Zhen was devious and clever. He would lay some kind of trap. There's no way he'd just run and hide. If he tried, Byrn would simply wait. Zhen may delay his death for a short time, but not elude it.

Byrn found the thought amusing. Clearly, no one could postpone death permanently. As a man who operated within the industry, Byrn appreciated that more than most. Most of his victims pleaded for a stay of execution. It was the natural thing to do. Byrn rarely granted their wish, although he'd always, where possible, explained to them the exact reasons they were going to die an early death. The assassin thought that only fair.

But what about his own death? It wasn't a notion that haunted Byrn. He couldn't perform his professional duties while living with the paralysis of fear. Byrn devised a simple solution that virtually enabled him to eliminate fear as an emotion altogether. Ironically, the answer had been inadvertently provided to him by his Chinese captors in the dank underground prisons cells he called home for several years.

Every day of his life, Lachlan Byrn expected to die. If he didn't, he regarded it as a bonus.

Simple.

As he strolled down the busy sidewalk, Byrn eyed the faceless passersby. They meant nothing to him, apart from providing the necessary camouflage. Of course, the camo effect was limited. Even with numerous western visitors in Beijing, he stood out as a rarity. He'd best make his way to an environment frequented by westerners.

At least for now.

Then he would decide how to approach the mysterious female who appeared to have an inordinate interest in his activities.

Chapter 7

Unpredictability was the key to Lachlan Byrn's survival.

Without doubt, Zhen Su would be undertaking two primary strategies. First, he would have his team, or what's left of them, scouring the streets of Beijing, searching every likely bolt hole around the city for the assassin. That would include hotels and hostels utilized by westerners, plus numerous other locations, such as bars and clubs.

They wouldn't find him because Lachlan Byrn had gone on vacation.

Unpredictably.

Byrn surveyed his surroundings. The *Fuxinghao* bullet train provided a spacious and comfortable first-class cabin. The seats were well spread out, and the train offered suitable internet connections and reasonable food. Byrn glanced at his watch. They would arrive in Xi'an in around ninety minutes.

The assassin smiled as his eyes met those of his fellow travelers. He'd been pre-booked on the tour and was expected to rendezvous with his guides and travel buddies at the airport. He'd messaged them, explaining that he'd missed his connecting flight and would meet them at the Beijing train station in time for the rail journey. The organizers weren't happy. But they tolerated the disruption. The ruse had allowed Byrn to collect his weaponry.

As events played out, the delay also provided the opportunity for the assassin to impact Zhen's team in a most negative manner. Message sent.

So, while Zhen searched the urban landscape, Byrn hid in plain sight with a tour group of fellow westerners enjoying the sites China had to offer. Additionally, he had a long-standing desire to visit the Terracotta Warriors in Xi'an. Byrn was engrossed by the history of human warfare. The truth was, he thrived on conflict… and death. The assassin was fortunate, not that many people could turn their passion into their profession.

Let Zhen search to his heart's content. And find nothing.

Byrn concluded that Zhen's second strategy would be to set up an impregnable line of defense. Byrn knew where the Chinese agent lived, although the information had been provided by Zhen to Byrn previously, deeming it unreliable intelligence.

Now that Zhen had confirmed Byrn's presence in China, the assassin wanted to give his former handler time to fully prepare his defenses. Of course, Byrn understood that Zhen's methodology would have a dual purpose. More than solely creating a secure position for himself, Zhen would be setting a trap for Byrn.

And Byrn planned to walk right in … kind of.

Byrn's strategy of leaving Beijing also had a duality to it. He needed to draw his unwanted female follower away from the city. In a different environment, he'd have a greater chance of exposing and dealing with her. The woman played on his mind. Was she a part of Zhen's group, or was she something else completely? If so, what? And from where?

Whatever the answers, she would be dealt with.

Lachlan Byrn needed one less complication in his life.

He stared out the window. Even at nearly two hundred miles an hour, the landscape was clear and defined. Terraced hills gave way to gray city outlines as the train powered past. It wasn't as calming as his beloved sailing, but train travel offered a therapeutic rhythm that cars and buses couldn't match.

Byrn closed his eyes and reached into his pocket. Flipping open a container, he retrieved two small white pills and threw them into his mouth. Modafinil, the Night Eagle, had been another dubious bestowal from his Chinese captors. Byrn had tamed his addiction to the point he only used the medication to keep himself awake during active operations. Understanding that he couldn't afford any substantial sleep or rest until Zhen Su was dead, Byrn would need to watch his back constantly.

As he thought about it, Byrn realized that over the length of their relationship, Zhen and his masters had generously gifted him with so much.

He now fully intended to pay them back.

Chapter 8

The day passed without surprise.

Staying within the confines of his tour group, Byrn traveled the one-hour journey to the Terracotta Warriors Museum in Lintong District by coach. He even chatted freely with his fellow tourists, playing the part of a holidaying office worker enjoying a once in a lifetime trip. Method acting. For this performance, Byrn's character was Thomas May from Woking, England. The assassin felt as though he'd put on a decent show.

He'd visited all three pits on the museum site, taking in all the information the tour guides could offer. However, despite the role he played, Byrn never took his eyes off the crowd that milled about the tourist attraction. He marked nobody paying him undue attention. He paid due diligence in searching for the woman but didn't see her. Either she wasn't there or had excellent fieldcraft skills.

On the return journey to Xi'an Byrn sat near the front of the bus, close behind the driver, the assassin glancing frequently in the vehicle's large rearview mirrors. At no point did he note any car following them.

As the countryside flew by, the assassin wondered how Zhen's search of Beijing was progressing. If nothing else in this world, Lachlan Byrn had learned that controlling the timing of any situation meant controlling the situation itself.

Zhen and Byrn would meet at a time of Byrn's making, even if Zhen chose the location.

Returning to the bland but comfortable tour hotel, Byrn declined invitations from fellow travelers to join them for dinner and headed out to find a small private eatery to squirrel himself away. He'd heard that Xi'an's cuisine featured an exotic blend of Asian and Middle East influences.

A couple of hours later, after he'd finished the last of his *yangrou paomo lamb* and *pita soup* in a cafe on *Sajinquio*, he was glad he'd taken the trouble to go off the beaten tourist track.

He'd purposefully chosen a relatively obscure location to dine not only for the food but also because it allowed him a lengthy stroll. The assassin wanted to stretch his legs. He also needed to ensure he wasn't being tailed before returning to work in Beijing.

Byrn chose a different route for the return journey to the hotel, figuring that some of the quieter back streets may offer a greater chance to expose anyone following him. Although, like any major city, the side streets and alleyways of Xi'an lacked the assurance and safety of main thoroughfares, the assassin wasn't fazed. As recent events had proved, he could look after himself.

The assassin had no idea of the street name, but he hit a narrow street that was eerily quiet and framed in shadow. The only people in sight were a couple further along the sidewalk, fully engaged in conversation. The only footsteps Byrn made out were his own.

Perfect.

Twenty yards down the road, that changed. Then there was an echo, only it wasn't an echo at all.

Byrn avoided slowing his pace or stopping, but he did lighten his step. Without a doubt, there were additional steps behind him, some distance away. The footsteps didn't seem to be thumping particularly heavily on the cement sidewalk. It could be because the feet belonged to someone of light build, maybe even a woman. Conversely, it could signify nothing.

Either way, Byrn intended to find out. He sped up, heading directly toward the gloomiest area of the street. The couple were still some distance away. The footsteps behind him matched his increase in pace.

As soon as the assassin hit the deepest section of the shadow, he stepped sideways into a doorway. He would remain unseen by any passer-by unless they stopped and turned directly to face him.

The sound of the footsteps persisted.

Closer.

Several seconds later, a dark silhouette passed Byrn's hiding spot. The person was quite tall, slender and had long, dark hair. Byrn couldn't discern the face, but the likelihood of such a coincidence was zero.

The assassin craned his head around the doorway, waiting until the figure was at least one hundred yards away before stepping back onto the street. She had increased her pace and her attention scanned from side to side along the narrow road. Byrn leaned down, removed his boots, and proceeded after her. Matching his pace with hers, the assassin began processing his alternatives. Follow the woman back to her accommodation, accost her here on the street, or simply kill her. From Byrn's perspective, they were all viable options.

Ten seconds later, the decision was taken out of his hands.

He'd been wrong about the couple. They weren't a couple at all, at least not in the traditional sense. They were two men, not particularly bulky or tall, but closer inspection indicated they both had wiry, athletic physiques. As they heard footsteps approach, Byrn watched both individuals tense up and turn toward the sound.

The woman stopped ten yards short of their position before slowly backing up.

The men moved forward, each reaching into his jacket pocket. In an instant, their blades glistened under the streetlight.

Byrn was too far away to catch their whispered conversation, but the men's intent was crystal clear.

The assassin swiftly crossed the street and silently approached the group from the shadows. As he got closer, Byrn picked up the threatening tone of the gruff male voices.

"No point backing away, lady. There's no one to help you here."

Their accented English didn't disguise their menacing intent.

The woman paused.

"I don't require help, but I suggest you both just go on your way. It would be for the best," she responded.

Laughter.

"Who's best?" asked the second man.

Byrn swore he saw the white glint of the woman's teeth. "Yours."

More mirth. Then they both continued to move forward toward the woman. Like hungry wild dogs.

Byrn stopped and stared. The woman's stance firmed, each hand dropping to her side in readiness. Even if the men were too stupid to see it, the assassin recognized a fellow predator when he saw one.

The first man went down while still laughing. His knife dropped from his hand as the woman produced a blade from under her sleeve and thrust it upward through his gut.

His cry of surprise was brief.

The second man made use of his partner's demise to launch his attack. He swung his own knife wide in an arc. The woman ducked down as the man's blade swept less than an inch above her head. Her left hand shot upwards, clasping the attacker on his knife wrist, and parrying any return blow. The thug realized his mistake too late. As the woman sprung up, she sliced her knife vertically between his legs. Involuntarily, he leaned forward, screaming, his face an inch from hers. She tugged the blade from his groin before leaning back and slashing him fiercely, right to left, across the throat.

After the second man hit the ground, the woman shunted backward and paused. Crouching, her hands resting on her knees, she fought to regain her breath. A moment later, she scanned up and down the street.

But she failed to examine the shadows behind her.

Maintaining a safe distance, Byrn stepped forward into the light, his QSZ-92 pistol aimed directly at the nape of the woman's head.

"Extremely impressive, but please make no further move. Your life is now in my hands, and I won't be as foolhardy as those two."

Chapter 9

"You have approximately one minute left in this world unless you provide an exceptionally good explanation for your presence here."

The woman turned around slowly, her disbelief evident. Her mouth slightly agape, Byrn also noted that her eyes widened like saucers. Fear or surprise.

Judging from what he'd just witnessed, Byrn figured it wasn't fear.

But she didn't speak.

"Okay then, this will be quick. About forty seconds left. I presume you work for Zhen Su?"

"Well, that's fairly typical, isn't it? You see a person of Asian appearance and immediately begin making assumptions."

Byrn was perplexed. Up close, it was obvious her accent was American.

"You're not Chinese?"

"No shit, Sherlock," she responded.

Byrn allowed himself a half smile. She had gusto. Most people quivered when faced with the wrong end of his gun.

The woman glanced at her watch. "You're not much of a timekeeper, are you? My forty seconds lapsed around fifteen seconds ago."

Was she daring him to shoot her?

"If not Zhen, who do you work for?"

The assassin was aware that a passerby could come across them anytime. The two bodies on the sidewalk were glaringly obvious.

"Well?" he said.

"I'm not at liberty to say," she replied, a small smirk appearing on her face.

"But you're at liberty to die?"

"It is what it is."

Byrn was starting to like the woman. He decided to allow her a little longer to live.

"You have skills," he stated.

"We all have skills," she replied. "Even a bricklayer has skills."

"You know what I mean."

Likeable but irritating.

The woman nodded.

Taking a moment, Byrn absorbed the situation. She was certainly beautiful. Up close, even in the shadowed light, her eyes were dark and penetrating.

"You'd best drop that knife," he commanded.

"But that would leave me vulnerable."

"I have a pistol pointed at your head, and you can't reach me with your blade. You're already vulnerable, so release the damn knife."

She loosened her grip, and the weapon clattered to the sidewalk.

"As I mentioned, you possess skills. You've been trained. Special Forces?"

"Ranger."

Byrn sensed his eyebrows raise.

"That's tough training…"

"For a woman," she completed his sentence.

"I didn't say that."

"You didn't need to. I've seen the look before. A whole lot of times."

"You're still active in the service?" Byrn decided to take another approach to get his answers. Elimination.

"No."

"Why did you leave?"

She smirked at him. "Is this some sort of job assessment?"

Byrn glared at her.

"No, it's a survival evaluation. Why did you leave military service?"

The woman glared straight back at him. No hesitation was evident in her mannerisms. No alternate clenching and opening of her fists. No apparent rapid breathing. She seemed calm.

"Limited job prospects in the field. Besides, I got a better offer."

"And that brings us right back to square one. If it's not Zhen, who is your employer?"

She shook her head. It was a standoff.

Byrn continued. "I figure you know something about me; therefore, I assume you're aware what I'm capable of. Yet still you refuse my questions."

The woman smiled. "Not only do I appreciate what you're capable of, I've seen you at work."

"The laneway in Beijing?"

"Yes, very impressive. Astounding really."

"Nevertheless, you're not scared."

The woman stared deeply into Byrn's eyes before she began to speak.

"In the next minute or two, you will decide whether I live or die. I've no control over that. I'm under oath to my employer not to reveal his identity, so that option is not available to me. The decision as to my future remains exclusively yours."

Byrn sighed. Frustration or admiration, he wasn't certain. Thirty wordless seconds passed before Byrn broke the silence.

"Turn around."

The woman remained steadfast, but a fleeting expression of disappointment passed over her face. A small down turning of the lips.

"So be it. But I thought you'd be the kind to shoot someone from the front."

She turned her back to Byrn.

In a split second, Byrn swiveled the pistol in his hand and slammed the weapon into the back of her head. She crumpled to the ground.

Byrn sighed again.

So, what the hell was he going to do with her now?

Chapter 10

"Goddamn it, my head is throbbing."

"At least you're alive to feel it… for now," Byrn responded.

The woman sat in a brick doorway propped against a shop door. Byrn had utilized the preceding fifteen minutes to clear the debris in the alleyway. The trash had been disposed of.

The woman rubbed the back of her neck, screwing her eyes as she winced in pain. Eventually, she looked up at Byrn.

"You don't pull your punches, do you? You could have been a gentleman and politely offered me a seat."

"Number one, I don't really regard myself as a gentleman. Number two, I couldn't keep an eye on you and clean up the mess you made simultaneously."

"Fair point," she replied. "So, what now? Has the jury in your head finished their deliberations?"

Byrn chuckled. The jury. It was a metaphor Byrn had used many times. It frequently signaled the precipitous end to someone's life.

"Still deliberating. At this stage, you're only alive because you've been directed to pursue me by a third party. To kill you without gaining that third party's identity would leave me none the wiser. I prefer to be fully informed."

The woman wriggled, running her hands down her legs.

Byrn smiled.

"It's gone," he said.

"What's gone?"

"The flick knife you had concealed in your pants."

"Intrusive pervert."

"I did what had to be done," Byrn responded. "So, moving forward. Perhaps we can come at this from another angle."

Byrn's captive crinkled her brows.

"Maybe if you tell me what your employer's interest is in me, we can progress from there."

The woman considered the proposal before responding.

"I suppose I can tell you that my instructions were to follow and observe. My boss wants to determine if you are authentic."

"And?"

"I wouldn't be in this position if you weren't."

"Fair point. Okay, we're making some progress. Is your employer well resourced?"

"Exceptionally."

"Does he or she work for a government, *any* government?"

A small snicker burst through her lips.

"No, it's more likely governments would curry his favor."

Byrn tilted his head to the side, absorbing all her words. A full minute transpired.

"All right. Let's assume your mysterious employer wants to hire me for a job and was simply testing my credentials."

"That may be a fair assumption. But I don't have the intel to confirm or deny it."

"Then I gather you are unaware of the details of the proposed assignment?"

"Correct."

The woman sighed.

"Look," she continued. "I've told you all I can. Just make up your damn mind and do what you've got to do, will you?"

"Trying to rush your own execution. That's new."

Silence.

"One final question," said Byrn. "Is it possible to get your employer on the phone so I can talk with him?"

"There's no chance. Our communication protocols don't work that way."

Decision time.

As Byrn analyzed the data at hand and considered the options available, he stared at the woman. Eyes closed, she leaned her head back on the door, her body lay relaxed and easy. Most people would have been trying to read the expression on his face. She just didn't seem to care.

"I lied. I have another question," he said.

The woman shrugged her shoulders. "If you must."

"Does your presence here in China threaten me or my mission?"

She smiled.

"I don't think too many things or people would threaten you or any objective you had in mind. But to answer your question, no. I pose no immediate threat to your work."

Byrn paused a moment longer. The jury had handed down their verdict. The judge was considering it.

"All right, on your feet," he ordered.

She seemed surprised. "Am I going somewhere?"

"*We're* going somewhere. Tomorrow you're returning to Beijing with me on the fast train. Then I'm taking you to the airport and seeing you on the next flight to wherever the hell you want to go, as long as it's out of the country. You can report back to your employer in person. Inform him that I have no interest in his proposition and that if I encounter you or him again, your lives will end at that moment."

Byrn understood that the woman would recognize the sincerity in his tone. People usually did.

"Nice, but you don't know who he is."

"You can be sure that as soon as I finish in Beijing, I'm going to go out of my way to find out. You might as well pass that information on to him too. Tell him that if he, and you, for that matter, play this smart, you've just dodged a bullet, literally."

"What about tonight?" she asked.

"You're coming back to my hotel with me."

She smiled.

Byrn looked her straight in the eye.

"Don't flatter yourself."

Chapter 11

"What's your name?" Byrn asked.

They were in the hotel elevator and had almost reached Byrn's floor.

"Regan Dia," she responded.

"Is that your real name?"

"Yup."

Byrn didn't shake her hand, but he did keep a firm grip on the pistol in his jacket pocket. The thugs back in the alleyway had underestimated Dia's skill set. He wouldn't be making the same mistake.

The doors opened, but Dia turned to Byrn before stepping out.

"So, is Lachlan Byrn your real name?"

He looked at her.

"You'll have to come to your own conclusions about that."

The assassin ushered her down the passage to his door. After swiping the card, he guided her through the doorway. Once inside the room, he pulled the pistol out of his pocket, motioning toward the bed.

"You take the bed. I'll stay on the couch. I won't be sleeping tonight, so don't get creative with any escape plans. And by the way, the bathroom has no exterior window, so that avenue of egress is unavailable."

Dia shrugged and disappeared into the bathroom. Byrn sat on the couch by the floor to ceiling window. He gazed downward to the parkland opposite the hotel. For such a populous nation, Byrn was impressed by the Chinese government's ability to create vast parkland areas within such busy cities. He supposed the parks provided one of the few avenues of escape and relaxation in a country where rules and regulation dominated and were enforced without mercy.

The assassin guided his focus back to the current situation. It certainly would have been more straightforward to shoot Regan Dia then and there in the street. At that point, there were no ties leading back to him. Her death, however, seemed unwarranted. Byrn wouldn't have hesitated to kill her if he had a clear reason, but the circumstances appeared to dictate she receive a second chance. Not utilizing her reprieve would have consequences. Unfortunately, he now had to waste twenty-four hours being a nursemaid. It was an inconvenience.

The bathroom door swung open. Dia appeared silhouetted against the light; a hotel robe wrapped around her.

Provocative.

Byrn dismissed any inappropriate thoughts before they even began.

"The bed," he said gruffly with a hint of sarcasm. "Make the most of your downtime. Sweet dreams."

Dia took notice of the pistol, which was still tightly held in Byrn's grip. Taking the path of least resistance, she headed to the bed before pulling down the sheets and climbing in, still fully robed.

"How can you be sure you'll stay awake all night? It's not

like we're out in the field."

"I'm sure," he replied. "And for what it's worth, for me, this is the field. Assassination is a different line of work than special ops. It requires alternate skills and unique sensitivities. If you plan on staying out of the military, you may want to develop some of those proficiencies. Particularly covert surveillance. Had you been better at it, you wouldn't be in this situation now."

"Screw you," Dia replied before turning over.

Byrn reached into his pocket, found his container, flipped the lid open, and retrieved a couple more pills. Let the Night Eagle resume its shift.

Byrn didn't rest at all. He spent the first hour maintaining vigil over his prisoner, ensuring her attempt at sleep was genuine. By 1 a.m. the assassin was satisfied. Once more, he turned his gaze to the park outside. Retrospection was not a pastime he entertained willingly. Particularly not while ensconced in a hostile environment. Doubly so because it was China.

His relationship with the country was profound… and not in a good way.

"I don't believe you Lachlan. It's too easy to lie. You know, people lie to improve their circumstances. It happens all the time."

Byrn sat chained to the chair, his feet immersed in six inches of water. He would have been angry if there had been any point to it, but the anger had been beaten out of him over the past months and years. He cast his eyes down to his torso. A pastiche of fresh blooded wounds, many still open, numerous older injuries etched in deep blue and black bruising, and historic scars their source long forgotten, lay exposed in the dim night. The fresh blood glistened, a deep crimson stream, vying for sunlight that would never come.

Byrn considered it ironic that the only sign of life within him was his own blood exiting his mutilated body. Like a current of rats abandoning a sinking ship.

"Well?"

Byrn looked up at his interrogator. Seated at a small desk on a wooden rise, the man kept his feet dry and clear of the water. In the shadows behind the light now focused on Byrn's face, Byrn caught the flash of teeth as the man smiled. They'd met, many, many times. But on bad days like this, Byrn couldn't even remember the man's name. Nor did he want to. For a millisecond, he wondered why the man was grinning.

Suddenly, a spark arced across the room as the pain ravaged Byrn's body. It was as though rods of steel had replaced his veins and were piercing every nerve within him like an array of electronic spears. An agonizing shriek permeated the air, an almost inhuman cry of torment. It took him a full five seconds to realize the cry was his own.

A second scream died midway through. The man raised the prod out of the water, sparks still emanating as he rested it beside his dry feet.

"You don't answer my questions, Lachlan. In those circumstances, how can I provide relief?"

The pain had given way to a dull numbness. Byrn's body welcomed it like a liberating army.

His mind acquiesced to the nothingness.

His mind.

Was there anything left to liberate?

Byrn took a deep, painful breath.

"You asked me a question... you sought my cooperation." He felt

himself stumbling over each syllable. He'd had minimal need for conversation over the last few years. "I answered... I gave it... what else do you expect?"

The man leaned to one side, showing more of his face in the half light. What was his name?

"Lachlan, you're telling me what I want to hear. That's not good enough. I require honesty. I need to know what you feel."

Byrn felt his body go limp. A physical reengage ignoring the broken mind held captive within.

"I... I..."

The interrogator reached forward, raising the prod in the air.

"No, no..."

"Yes Lachlan, I'm afraid it's yes... until you can learn to be honest with me."

The interrogator plunged the prod into the water.

Byrn wanted to pass out. He fought to be unconscious. Yet he knew it didn't work that way.

Unbelievably, the next cry cut even deeper into his soul; a soul driven too far beyond its limits. The steel rods sliced through his sinewy body like poisonous snakes of lightning, impaling, contaminating, invading.

The scream grew louder. A soul crushing crescendo.

Byrn's eyes snapped open.

That decimating acoustic. From his half-awake daze, or memory, or whatever the hell it was. The roar seemed so real.

Byrn stared out the window.

Shit. It was real.

The pulsing of the helicopter's engine echoed through the room. The bird was setting down in the park opposite.

Byrn leaped off the couch.

"I'm awake. What the fuck is that?" shouted Dia.

"Get dressed. We're getting out of here," Byrn responded.

They'd both grabbed their kit and were bolting down the hallway within sixty seconds.

"The stairs," yelled Byrn. "We can shoot our way down a stair well, but an elevator is a canyon with one entrance. We'd have no chance."

They burst through the door. Dia began to head straight down the stairwell.

"No, up," yelled Byrn. "Let them find our room. We'll go down while they're searching the floor."

Dia raised an eyebrow but followed Byrn.

They'd perched in the stairwell two levels above for less than three minutes when the commotion of boots on the concrete echoed up the stairs.

"You were right," whispered Dia. "They would have finished us on the way down."

They held position for another two minutes until the clatter had died down.

"Now," instructed Byrn. "If there're any operatives lagging behind, we take them out on our way down."

Four minutes later, they were dashing across the parking area at the rear of the hotel.

"Where to?" asked Dia.

"Anywhere but here."

They'd almost made the fence on the far side of the lot when Byrn heard a male voice shouting out from the rear. It was followed by the mechanical rattle of automatic fire tearing up the asphalt.

"Don't look back, just go," shouted Byrn as he and Dia

scrambled over the fence.

Once they'd escaped the immediate lights of the hotel parking area and the gunfire, Byrn led them northward. Two hundred yards down a dead-quiet street, the assassin stopped.

"You keep going," yelled Byrn. "Do whatever the hell you can to get clear and then get out of the country. It's me that Zhen's after. You've got a chance on your own."

"What will you do?"

"I'm going to trim the size of Zhen Su's personal hit squad some more. Now get out of here."

The woman hesitated.

Byrn pushed her forward.

"Just go, damn it. The longer you hang around, the greater risk to us both."

Dia nodded, then turned and fled into the darkness.

The assassin figured he had around a minute to secure his position. He scanned the area. The only cover was an industrial dumpster at an intersection twenty yards ahead. It wasn't much, but it was better than remaining exposed on the open road. In his mind, he'd already allocated that position to his attackers.

The circumstances had changed. Byrn was in control, and his pursuers were now his prey. It was time for the assassin to do what he did best.

Kill.

The first wave came in a group of three. One operative on each sidewalk and one down the center of the road. They were all running. It amazed Byrn how hunters often overlooked their prey's changing tactics. Either way, the man in the middle of the road would live the longest... just. The two on the flanks needed to be taken down quickly before they could make cover.

Byrn crouched down behind the bin. He trained his QSZ-92 at the man on the left side of the road. He waited until all parties had crossed a small side road, leaving them nowhere to run. The assassin then arced his gun around to the man on the other side, pre-establishing the angle of his second shot. His shots would be rapid fire, making round two an automatic reflex.

He then returned his aim to the first man.

Three, two, one…

Byrn fired. The operative went down, but the second he squeezed the trigger, Byrn shifted his aim. As the first man hit the ground, the second operative met the same fate, with a bullet in his forehead, both crumpled on the sidewalk.

The guy in the center of the road stopped dead in his tracks. He turned and bolted to the left. Byrn followed him with his barrel, firing just before the fugitive crossed the gutter.

Temporarily satiated, the assassin waited.

There would be a second wave. But how many? The chopper wasn't that big, yet Byrn figured that Zhen wouldn't employ local police to join in this type of operation. The next wave would be two people, three at most. They would have noted the gunshots and would be moving forward at a circumspect pace. Byrn considered the options. If he was in charge, he'd send the two men forward carefully, making use of local cover and shadows where possible. If there was a third operative, Byrn would dispatch him or her to approach from behind. But that would take some time.

Byrn planned the scenario out in his head.

If the commander was clever, he would instruct any third player to wait, only coming up behind the assassin while he was preoccupied with firing at the other two targets.

The seconds ticked by. There was nothing. No sound. No movement.

Byrn reconsidered the option of the first wave being the only attack before quickly discounting it. No point second guessing himself. He'd wait it out.

The assassin crawled along the sidewalk, maneuvering his location to the opposite end of the dumpster. His view of the road was limited, but the location offered more protection from a rearward advance. Enough time had now passed for the third operative to have gained position.

The clock was ticking.

Twenty seconds later, Byrn caught it. The slight movement of a shadow on the right-hand side of the road ahead of his location. He scanned the opposite side but saw no corresponding motion. The assassin maintained his vigil.

The first shadow moved in and out of view. He wasn't easily identified, but a professional could pick him out. There was still no activity to the left.

Byrn let the time run on, still drawing a visual blank to the left.

Then it hit him. He was searching for a shooter who wasn't there. Probably with only two operatives remaining, whoever led the team was ruthlessly sacrificing the first operative. In an instant, the assassin realized why. He swung himself around, throwing himself flat on the cement. He pegged the second operative in the shadows near a streetlight fifty yards down the road behind him. A rifle perched on his shoulder, ready to fire.

Nice move.

Almost.

Byrn got off three rapid rounds into the man's torso.

Nicer move.

As he squeezed the trigger the final time, a metallic thud just above Byrn's head indicated he was now under fire. He crouched low as a second round hit the bin precisely where his head had been. The first operative was swinging around.

Byrn flung himself down and scrambled along the length of the bin, coming out low along the adjacent side to his original position.

Emboldened by his successful surprise attack, the operative moved forward across the road, maintaining continuous fire on Byrn's position.

Only it was the wrong position.

Byrn reached around the dumpster and put two slugs into the man's face. He died emboldened but ineffectual.

The assassin withdrew down the street and waited. Thirty minutes later, he heard the roar of an aero engine revving, then the whirring of helicopter blades. Whatever was left of Zhen's hit squad was retreating, leaving the locals to clean up their mess.

An hour later, Lachlan Byrn had stolen a small Toyota and headed northeast on the long drive to Beijing. Night travel was less conspicuous for a foreigner. Now was the time to counter the pressure on Zhen Su. Byrn grinned at the thought.

As he drove, the assassin popped a couple more pills and considered the evening's events. The situation had been dealt with promptly and efficiently, as was Byrn's way. The bonus was another clear message sent to Zhen. What concerned Byrn was how Zhen discovered his location so quickly. The

Chinese agent should still have been scouring Beijing for him. Clearly the man had inside intelligence, but from where? Byrn's presence in Xi'an wasn't known to any of his network.

Two hours into the drive, Byrn had reached an unimpeachable conclusion. The betrayal of information hadn't come from within the assassin's own ranks. There was a connection between his real-time location every time Zhen Su's men had attacked him and an external factor.

That factor was the clear common denominator. And Lachlan Byrn didn't need to perform any mathematical calculations to know exactly who she was.

Chapter 12

The trouble with the obvious was judging the reliability of the source.

Without doubt, the information provided to Byrn was a ruse. Now the ruse was being used to lure the assassin into a trap. Byrn couldn't help but admire the forward planning. Zhen was at the top of his game. Still, Byrn decided to play along. He'd walk right into Zhen's ambush, but not in the manner the Chinese agent anticipated.

Zhen Su had previously supplied Byrn with a photograph of a woman and two young children, girls. At their last meeting, prior to the shit fight in Estonia, Zhen gave Byrn the picture, promising the assassin that Estonia would be his last job for the Chinese. He claimed his conviction was so strong that after the hit on the Russian president, if he or anyone in his government ever called on Byrn's services again, then Zhen would sacrifice his own family. He'd referred to it as 'skin in the game'.

Of course, Zhen Su was a liar by profession. At the time, the Chinese agent would have been convinced that Byrn would die on the mission, either in action if Byrn failed, or during the extraction if he happened to succeed. Zhen orchestrated the circumstances, but the attempt to eliminate Byrn had floundered.

And Byrn was pissed.

The assassin flipped the picture over, revealing the address scrawled across its back. He then raised his eyes and stared down the street. The house was larger in real life.

It was midafternoon. Byrn drove straight here from Xi'an. After dumping the car some distance away, the assassin completed the balance of the journey by foot. Canal Bank was a gated enclave just east of Beijing, in the Tongzhou District, although the gates had presented no issue for Byrn. The district was a secondary point for Chinese government operations as they attempted to move some of the populace out of the hectically cluttered Beijing. But in this specific location, the neighborhood reeked of money.

It made sense. Zhen was a high-ranking official these days, and knowing the man's total lack of morality, he would have his fingers in several lucrative operations outside his main line of work.

That was what worried Byrn. It made too much sense.

The address given to Byrn led to a majestic, European-influenced home. It was two stories, with Romanesque pillars supporting a solid portico at the front. A pair of balconies overlooked the luxurious neighborhood, with vast parklands and the Grand Canal in the distance. The Chinese architectural influence was evident in the ornate railings and uniquely Asian roof tiles.

Zhen had done well for himself. If this really was Zhen's house.

There was no obvious movement in and out of the house, but three armed guards clutching Type 56-4 assault rifles, dressed in neutral black, wearing fully equipped tactical vests, stood right outside the home. One on either corner, one at the front gate.

Overkill or prudent protection. Or perhaps simply a skillfully executed performance for Byrn's benefit.

Byrn lay wedged under a low-lying shrub three houses up on the opposite side of the road. It took him some time to reach the position as he sidestepped to avoid multiple foot patrols and a succession of dark vehicles with blacked-out windows roaming the streets. While it may have been easier for the assassin to insert himself at night, he figured that's when security teams would be on highest alert. Carefully working his way through the large back yards and across a series of high protective fences, he'd eventually got himself to ground zero.

Yet there was nothing to see.

Perhaps that was the point. Or maybe Byrn was overthinking. He needed more data.

Around 4 p.m., that data arrived.

A dark limousine pulled up directly in front of the house. The driver appeared, circled the car's hood, and opened a rear passenger door on the sidewalk side. A few seconds later, a woman climbed out of the car. Her bob cut black hair fluttered in the breeze as she surveyed the area. Three seconds later, two young girls emerged from the same door. They also glanced up and down the sidewalk. The driver then quickly ushered the three of them through the front gate. Byrn scanned the length of the home's front fence. The guards were now standing straighter, clutching their weapons more tightly.

Glancing at the photo in his hand, Byrn confirmed it was the woman and children he had just seen.

What a show. Byrn was impressed. Had Zhen Su gone to all this trouble just for him? It was a shame the play lacked a stronger script. The woman looking around was almost convincing, but in reality, the two young children would have just skipped out of the car and headed toward the main gate. The director should have paid more attention to authenticity rather than messaging. Of course, the *pièce de résistance* was the fact the limo pulled up on the street at the front of the house instead of proceeding down the driveway behind the walls. Byrn supposed those producing the show could only work with the parameters they'd been set.

Either way, Byrn got a message, but probably not the one Zhen intended.

The afternoon shadows morphed into early evening by the time a dark SUV edged its way slowly down the road. Byrn struggled to identify the occupants as the vehicle stopped outside the house. The driver performed a routine similar to the one performed by his predecessor earlier in the day, making his way around to open the rear passenger side door. On cue, a male figure emerged from the car. Even in the dulling light, identification was easy.

Zhen Su.

Like the woman and kids before, he looked around, taking a moment to exchange a few words with the driver before heading across the sidewalk and through the main gate.

Byrn supposed that this was the point that any normal person bent on revenge would feel their blood pressure rise and perhaps even break into a sweat as rage filled their bodies, the target of their fury suddenly within reach.

Byrn was not that person.

A wave of calmness swept through him as though someone had injected ice into his veins. He was on alert; the sense of anticipation aroused him but did not distract from his task. This was now all about methodology and engineering. The joy would come later. The assassin had a kill to choreograph. The stage may have been set by Zhen Su, but as ever the timing and the mechanics would be completely controlled by him.

Lachlan Byrn was in his element.

Chapter 13

Byrn spent the next few hours extracting himself from the neighborhood. He'd been correct about the extra manpower after the sun went down. More than once, he'd nearly been exposed by patrols. Despite the whole operation appearing burdensome just for a recon sortie, the assassin recognized the significance of intelligence substantiated through observation.

By sunrise, Byrn was holed up in a small boarding house in Dazhalan, a downtown slum area of the city. No questions asked, anonymity encouraged.

The assassin lay back on his compact metal framed bed. The room, like many others he'd stayed in, contained his basic essentials. A deadbolt on the door, a window opening on a different wall from the door, and some sort of facility to make coffee. Byrn was tiring but had no intention of sleeping. He wouldn't sleep again until he was out of China. He popped two more pills and contemplated his next move.

The assassin mulled over the intel that he had gathered. Zhen's connection to the address in Canal Bank was confirmed, but what about the other players? Were those people genuinely Zhen's family? Byrn had doubts. Overplaying their hand in the acting stakes gave nothing away. Badly directed paid actors and individuals with no professional skills could have delivered the same transparent performance. Also, would Zhen really risk his own family, if he had one, in a covert operation? Byrn knew of no one else in the game who would even consider that, but Zhen was a different kind of ruthless. Was the man that desensitized? The assassin figured that nobody on the planet knew Zhen Su's darker side better than him.

He'd experienced it up close....

"Lachlan, I intend to own you, and I'll settle for nothing less."

Byrn looked up from the rusty iron frame he was chained to. He rolled his head to look his interrogator square in the eye. It was the only part of his body that had mobility. As he began to speak, the fragility of his own voice surprised him. He didn't think there was anything left in this world that could be a new sensation.

"If... if I ever get out of here, I will come for you..."

The prisoner heard his voice trail off to nothing as his energy evaporated.

"You see Lachlan, that's exactly what I mean. While you keep making statements like that, warrants of rebellion, I know my work here is unfinished."

Byrn closed his eyes.

"And that is no escape, my friend. You can close your eyes all you like, but when you open them, I'll still be here."

Zhen allowed an extended silence to pervade the musty air.

"Open your eyes, Lachlan. I'm asking as a friend."

Byrn didn't move.

"Open your eyes Lachlan. You need to do as I say."

Nothing.

Byrn almost sensed the force of the weapon as Zhen brought it to bear. The sharp point of the jian pierced his bruised skin. As the blade plunged deeply into his left thigh, Byrn's eyes burst open involuntarily. A raspy cry emanated deep inside his body, its lifeless tone belying the depth of the pain.

He just caught the dry smile on Zhen's lips as his inquisitor twisted the double-edged sword within his bleeding flesh.

"You know Lachlan, it is better when you do what I ask. It's better for me, and it's most certainly better for you."

Zhen looked down on his prisoner with the relaxed mannerisms of a patient teacher repeating an important lesson to a struggling student. He shook his head slowly and allowed his shoulders to sag. Yet he kept the blade in Byrn's thigh.

"Make no mistake Lachlan, I will own you. I'll own your behavior; I'll possess your soul in its entirety, and I suspect the aspect of our future relationship that may currently seem the most abhorrent to you is that you will be begging me for my friendship."

"Well fuck you, you son of a bitch." The words exploded out of Byrn's mouth.

Zhen shook his head once more, another slight grin forming on his face.

"So be it, Lachlan. Sadly, there are still many lessons for you to learn."

The Chinese agent withdrew the jian from Byrn's jagged flesh with one clean upward stroke. A millisecond later, he plunged it down with such force it penetrated Byrn's right thigh completely, impaling it on the bed's rough wooden slats.

Byrn only heard half of his own anguished scream before the darkness mercifully enveloped him.

They happened so often, particularly when he was riding on the wings of the Night Eagle, that Byrn wasn't really phased by them anymore. To anyone else, they'd seem like harrowing nightmares. To Byrn, they were just vivid recollections. If he had any available emotion, the assassin supposed he could be celebrating the fact that these events were now in his past. Yet he knew that once you'd survived that hell, the memories were just a part of your daily existence. A life sentence of relived torture.

Byrn exhaled deeply and swung his legs out from the bed, his feet landing on the hard floor. In the back of his mind, a plan was beginning to emerge.

The information that he had collected was valuable, yet it wasn't everything. The assassin appreciated that the art of prediction was what separated him from his peers. For some reason, Byrn managed, in most cases, to predict the behavior of his targets. He supposed it partially came from experience, but there was something else. Lachlan Byrn understood evil. He breathed it, he slept with it, and it was part of his substance. A dark driving force within.

By the time the first rays of sunlight lit the alleyway outside his small window, the assassin had figured out how Zhen Su would play this out.

Darkness reading darkness.

Within twenty-four hours, Zhen's 'family' would either be mourning his death or collecting their final paychecks.

Chapter 14

The next morning, after drinking too much coffee and downing some additional tabs of modafinil, Byrn headed back toward Canal Bank. The assassin mixed his modes of travel between taxi, public transport, and foot. No one person would be able to identify where he began his journey or where it ended. As expected, once he reached the outer edges of the residential enclave, his task became more hazardous.

He started by following the canal's banks as it wound toward the closest point to Zhen's home. He then headed north, through some curated parkland. The assassin's research had suggested that some of the majestic trees he walked by were over a hundred years old and had been transplanted here at an enormous cost to the developer. Byrn didn't give a shit. As far as he was concerned, they formed adequate cover, end of story.

Byrn neared the park's edge when a dark SUV resembling the one from yesterday, approached along the road. He quickly tucked himself in behind the nearest tree. The doors opened and four solidly built men emerged. Like the security personnel at Zhen's house, they were well-armed and appeared ready for business. They fanned out from the vehicle and strode purposefully amongst the trees, their eyes scanning the surrounding parkland.

Byrn projected the search based on the pattern he'd seen guards begin. He noted that there would be an opportunity to take them down one at a time, but that would send a message to Zhen that Byrn wasn't yet ready to deliver. As he heard footsteps approach his hide, Byrn withdrew the knife secured in a holster on his ankle. The footsteps grew louder, indicating an operative nearby. If he remained where he was, Byrn would be seen. If he ran for it, he'd be seen. Now was the time for a calculated judgement. The greatest likelihood was that the guard was headed toward the canal bank. If he was taking the most direct route, he would pass to the left of Byrn's tree. If his plan was to gain the maximum visual coverage of the park, he would veer to the right.

The assassin had roughly two seconds to make the call. It was daytime. Accordingly, Byrn figured the guard would see less need for a thorough search, so he voted left, and gradually edged his way around to the opposite side of the tree. Gripping the knife firmly, Byrn held his breath.

Heavy footsteps retreated toward the water beyond the hide. It had been the right call.

This time.

Byrn waited until the park was clear, adjusting his position around the massive tree trunk as required. Fifteen minutes later, he heard the SUV's engine spring to life. He risked a glance and saw the vehicle receding up the road.

Daylight infiltration had its issues.

The assassin spent the next hour slowly winding his path toward Zhen's purported home. He'd had to stop and take cover three times along the way. It seemed the presence and alertness of the guards were increasing.

By midafternoon, Byrn was in position. But it was a different spot from the previous day. The assassin lay covered in dense foliage in the front corner of a large garden across the road from the house behind Zhen's. At the entrance to Zhen's house, Byrn was certain the show from the day before would be repeated in an identical manner. He had no need to see it again.

This time he would be at the stage door, waiting for the actors to exit post-performance.

Byrn's logic was simple. If he'd been in Zhen's position and was planning to ambush an experienced operator, he would leave nothing to chance. Firepower and a clear range to use it were the key elements. Byrn had noticed zero activity in the houses on either side of Zhen's the previous day. In normal circumstances, that would be unusual. In the scenario playing out in the assassin's head, the absence of movement was mandatory. Byrn figured each adjacent dwelling would be stacked with armed operatives, biding their time. When Byrn was spotted trying to access Zhen's house, and given so many eyes on the location, he would certainly be spotted, they would pounce. As Byrn entered the premises, he doubtlessly would be greeted by a similar entourage of killers waiting inside.

Unlike special ops teams tasked with rescuing hostages who had to take great care and target carefully, the assassin knew that these people's combined firepower would be unleashed with abandonment in a frenzied lethal attack. Anyone caught in the middle would stand no chance. They could fire recklessly because no innocents would be there. They would have left.

By the stage door.

It was a solid plan, and Byrn was sure Zhen would have every confidence in its successful implementation. It probably would have worked too if it wasn't for the previous day's substandard acting.

So Byrn stayed put. Let the actors go through the motions before a nonexistent audience. Allow Zhen to play his part as the bait in the snare before exiting to safety, like the coward that he was.

When it came to the precise execution of the plan in his head, Byrn employed his key strategy.

Patience.

Lachlan Byrn simply waited.

Chapter 15

Confirmation.

At around 4 p.m. a black limousine, identical to the one that had dropped off Zhen's 'family', pulled to a halt outside the house directly behind Zhen's. Three minutes later, guided by two armed men in combat black, the woman and the two children came scurrying down the driveway before climbing into the rear of the vehicle. The limo sped off.

No stagecraft required.

Byrn took note of the surrounding firepower. There were the two men, plus presumably the driver and one more guard in the car, although the driver could well be alone given that he'd had to get out yesterday to open the back door to let everyone out.

Nobody else was in sight.

So, three, maybe four armed operatives.

The question was, would it be the same scenario for Zhen's departure?

Within a few short hours, Byrn would find out. In the meantime, he had to move.

There were two key components to Byrn's plan that presented a challenge. He needed to make his way undetected across the road, and he had to time the moment of his assault to the minute, if not second.

Patiently, the assassin waited for the first signs of nightfall.

When the shadows became long, casting a dark mishmash of shapes across the asphalt, Byrn made his move. Sliding along the grass inside the fence line, he reached the garden's driveway unseen. Then, using the lengthening shadows as his cover, Byrn scampered across the road, taking the low fence of this target house in a single swift leap. He honed in on the protection of a low-lying bush next to the house.

Again, Byrn waited, figuring that if he'd been spotted, he'd be dead by now.

The assassin's next move depended on how precisely Zhen's movements would be timed. Knowing Zhen's tendency for total control, Byrn figured he would check on the preparedness of the troops in at least one, if not all, the houses. He'd want to keep his people on their toes. That would take time, time that would be impossible to calculate to the second. Accordingly, the guards allocated the duty of shepherding Zhen to his car would have to wait for him. Everything relied on the fence between the adjoining properties being at least six feet high. If so, the guards escorting Zhen on the far side of the wall wouldn't be able to see over it. They would essentially be passing Zhen, presumably on some kind of ladder, over the fence.

Byrn slowly made his way toward the property's rear boundary, following the side fence furthest from the driveway. As he reached the residence's back corner, it occurred to the assassin how close his proximity was to the thirty or more well-armed and highly trained operatives whose sole mission was to end his life.

Stimulating.

Byrn sensed his nerves pulse with anticipation. They were countered by his naturally steely demeanor. He'd woken up this morning expecting to die today. With each passing minute, that was looking like an increasingly likely outcome.

Whatever. So be it.

He craned his neck to peek around the edge of the house and through the trees that lay scattered throughout the garden. In the near distance, he saw the rear fence. Solid… and high. He scanned its length. In the far corner, there was a robust aluminum ladder bracketed to the fence. The points of a similar ladder on the other side visible over the top.

Perfect.

The darkness was increasing its hold by the minute. The lights came on in Zhen's house, but the buildings on either side remained shrouded in blackness. Byrn held no doubt that sentries, some with night vision glasses, would be scanning Zhen's front and back yards.

This was the point where the timing became crucial.

Byrn flattened himself against the wall of the house, engulfed by shadow. It could be anytime now.

The night was deadly still, no breeze, no other sound, as though the trees were in a trance…

"I'll do what you ask of me. I will work for you."

Zhen Su grinned, slowly exposing his yellowing teeth. Like a wolf in the wild preparing to make a meal of his prey.

"We both know that is not enough, Lachlan. I require more from you."

Byrn looked directly ahead, as though in a state of suspension.

"Come on Lachlan, you know what I want, and you must acknowledge that you won't come close to getting what you want

until my demands are fulfilled."

Byrn didn't flinch. The battle he fought was solely within himself. Self-respect challenged the need for survival. He was still breathing, so the victor was clear. He felt his body quiver. There were forces at play here that he no longer controlled, and they wrestled like ferocious and immoral armies beneath his skin.

"Come on, Lachlan. I truly believe you are almost there. You have made much progress in the last twelve months."

The shaking continued. Byrn felt the saliva dribbling down his chin. He was searching for a thought... he found nothing.

That was the moment, the actual moment in time that Byrn realized he was no longer the man he once was, and never would be again. He knew they could control his body, but he'd considered it impossible that they could take his mind.

He'd been wrong.

The reality was he'd been wrong in every respect. There was nothing left to fight with. Lachlan Byrn was gone and whatever now existed within his flesh was owned completely by the man before him.

"Come on, Lachlan. You can do this. I know you can, but do you?"

Byrn began to nod, imperceptibly at first and then with increasing vigor. If a mannerism could be a white flag, this was it.

"I... I...I..."

"Come on, Lachlan. Your pathway is clear. I have cleared it for you."

The nodding continued, as did the drool.

"I... I would..."

"Yes, Lachlan, what would you like?"

Byrn's head slumped down. A moment later, the prisoner willed it upright, staring his opponent straight in the eye.

"Zhen Su, I would like you to be my friend. I offer you my devotion and loyalty."

Zhen sat back in his chair, a broad grin appearing on his face. His eyes glowed in victory.

"Welcome Lachlan, welcome. I would be most honored to be your friend and ally."

Immediately, coarse canvas scraped against Byrn's face as the hood was yanked down from behind. Then, a force as powerful as a locomotive train slammed into the side of his head. His neck snapped involuntarily to the right. The pain screamed at him, screeching like a devil within.

He remained barely conscious.

"And remember Lachlan, for we have spoken about it many times, that if you betray my friendship, these last few years will seem like a pleasant vacation. Remember that my new friend."

Again, the locomotive, and then the darkness of the tunnel.

Byrn squinted. His skin felt hot, burning. The heat scorched his face like a flaming cloth. Surely not. It couldn't be.

The sun.

He hadn't seen it for years.

No, he must be dead.

He opened his eyes. The glare blinded him, searing his eyeballs. He squeezed his eyelids shut.

Defense.

He tried again, a little longer.

And again.

The blinding light was surrounded by a deep blue hue.

Once more, the sky.

No. Not possible.

He looked from one side to the other, his head still lying flat on the ground. On the grass.

Grass.

Struggling, he leaned himself up on an elbow, scanning his environment in awe.

He lay in a paddock. No walls, no guards. No one.

It was because of his new friendship.

Lachlan Byrn was free.

He'd been released... into a brand-new kind of hell.

Shit.

It had never happened on an operation before.

The vivid recollection had interrupted his workflow. Byrn supposed that somewhere deep in his psyche, he'd have to deal with the issue... later. It wasn't too surprising that the convergence of forces coming to China, being in such proximity to Zhen, and the prospect of a final confrontation was playing havoc with the assassin's already damaged mind.

Yet something had snapped him out of his trance like state. Voices.

Byrn heard two male voices, and they were making no attempt to control their volume. A door slammed, and the assassin picked up footsteps coming down the property's rear stairs not ten feet away from where he hid. Although half concealed in the dim light, the outline of two figures was visible, as was the shape of the Type 56-4 assault rifles strapped over their shoulders. That was the key. These men needed to be ready to help their boss over the fence. They couldn't do that and hold their weapons at the same time.

Lachlan Byrn was a detail man. This is exactly as he expected.

Zhen could arrive at any time and Byrn had no way of

knowing precisely when he would front up. He opted to wait for an auditory sign of commotion, a noise that would expose Zhen's presence.

Yet again, concealed in the darkness, the assassin plied his game of patience.

Thirty-four minutes passed before he heard it. The distant sound of a car door slamming, then a second one. Several sets of footsteps on concrete, some distance murmurs of additional voices and perhaps the whack of a front or side door shutting noisily.

This was it.

The biggest tell of all. The two guards on Byrn's side of the fence, whose mannerisms had been relaxed and casual, abruptly changed their posture. Shoulders tightened and chests thrust forward, the men suddenly seemed prepared.

Several minutes passed. Then Byrn heard a crackle. The man on the left of the ladder reached down to his belt and retrieved a radio. He listened briefly before issuing a brief response.

"*Shì de.*" Yes.

Now was the moment. Zhen was on his way.

Speed, silence and efficiency. If one facet faltered, the mission would be over before it began.

Byrn stooped down to his right ankle and grabbed his knife. He then bent over to his left and retrieved another similar weapon. Both guards stood with their backs to him, staring expectantly at the fence.

Byrn covered the distance in less than five seconds.

The guard on the right started to pivot, sensing something behind him. Before he'd completed the motion, Byrn raised his right arm and slashed the man across the throat. Simultaneously, the left guard swiftly turned and reached for his rifle. Byrn lunged forward, his left hand stabbing the man in the side of his abdomen. The man bent forward. Without hesitation, Byrn swept his right hand in an arc slashing his throat.

Two seconds, two deaths.

Timing was now everything.

Even as he reached down to the man on the left, whose physique was slender like Byrn's own, the assassin heard an engine rev as a car drew up in front of the house. Zhen's ride. Fortunately, Byrn's position at the rear of the property was well concealed from the roadway by the residence and thickly populated garden.

Byrn heaved the man's assault rifle from his shoulders, carefully positioning it on the ground. He then unzipped his vest and jacket before putting both over his own dark clothing. After grabbing the guard's fallen cap from the path and placing it on his own head, he dragged the first guard behind a nearby bush. He repeated the movement with the second man.

The assassin knew his disguise would fail scrutiny in the glare of daytime, but in the failing evening light, he hoped it was enough.

Two and a half minutes after the initial stab of metal had penetrated his first victim's skin, Byrn was prepared and waiting to receive his guest.

Footsteps.

Closer.

Almost at the back fence.

"*Zhǔnbèi hǎo?*" Ready?

"*Shì de Xiānshēng,*" Yes, sir, replied Byrn. Keep it simple.

Then, like a second coming, a man's head appeared over the fence line. Zhen Su. Byrn reeled in every possible intuitive reaction, simply reaching out a hand to help Zhen over. Just as any subordinate would do.

Zhen ignored the offer without comment. As the Chinese agent set foot on the grass, Byrn turned and bowed his head, the visor easily covering his face in the darkness.

"*Zhǐyǒu yīgè rén?*" Only one man?

"*Shì de Xiānshēng.*" Again brief. This time Byrn accompanied his response with a hand on his stomach and feigning leaning forward to vomit. He led Zhen forward as he made the movement.

The assassin sensed Zhen tense up. Any deviation from standard practice would alert him to potential danger. Fortunately, as they progressed, the small bend in the driveway revealed Zhen's SUV waiting for him on the roadway, its driver silhouetted in the shadows standing by the open rear passenger door. That seemed to placate the Chinese operative.

He continued forward.

Byrn led the way, keeping his head down. As they approached the SUV, the assassin stepped to one side, his face still concealed by the combination of hat and darkness.

Without any acknowledgement of either Byrn or the driver, Zhen climbed into the vehicle. The driver closed the door without acknowledging Byrn and proceeded around the back of the car. Over the vehicle's high roof, Byrn saw him examine up and down the road before settling into the driver's seat.

In a lightning-fast move that surprised both driver and passenger, Byrn, knife in hand, stepped to the left, opened the front passenger door, and climbed in. Within a second, the driver lay slumped across the wheel, a river of blood pouring over the SUV's console from his slit throat. A second after that, Byrn had his QSZ-92 trained between Zhen Su's eyes.

Zhen's jaw dropped, his eyes widening in alarm.

The assassin sensed a tightening on the edges of his lips as he spoke. "I've waited a long time for this moment, Zhen. Welcome to your execution."

"No, Comrade Byrn," came the voice from behind. Byrn felt the cold steel of a barrel pressing against his neck. "Welcome to yours."

Chapter 16

Byrn figured it would happen this way. His demise. There would be one small component, some random act of chance that would turn the game against him. No matter how meticulous the assassin's planning, the threat of an arbitrary event always lingered.

So, this was the day.

He'd do what he could to influence the circumstances toward a different outcome, but he didn't really hold much hope. He was wedged in the car, no room for a physical maneuver, little or no chance of a counterattack. Still, he'd continue the process of examining the options.

"Hello Lachlan," said Zhen, quickly resuming control of the situation. "This is no way for you to greet an old friend." The man's newly acquired broad grin was mocking, yet his eyes remained dark and emotionless.

"Here's how this will play out, Zhen," announced Byrn. "I will shoot, you will die. Granted, it wasn't part of my plan that I'd be taking leave of this world as well, but as they say, it is what it is."

"I doubt that you'll get your bullet out of the barrel before your brain ceases to control your bodily functions, Lachlan. No… I believe you will die today, and I'll be home in time for dinner."

Again, the smile. The snarl of a wolf. The little prick was regaining his confidence.

"Besides, Lachlan. You should be well aware of the basis of our friendship. I'm the one who manipulates our interactions."

Byrn hadn't moved an inch. He wanted whoever was behind him to keep the barrel's pressure on his skin constant. Sensing a subtle tension tremor was the only way he could anticipate the shooter's imminent fire. Byrn intended to put a slug into Zhen before his own brain was blown out of his head.

The assassin didn't mind dying, but he was pissed he'd turn up his toes in China, of all places. It was as though he had never left. Still, if he was going to go, he may as well do it in style.

"You know, Zhen," he began. "There is a kind of poetry in this. You and I checking out together. What could be more appropriate than the two of us descending the stairway to hell hand in hand? To be honest, I should probably lead the way. You see, thanks to you, I've been there before."

"Drop the gun, comrade asshole." The voice from behind. "I won't be saying it again."

Byrn's senses ran on full alert. Every time his assailant spoke, a slight tremor ran through the barrel pressing against him. If the man talked either just before, or while he was in the midst of firing, Byrn wouldn't get a read on it.

Zhen's confidence appeared to falter. He'd begun fidgeting with his hands, a giveaway sign. The agent glanced over Byrn's shoulder at the man behind. Was Zhen trying to send him a signal? The Chinese agent's left hand gradually eased along the leather seat toward the door handle.

"No," snapped Byrn.

Zhen froze.

"You're right, Lachlan. This situation is somewhat volatile. Your death is assured, but mine could go either way. In all honesty, I do believe the odds are weighted heavily on my side."

"Enough," said Byrn. With his hand as steady as a rock, he began to squeeze his trigger gently. Imperceptibly.

The assassin maintained complete control of his features, his expression betraying no emotion. It wasn't that difficult to portray a frozen portrait on the outside when your soul ran as cold as an icecap. Byrn allowed himself a final thought.

'Goodbye, Zhen, you motherfucker, and so long bitch of a world.'

Byrn's grip on the trigger hardened.

In the same split second, three things happened simultaneously.

First, Byrn noted Zhen's forehead furrow. Expected when facing certain death, but the Chinese agent directed his gaze behind Byrn, where there should be no threat.

Second, the cold, hard press of the barrel fell away from the skin on the back of Byrn's neck.

Third, there was a dull thud on the ground at Byrn's rear.

Byrn eased his finger off his trigger.

"Not today, my friend," came a voice.

It wasn't the man who'd had the gun trained on him.

"I hope you don't mind. It seemed an appropriate time for a decisive gesture," the voice continued.

Keeping the QSZ-92 and his eyes trained on Zhen, Byrn smiled.

"You," he responded.

"Yes, Lachlan. Me."

Chapter 17

REGAN DIA

Despite her military training, Regan Dia didn't always do what she was told. When Byrn ordered her the hell out of Xi'an, and the country, she'd fulfilled part of his request. It made sense to leave Xi'an. After witnessing Byrn in action against Zhen's squad in Beijing, she held no doubt who would emerge victorious from the ensuing street battle in the regional city.

The next question was where to now?

Dia caught the high-speed train back to Beijing. No one was looking for her, and unlike Byrn, her Asian features allowed her to blend easily into the human panorama. Once in China's capital, Dia decided to continue her mission. Her boss had instructed her to keep tabs on Byrn and, where possible, observe him in action. That was exactly what she intended to do.

It was a given that Byrn would disappear again, and no amount of hunting around the city would locate him, so Dia needed another strategy. Fortunately, she had one.

Dia's employer was a man of almost infinite resources. He'd been able to supply her with Zhen Su's home address. Dia was unsure if Byrn possessed the same intelligence, but if he did, she knew he would eventually appear. Utilizing her increasingly broadening skill set, she stole a car and made her way out to the Canal Bank enclave in Tongzhou.

The former ranger parked a few hundred yards and several streets away from Zhen's address before proceeding on foot to a point where she could monitor the agent's house. Upon passing through the estate's gated entry, Dia had presented forged papers from the Ministry of National Defense which, as normal, allowed her access almost anywhere she wanted to go. Accordingly, no one took particular note of her. To ensure she fitted in with her environment, she'd stolen an upmarket Mercedes from the Beijing Capital International Airport long term parking lot.

Just another rich bitch in a suburb swarming with them.

On the first day of her surveillance, she'd seen no sign of Byrn. She figured that had no bearing on whether he was there or not. The man knew his shit. Dia witnessed the arrival of both Zhen's supposed family in the afternoon, and Zhen himself in the evening. What surprised her was that when she arrived early on the second morning in a different upmarket stolen vehicle, she noted no sign of Zhen or his family leaving the residence. In Dia's world, what goes up must come down, or in this case, who goes in must come out. It didn't take her long to figure out what was going on.

When she shifted her first surveillance to the street behind Zhen's house later in the day, Dia struck pay dirt. She saw the woman and children leave and climb into their limo. Moving positions, she found a well-camouflaged spot in a garden further down the road and waited for Zhen.

Dia literally almost fell out of her tree when she recognized the familiar outline of a figure zig zagging through the evening shadows before crossing the street. If she didn't have night vision field glasses, she would have missed him altogether. Byrn amazed her. He glided with the stealth of a cat and the visibility of a ghost.

After some time, when the SUV pulled up, and she saw Zhen being led toward it by an armed man, she recognized the leading figure immediately.

Amazing. What gall.

Feigning a rich bitch out for an evening walk, Dia moved in for a closer look. After all, her brief was to observe. She'd made it about thirty yards down the street when the SUV's internal light flicked on. Dia halted her steps and witnessed Byrn, performing at his lethal peak, eliminate the driver, and shift his attention to Zhen. She'd been surprised when another armed operative appeared from the front door of the house before approaching Byrn with considerable stealth. In mere seconds, it became evident that the tables had turned and Byrn was in trouble.

What to do?

Her instructions were clear. Observe and, in no way, become involved in any of Byrn's precarious scenarios. It occurred to Dia that she'd probably already disregarded her boss's expectations through her interaction with Byrn in Xi'an.

She paused and considered the situation.

Byrn seemed clearly unable to free himself from his predicament, and after all, he had saved her skin in Xi'an.

Eventually.

What the hell, 'in for a penny, in for a pound,' as the British loved to say.

Dia moved forward, down the sidewalk, close to the fence line. With the car light on and Byrn's assailant poised with his back to her, she managed to approach the vehicle unnoticed. This was a one-shot deal. If her actions didn't turn the situation around immediately, she would be under no illusion as to the outcome. She would be joining Byrn in drawing her final breath.

The last fence she passed featured a rock lined flower bed out front. The Chinese loved their ornate gardens. Dia scooped down and grabbed a sizable stone. One that was heavy enough to do the job but that she could still manipulate easily.

In three steps, she reached the car, standing directly behind the guard with the pistol pressed against Byrn's neck. She raised the rock. Some part of it must have glinted in the cabin light because Zhen suddenly wriggled in the rear seat looking directly at her, his face betraying his alarm.

Now.

Dia used all her strength to bring her impromptu weapon down on the back of the guard's head.

For a split second, her victim didn't move.

Then he collapsed into the concrete gutter.

Chapter 18

"We'll talk later. Right now, we've got to get Zhen, and us, out of here," said Byrn.

"If you're going to kill him, why not just do it right away? You could use a blade. No one would hear," Dia responded.

Byrn climbed out of the vehicle without taking his eyes off Zhen. The Chinese agent sat despondently; head slumped forward in the rear seat.

Byrn glanced briefly at Dia.

"It's complicated. Way too complicated to explain now. Zhen Su and I need to have a good long talk and he needs to experience a good long death."

"Personal, huh?"

"In the extreme," replied Byrn. "I'd kill him now if I had to, but for me, that would be a disappointing result."

Dia nodded.

"Drag that driver out of his seat and get in," the assassin ordered. "I'll keep an eye on our friend here. That is, if you're happy to be part of the situation you've interrupted?"

"Interrupted," Dia responded, laughing as she ran around the front of the SUV. "I just saved your skinny British ass."

"Point taken. Now let's move. More of Zhen's squad could arrive at any time. I'm surprised they haven't twigged to what's happened yet."

Byrn shoved Zhen over and climbed in beside him, his weapon unwavering. The Chinese agent was smart enough to know that Lachlan Byrn was not a man you challenged physically, unless you were extremely sure of your ground. At this point, Zhen was anything but sure.

"I've got a car around the corner. They won't be familiar with it. We should transfer to that," said Dia.

Byrn considered the option as Dia pulled away from the curb.

"Yes, but not yet. There'll be eyes all over this place. If they don't see this car leave within the next couple of minutes, all hell will break loose. The longer we can delay that, the better. You change over to your car; I'll take Zhen in this one for another couple of miles until we get clear. After that, we'll join you in yours."

"Won't he cause you trouble if you're alone with him and driving?"

Byrn smiled as he flipped the pistol over in his palm and hit the Chinese agent in his temple with such intense force that Dia thought she picked up a bone crack.

"That won't be an issue," replied the assassin.

An hour later, with Dia still at the wheel of the stolen Audi, the trio headed east along the Jingping Expressway. Byrn sat in the back next to Zhen Su, who had regained consciousness. His hands and feet were bound tightly.

"Turn off the expressway right after Liqiao," commanded Byrn. "We've gained as much distance from Tongzhou as we dare risk using the main roads. The Chinese are as proficient in the use of CCTV as any other nation. It's time to go off grid, and where we're going, I don't want to be disturbed."

Dia steered them down an endless series of sideroads, as directed by Byrn. An unsettled silence dominated much of the journey.

Eventually, Byrn decided to sort through some pressing issues.

"You don't give up easily, do you?" he asked.

"You're welcome," Dia responded.

Byrn smirked.

"I won't mince words here. I had you pegged as a problem. Whenever Zhen's goons got a hold of my location, you seemed to be somewhere on the periphery."

"Food for thought," she responded.

"You're not denying it," said Byrn.

Dia glanced at Byrn in the rearview mirror.

"I can't deny facts," she said succinctly.

"Are you admitting you informed Zhen's team of my locations?"

Dia eyeballed him again.

"You can't deny facts either, Lachlan. You tell me. What potential motive could I hold for reporting on your location and then jeopardizing my own safety to protect yours?"

"Protect me?" Byrn sighed. "Your assistance proved helpful, but I would have managed just fine without it," he snapped.

"Define fine."

Byrn didn't comment.

"You know what troubles me?" asked Dia.

Byrn remained silent.

She continued.

"I think you really would have been okay with a bad outcome. The prospect of death doesn't seem to bother you at all."

Byrn pressed his lips together tightly before replying.

"Comes with the job."

Once more Dia eyed him in the mirror.

"No, Lachlan. It comes with the disintegration of your soul."

"Well, hallelujah, praise the fucking Lord. Just drive, will you?" he snapped.

Once again, the silence descended like a cold, damp blanket. They drove on into the night.

Thirty minutes later, still on a reasonably main arterial road, they passed an aging train station.

"Stop here," Byrn ordered.

Dia pulled the car to a halt.

"Do you have money?" he asked her.

"Enough."

"And papers?"

"Sufficient to get me most places I have to go within China and across the borders."

"Then get out."

"What?" she asked, her voice trailing higher in surprise.

"You heard me." Byrn pointed to the car door with his pistol to illustrate the point.

"You may need me."

"I won't. Just step out of the car, and this time, take a train and get the hell out of the country."

"You don't want a witness."

"You've seen enough already," Byrn responded. "No more."

"And how many times have witnesses to your work been allowed to walk free?"

"Not many," he replied.

"Why me?"

"I owe you."

Dia turned to the rear of the car, catching Byrn directly in the eye.

"At last, a thank you."

"Get out," he repeated.

Without a word, Regan Dia opened the driver's door and stepped onto the sidewalk. She strode purposefully toward the station entrance, not looking back.

Byrn waited a couple of moments until she'd disappeared from view. He checked Zhen's binds before stepping onto the street, around the hood of the Audi and into the driver's seat. At no point did the pistol in his pocket stray from his target.

Once settled into position, Byrn quietly revved the engine. He then turned toward his captive in the back seat.

"From now on, my friend, it's all about you."

Even in the dulled reflection of the streetlight, the assassin noted the minute tremor in Zhen Su's hands.

Chapter 19

The headlights' beam flashed across the façade of the old farmhouse. At first glance, Byrn wondered how the decaying wooden walls held up the weight of the ornate tiled roof. Still, he'd been assured by his contact that this property would suit his purposes. The assassin turned the engine off and opened the car door.

"Let's go check out some real estate," he said, turning to Zhen.

The Chinese agent appeared drawn. Dark bags appeared under his eyes and his body sagged, devoid of willpower. Despite that, Byrn gave him credit. Under the assassin's gaze, the man attempted to draw himself up in the seat, as if an assertive posture would disguise the dread he felt.

"Now come on, Lachlan. You've made your point. You know, I can provide you with as much wealth as you want. You'll be able to set yourself up anywhere and live any life you choose. All you need to do is take me back to Beijing and I'll make the arrangements, or at the very least, release me here."

As he spoke, the man seemed to energize himself, as if believing his own words.

Byrn ignored the plea. He climbed out of the car, opened

the rear door, and dragged Zhen out by his jacket collar. After dumping him on the ground, the assassin retrieved his knife from its scabbard and sliced through the ties that bound the agent's feet.

"Don't even think about running, Zhen. We're both aware that it would be a pointless gesture."

"But it might make for a simpler death," replied the captive.

Byrn looked at him, his features crinkled in amusement.

"Nope. Not a chance. A bullet in the ankle to stop you, but then I'd strain my back, dragging you up those stairs. That would make me even more pissed. Is that the result you're chasing?"

Zhen shook his head.

Byrn dragged Zhen to his feet and shoved him forward. "Move."

The assassin took care as they ascended the stairs. He lagged behind Zhen, well aware that the Chinese agent had an arsenal of tricks up his sleeve. He didn't intend to cop a boot in the chin if the man decided to employ his well-honed traditional fighting techniques. Byrn had switched from the blade to the QSZ-92 as insurance.

The timber verandah appeared fragile, the floorboards bending underfoot. Byrn shined his flashlight from his burner phone along its length.

"Through the front door, it's open. Straight ahead, then turn left down the internal staircase."

Byrn had never set foot in the place before, but he'd seen plans of the building and his almost eidetic memory had stored them for ready recall.

Zhen Su walked forward. Slowly. Byrn would have done the same. Every second gained may provide some yet unseen opportunity for escape. Only in this case, the assassin would ensure that any latitude remained out of sight and unattainable.

The internal stairs were only marginally more solid than the external, but they led to a cement landing. Byrn shined his light in a decaying wooden trap door to the right of the space.

"Open it. It won't be locked."

Zhen glanced behind him, catching Byrn's steely glare. The assassin knew that his captor understood that every step forward brought him closer to not only to death, but a level of pain that would frighten the devil himself.

"Move."

Zhen leaned down and yanked the hatch open, laying it over on its hinges to the right. Byrn immediately stamped his foot down on the wooden structure, ensuring Zhen couldn't flick it closed behind him.

"Down."

Byrn cast the light on a rickety timber ladder that disappeared into the darkness. The assassin figured this was probably the most difficult part of the operation. If he let Zhen go ahead, the man could vanish into the blackness below before returning to surprise him. If Byrn stayed too close on the ladder, it wouldn't take much for the Chinese agent to reach up, twist his ankle, and send him spiraling downward.

Lachlan Byrn, however, was a man who thrived on finding solutions to seemingly insurmountable problems. In this instance, the remedy was clear-cut.

The assassin followed Zhen closely down the ladder. He waited until he had a firm grip on the open trapdoor, now at waist height, before thrusting his foot downward like a steel capped torpedo. A surprised cry of pain emanated from the darkness. Byrn stabbed again, this time with his heel. The next sound was a dull thud echoing through the near empty basement as Zhen Su hit the cement floor, totally unconscious.

Brutal but effective.

Byrn descended the remaining rungs of the ladder before reaching the basement floor. He flashed his light toward a wall to his right. As expected, a kerosene lantern hung precariously, attached to the withering stone by two rusty bolts. Byrn shined the light down on the comatose Zhen, currently splayed on the floor. He then strode over to the lamp, pulled a lighter from his pocket, and lit it. After adjusting its wick, the assassin pivoted to survey the room. What he saw pleased him. Once again, the professionalism of his network hadn't let him down.

Byrn was aware that perfection came at a high price, but what the dim light revealed was just that.

Perfection.

Chapter 20

Byrn sat cross-armed on a wooden kitchen chair in the middle of the room and waited. The assassin wasn't in a rush. He'd allocated the remainder of the night and all the next day to the task at hand. He didn't plan to exit the country until the following night. He knew that sooner rather than later, Zhen Su would regain consciousness, and Byrn wanted to be there to welcome him.

Back to his own kind of hell.

The minutes ticked by...

The prisoner didn't understand. He was a free man now. Surely that wasn't a dream. Perhaps it was some sort of trick. They'd plagued his mind with the seeds of bewilderment and confusion before.

Monopolization, isolation, debilitation.

They were masters of the game.

No... not they... him... the interrogator. He was the master.

Was this the ultimate taunt? Set him free only to rein him back in. Remind him of all that he missed and then steal it back. Embed the sensation of breathing fresh air, only to refill his lungs with the dank, putrid dampness of his cell.

Somehow it all seemed wrong, skewed. He'd given them... given him, the interrogator, everything he asked until there was no part of his being left to offer. Why would the man do this?

What more could the prisoner give?

Footsteps. The creak of the heavy door opening. The screeching of the rusty hinges. More footsteps before the predictable clunk as the door swung closed, bolted.

They were only sounds, but to the prisoner, to Byrn, they were more. In sequence they shaped an overture. A clear invitation of expectation. An invitation to hell.

The footsteps grew closer. Then, as always, the interrogator stepped out of the shadows. Any faint hope that it could be someone else was extinguished the moment his features loomed out of the darkness.

The prisoner didn't raise his head. It was an act of futile rebellion. He knew he'd look up in the end. Either that, or the pain they delivered as punishment would tear through him like a ravenous tiger. But he'd wait. He always waited, living in forlorn hope until the last possible moment.

"Lachlan. We've spoken about this. Lachlan, you need to look at me."

The prisoner slowly raised his head, each second he took, providing some perverse kind of sanctuary.

Finally, he opened his eyes, waiting for the disappointment to flood through his broken body.

Suddenly.

No.

This was not the expectation.

No.

What the hell?

The prisoner stared the interrogator directly in the eye, alarm clawing at his skin.

The face.

The interrogator's face... was his own.

Byrn broke the spell.

Well, that was new. The assassin popped a couple of pills and glanced about the basement.

Three feet in front of him, Zhen Su remained chained to a metal chair. Byrn had insisted the chair be metal and there be chains, not ropes.

Authenticity was everything.

Zhen grunted, then began breathing heavily. He pulled his head back, swiveled it around, as if evading something.

Some more grunts. A drawn-out moan. Pain.

Finally, his eyes opened.

Byrn stared at him. The assassin felt his jaw set hard and his lips pressed together in anticipation.

"Hello, Zhen... and welcome."

The assassin allowed his prisoner a couple of minutes to scrutinize his new environment and soak it up. Maybe even appreciate the effort.

He watched patiently while Zhen's lower lip began to quiver. Fear at this level was difficult to conceal.

Byrn wasn't sure whether it was the array of blades laying on the side table next to him, or perhaps the double edged *jian* leaning against it. Of course, it could have been the metal prod in his hand, his grip protected by thick rubber, the other end exposed. The prod alone wouldn't have been enough to provoke Zhen's reaction. The heavy electrical cords leading from the prod to several fully charged batteries would have done the trick. That and the fact the Chinese agent's chair sat perched in a small child's wading pool, full of water.

Byrn smiled as he watched Zhen lift his head.

"It doesn't need to be like this, Lachlan. Please reconsider."

Byrn paused before answering. He and he alone would control the dialog.

Ten seconds dragged past.

"You're requesting me to reconsider, Zhen. And when you were sitting in this chair, how many times did you 'reconsider'?"

Byrn could see his nemesis' brain hard at work behind his eyes. The eyes never lie. The dilation of his pupils betrayed the fear.

That pleased Byrn.

"I set you free," said Zhen. "Others wanted to kill you. I said you would have uses."

"You should have listened to the others, Zhen. Then you might have seen your next birthday."

Again, the assassin paused.

"And that freedom thing, I'm surprised you brought it up. A dog on a chain is not free, no matter how long the chain."

"I have my masters, Lachlan. I must do what I'm told."

Zhen seemed to be mustering strength in his voice, attempting to sound resolute. He hadn't descended to the point of pleading yet. The assassin understood that it was inevitable that time would come. Zhen would know it too.

"I'd like to laugh, Zhen, but I'm afraid it's just not in me right now. You'd be aware the 'simply following orders' defense didn't work at Nuremberg. And I can tell you that I'm a significantly harsher court than they ever were."

The men stared at each other. A comfortable silence for Byrn, less so for Zhen.

Eventually.

"Shall we begin?" asked the assassin.

"I implore you Lachlan…"

Byrn raised a hand.

"I'm going to use a metaphor that I've used before Zhen. I'd hate you to think that I don't have some special experience designed just for you, I certainly do." The assassin waved his free hand across the room as he spoke. "But this particular metaphor always seems so appropriate for an individual who has built his or her own success on the graves of others."

Zhen's shoulders slumped.

The assassin continued.

"Think of me as holding a full-length mirror before you. You are not looking at me, but rather at yourself. Do you see the image? Can you see yourself clearly?"

Zhen remained silent.

"No matter, I believe you can. And you know, you evil prick, that I've sat in your chair and seen exactly what you are staring at many, many times."

Zhen cast his eyes downward.

Byrn raised his voice.

"Don't avert your eyes, you gutless bastard. Face yourself, breathe it in, or there will be consequences." Byrn rolled the prod around in his hands.

Message sent.

Zhen lifted his head but made no comment.

"Now ask yourself Zhen, literally ask yourself, the man you see in our imaginary mirror. Ask him for mercy. Plead with him. Make your case."

More silence.

"There is no point," Zhen's words were barely whispered.

Byrn sat back in his chair.

"No, Zhen, there is no point. I only wish I knew that the moment we first met. Do you remember that time?"

The Chinese agent nodded.

"You professed to have my interests at heart. You said you could help me if I gave you what you wanted. You even offered me friendship. That became a bit of a theme later on, didn't it?"

Zhen nodded again.

Byrn waited. His goal was to ensure the man recognized and valued every moment and nuance of this experience. Zhen had to embrace the anticipation. Fear must become terror.

"Would you like to ask me for my friendship, Zhen? Perhaps offer me your loyalty? Check the mirror. Do you see a man who understands loyalty?"

"I have supported you Lachlan."

Byrn snorted.

"You used me Zhen. You tore me apart physically and then mentally extracted every independent thought and emotion from my being. After that, you sent me to work for you. To do the jobs your people couldn't or wouldn't do. Is that your understanding of loyalty?"

"I was your friend, Lachlan. I am your friend."

The assassin sensed a tremor in his knee, the rumble slowly spreading through his gut. He didn't respond to Zhen's words.

Suddenly, out of nowhere, a torrent of emotion overwhelmed him. Wave upon wave of darkness flooded his thoughts, overpowering his consciousness.

Black. White. Light. Darkness. Rage. Resolution.

Then, nothing.

Zhen Su's anguished scream filled the basement as his cry of pain shook Byrn awake. The assassin's eyes jerked open as he looked down at his prisoner, the *jian* protruding upward from the man's upper thigh, near his testicles. Blood seeped through the jagged cut in his trousers, trailing down his leg and turning the pool of water into a crimson bloodbath. Byrn glanced across at the table beside him. The *jian* wasn't there.

How?

The assassin had no recollection of standing up. He also had absolutely no memory of attacking his prisoner with the sword and plunging it into his flesh.

Zhen continued his wretched wail. Byrn cast the sound aside, out of mind. Inconsequential.

This new issue was unexpected and likely debilitating.

Standing there, shaking, laboring, perspiration oozing from every pore in his skin as he towered over the flailing body of the man who was the root of the assassin's own desolation, led to a single inescapable conclusion.

Lachlan Byrn was losing his mind.

Chapter 21

Neither man spoke.

Zhen, because he couldn't.

Byrn, because he didn't trust himself to.

Finally.

"Well Zhen, I guess we both learned something from that. It appears the term 'friend' coming out of your mouth is somewhat of a trigger word for me."

Zhen's face was a sweaty mess of crinkling skin and bared teeth as he struggled to fight the pain.

"Here, allow me," said Byrn as he leaned forward to withdraw the sword. "Oh, it seems to be stuck in some sinew or something. I might have to jiggle it around a bit."

The anguished cry from Zhen's lips made his first reaction sound like a love song. As Byrn retrieved the blade, the man's tone became deeply, angrily, guttural… just before he passed out.

Byrn sat there, transfixed, not on any object, but on the trappings of his own mind.

There were behaviors going on here which had never happened before on the job. The flashbacks. First while he lay in wait to kidnap Zhen in the garden at Canal Bank, and then here, while he waited for Zhen to come around.

Unacceptable distractions.

Now this impulsive, impromptu attack. The violence of Byrn's action didn't appall him at all. His issue was with the execution. Specifically, the fact the assault was unplanned. He'd simply snapped. Blacked out. It was clear that he'd lashed out yet had no recollection of the event. Byrn just didn't work that way. He controlled every professional situation. Impulse wasn't how he rolled. So, what the hell had just happened?

Glad that Zhen's unconsciousness offered some respite, Byrn considered the implications.

Ten minutes passed before the assassin attempted to draw any conclusions. Clearly, he was too close to this. He hadn't lost control like that since the moment he murdered his father when he was a kid. Back then, the cruel bastard had been brutally attacking his sister. Byrn had done what he needed to do, without thought or planning. Byrn chortled to himself as he considered the field day a psychiatrist would have comparing the two relationships: Zhen, his father. What a swamp.

Did this change things? Was Zhen Su still so immersed inside Byrn's head that the assassin couldn't move forward in his usual controlled manner?

Borderline call.

Should he proceed as planned?

Too fucking right. He'd come too far to back down on any level.

'All right, get a grip on yourself and proceed,' he told himself.

Perhaps Zhen, even when facing certain death, was still

attempting to control Byrn, to influence him. Okay, caution required.

Byrn took a few moments to steady himself. It was a new sensation. Eventually, he felt ready. It was time to do what he did best… kill.

Again, the process was repeated. Zhen groaned himself into consciousness. Byrn tapped his foot impatiently. He wanted to get on with this.

While his prisoner had been comatose, Byrn had wrapped an old rag tightly around the man's upper leg to stem the bleeding. Infection was of no consequence.

"So, shall we move forward? I fear we'll both have to choose our words carefully."

Now fully awake, Zhen stared into Byrn's eyes.

"Kill me."

"Ah, acceptance. That's good progress my fr…. old chum," Byrn replied. "However, in response, I would refer you back to our period of reflection. How often did I ask you to kill me?"

Silence.

"Answer me, you scum," spat Byrn, his simmering anger evident. "Back in those dark putrid cells, through endless interrogations, how many times did I implore you, beg you, plead with you to take my life?"

Nothing

"Answer."

Byrn stared down at Zhen's fresh wound, as did his captive. The assassin began to lean forward.

"Many", Zhen responded.

Byrn sat back.

"How many?"

"More than I can remember."

Byrn leaned forward again, this time slapping the man on his injured thigh with the palm of his hand. Zhen's broken scream penetrated the room.

"Well, I can remember. I implored you every single day for nearly three years to kill me, to show some level of mercy."

Zhen nodded.

"Look in our mirror," Byrn ordered. "How frequently did the man you see display any form of compassion?"

Zhen tilted his head and inhaled deeply.

"Whatever I say will make no difference to the outcome here."

"Perhaps not. In fact, definitely not. But your words may have some impact on the levels of pain you are exposed to."

Zhen nodded slowly.

"I showed no humanity, no mercifulness."

"Got that in one, bucko. At last, a morsel of truth."

Byrn sensed a familiar unsettling swell within his own gut.

He waited a full two minutes before continuing.

"Zhen, I want you to look around you. Absorb your surroundings. When you are ready, I need you to describe this environment for me."

Now, somewhat malleable from the pain, Zhen complied with the direction. His gaze wandered across the basement, taking in the array of blades next to Byrn, the *jian*, now laying on the concrete floor, the prod, the batteries and the hammer and small axe underneath his captor's chair.

"I see implements capable of great pain and torture, tools that, if employed in the right manner, could break a man's soul."

Byrn allowed the edges of his lips to crease.

"I'd put it more simply. I see symmetry."

Zhen nodded imperceptibly. Reluctant acceptance.

"So, where to now? If you were in charge, Zhen, where would you begin?"

"You will do what you will do. You have no need for my direction."

Once again, Byrn sensed the fury slowly rising within him, but this time, he was aware of it. He would work with the monster, as he always did. He leaned forward, so close that Zhen would sense the breath on his face. While the man stared ahead, Byrn, unseen, reached down and picked up the hammer under his chair.

In a single, swift action, the assassin brought the tool down hard on Zhen's wrist. The snap of bone cracked across the room.

Zhen snorted rather than screamed. But he maintained his focus on Byrn's face.

"It is as I would have begun," Zhen gasped. "A sharp and painful cue, prompting the captive to understand to whom he has been subjugated."

"Thank you, master, you have taught me well," Byrn responded mockingly. Then he spat in the agent's face.

And waited.

Byrn understood. To his captor, the ensuing silence would be terrifying. The anticipation of extreme suffering, almost worse than the pain itself.

Soon, he would commence the second stage. The relentless waves of violence. Consistently approaching the verge of no return, then reversing course, only to restart the journey. Layering the suffering like a birthday cake. From now on, he'd ensure the subject remained conscious throughout. Byrn was aware that Zhen would not only appreciate the sensation, but it would eat at him, an aggressive cancer devouring him from inside his very being.

The interrogator had lived through it all before, only this time the perspective was crucially different.

Symmetry.

Byrn closed his eyes momentarily. As he did, the immediate disturbance of a throbbing darkness surging within him began to beat hard on his chest. From the inside, trying to get out.

Let the monster do its work.

Deep in Byrn's soul, the turbulence grew with surprising intensity. The assassin felt himself begin to shake. First a small tremor, then something more.

His skin burned hot, as though his own blood was boiling him alive. The rage, now developing into a blinding fury, escalated through him, rallying with each passing second.

What the hell was happening? Check yourself, man. Maintain your footing.

The reins were slipping through Byrn's fingers.

He gasped, inhaling deeply, hoping the fresh oxygen would bring strength. All he breathed was dank, stale air.

Sweat hemorrhaged from every pore, his life force fleeing its host.

Across from him, Zhen Su smiled. Suddenly, everything was different.

"Lachlan, look at me. I'm the only one who can help you."

Dependence. Even now, Zhen attempted to manipulate him, as though he alone could take Byrn's pain away.

Byrn fought hard. This was his party. He wouldn't allow

Zhen to crash it.

"Lachlan."

"Fuck you, Zhen."

"Lachlan, there is no one else here to assist you."

Isolation.

The interrogator's voice grew in confidence, sounding firmer, more assured.

No. Byrn was the interrogator here. *He* had quarantined Zhen from his comfortable world. What sort of mind fuck was happening to him? His brain seemed like a computer memory card where all the new data blended haphazardly with the old. He saw only gibberish. Sort the files, man. Get some order.

The assassin sensed himself rocking backward and forward in his chair.

Sit rep. He'd followed the plan meticulously. Zhen was alone and debilitated. Byrn owned the room. How the hell had Zhen Su suddenly flicked a switch inside Byrn's own mind? Maybe Byrn hadn't decanted the Chinese agent's programming as effectually as he'd thought. Had Zhen left a time bomb ticking deep inside his psyche?

"Lachlan, you must trust me."

Out of nowhere, the sudden explosion in Byrn's mind sent waves of searing agony catapulting through his head. He was blinded by the darkness.

Sweat streamed down his face.

Through squinted eyes, Byrn caught sight of Zhen's face. His captor's demeanor had changed. He now leaned back in his chair as far as possible, his expression open in terror. For a fleeting second Byrn thought, 'you should see it from this side'. There was nowhere to go. This wasn't an attack; it was an eruption.

Byrn pressed his hands against his head, as if the eruption could be terminated from the outside.

The pressure was building… building… in his head, his veins, every part of him. He felt himself gag as his airways succumbed to a vice-like pressure. Any moment now…

Byrn fought with every ounce of strength he could muster. He pushed the air through his lungs, a debilitated man shoveling a heavy load.

"Fuck it." The words barreled out of the assassin's mouth like a raging tornado.

"Fuck you all…"

Lachlan Byrn reached desperately into his jacket, probing for his pistol. It was the only way. His fingers touched the polymer grip. He yanked at it frantically.

Then it was there, in his palm. Yet, the man with the steadiest aim on the planet saw only the tremor of the barrel, yielding to his own quivering hand.

What the….

The pain gnawed at his brain like a drunken vulture. A cocoon of darkness enveloped him. The anger spewed from his open mouth, flames of torment.

Zhen screamed, "Lachlan, listen to me as your…."

Byrn raised the weapon, holding it to his temple, the cold steel pressed against his burning skin.

Through the veil of cascading sweat, Byrn caught a glimpse of Zhen's shoulders sagging, his wide-eyed terror transforming into a sneer. Relief.

Suddenly, in a blinding, frozen second, Byrn understood the fight. He could see the enemy. But it wasn't Zhen Su.

Then the darkness eclipsed him, vanquishing hope. Only

the tiniest speck of light lay ahead, just out of reach. Unattainable.

"No, fuck you. Not now."

The shaking erupted into convulsions, a killer out of control. Byrn had fought hard, but the battle was lost. Yet he examined the tiny glimmer, willing himself toward it. A warrior's imprudent determination.

Then, unexpectedly, a surge of strength empowered his forearm. He twisted his wrist and swung the pistol around, his finger still resting on the trigger.

He had just one job.

"You son of a bitch."

Lachlan Byrn squeezed the trigger, instantaneously a small red dot appeared on Zhen Su's forehead.

Then everything went dark… and silent.

Chapter 22

The drive to the border was long and arduous. The passing countryside and the intermittent towns faded into a distorted blur as Byrn pushed the car along the road. The vehicle's headlights showed the way forward. All Byrn needed to do was follow them.

The assassin had spent the day cleaning up the house and disposing of Zhen's body, now buried deep in a field a decent distance from the farmhouse. He'd waited until nightfall to begin his journey. That had always been the plan.

Back in a predictable routine, Byrn sensed his usual calmness return.

He'd regained consciousness slumped in the chair in front of Zhen's bloodied body. The assassin couldn't recall every detail of the kill, yet he recalled enough to scare himself.

Byrn thought he'd handled each psychological twist and turn that challenged him in his life. There had been a shit load of issues to deal with. He'd confronted most and discarded the rest as inconsequential.

After exhausting all aspects of normal human emotion from his soul, Byrn found his solace.

In the act of killing.

The assassin held no illusions. He was broken. But even

broken machines can be put to alternative uses. As a normally functioning human, he was obviously irreparable. But there were other roles he could fulfill. Roles that involved his unusual skills and controlled temperament. Killing people offered him everything he needed.

Job satisfaction.

A reason to exist.

Solace.

Besides, he just loved the work.

While his internal processes demanded some focus, Byrn remained aware enough of his surroundings to perform routine tasks. Like driving. As he approached another small community, Huajianzi Town, according to the sign, he turned left, skirting the main drag and following several deserted side streets until he rejoined the highway on the far edge of the community. The less attention, the better.

The detours were necessary, although time constraints loomed. The assassin needed to meet his contact before sunrise if he was to make it across the border without unwanted delay.

Back on the open road, he refocused. The human computer sorting the internal data.

But what of the attack? Zhen Su was now dead, but the process Byrn followed wasn't what he'd planned, and that almost never happened. Every kill was engineered to within an inch of its life. What the hell went wrong this time?

Byrn knew the answer, but equally he was aware he needed to take a few sideroads to arrive at his final mental destination.

Just like this road trip, in his head, there were borders to cross.

Byrn was fortunate to progress the kill to its rightful conclusion. Whatever the hell had gotten hold of him was a powerful and unpredictable beast. He hadn't experienced an attack like that for a long time, if ever. Yet for some reason he now felt exhausted but cleansed, as though some burden had been lifted from his shoulders.

Clearly, Zhen Su lived in Byrn's head far more than he realized. The assassin never sought professional help after his years of captive torture, nor would he ever. He'd gone cold turkey and dealt with the incessant darkness in his own way. Judging from the previous evening's events, he'd missed some crucial steps. Obviously, Zhen managed to maintain some sort of hold over the assassin without him even realizing it.

But that wasn't really the problem. That train of thought was just another sideroad.

Byrn had fought the overwhelming power to self-destruct. It hadn't been easy. If he was honest with himself, that fight never proved easy. Either throughout his earlier life or in that dark basement with Zhen.

Had the assassin been warned that whatever brainwashing techniques Zhen had brought into play over the years would have made it difficult for him to kill the man, Byrn would only have been mildly surprised. If he'd been told that he would overcome the difficulty presented and successfully take Zhen's life, he wouldn't have been shocked at all.

Any other outcome would have been bitterly disappointing.

The thing, the real issue that perplexed Byrn, was that the assassin discovered the war he'd been fighting was with himself.

It wasn't about Zhen living or dying.

It was about the way Zhen died.

Byrn briefly released the wheel and retrieved a bottle of water from the car's console. He flipped it open and took a long swig, his eyes never leaving the road ahead.

Resting the bottle between his legs, he delved into his coat pocket, his fingers touching the familiar plastic container. He flicked its lid, removed a couple of pills, and hurled them into his mouth before washing them down with some more water.

This wasn't a time to sleep. On any level.

The way Zhen died.

Byrn had planned a long and painful death for the Chinese agent. He'd gone to a great deal of trouble and cost to arrange for all the required implements to be in place. His intention was to recreate the hostile environment in which Zhen drove Byrn to incredible depths of horror and despair.

Conditions beyond a normal person's imagination. Whatever a normal person was.

The assassin acknowledged that he would only have twenty-four hours to implement a regime that Zhen took nearly three years to perfect, but he was certain he could do it.

Until he couldn't.

That was the issue.

As Byrn's intricate mental process unveiled itself through the murky swamp of his psyche, the assassin 'humphed' out loud.

Who would have thought?

Throughout his time in captivity, under Zhen's control, one idea, a single guiding light, provided Byrn with the impetuous to carry on, to survive.

He was better than Zhen.

He needed to be better than Zhen.

It was the only way that Byrn, a prisoner with no rights, no voice, no physical strength, could keep going.

Somewhere inside, he must be a better man than Zhen Su. The interrogator.

Byrn told himself that over and over again. In his sleep and during the sessions with Zhen when the agony became overwhelming, and the torment insufferable. When the guards threw him the minute scraps of food designed to sustain life at the most basic level. When every vestige of dignity deserted him.

He was better than Zhen.

Lachlan Byrn, or whatever the hell was left of him, was stronger than Zhen Su, master interrogator.

Byrn pressed his lips tightly together and gripped the steering wheel unyieldingly, like a lifebuoy.

The punchline.

That moment.

Somewhere amongst the torrent of conflict passing through his head the night before, Byrn experienced some sort of epiphany.

If he proceeded according to plan and subjected Zhen Su to the same level of torture, humiliation, and indignity that he himself experienced at Zhen's hand, then he would be no better at all. Byrn killed for information. He'd inflicted pain when his victims were reluctant to see where they'd erred, usually before he took their life. Byrn had done more bad things than he could recall, but he never tortured someone for a prolonged period just for the satisfaction of witnessing their suffering.

If he did that, Lachlan Byrn would have been the same as Zhen.

No reason to live.

No reason to survive.

A moral vacuum.

Byrn was a killer, but he was not Zhen Su.

Go figure.

The assassin pressed down hard on the gas pedal and drove into the night.

Chapter 23

As the first shafts of sunlight lit the neighboring mountains, Byrn pulled the Audi to a halt in the parking lot of a disused factory in an industrial neighborhood of Ji'an. The Yalu River bordered the town, separating it from its regional neighbor, Manpo, over the border in North Korea.

It was a tried-and-true route that Byrn had used before, back in the days when he worked for Zhen, yet still spent considerable time in China.

A world ago.

After walking for an hour in semi-darkness, the assassin waited in shadows at the designated spot, an out of service gas station on the edge of town. Eventually, Byrn heard the deep chug of a large diesel motor approaching along the road. He pressed himself back against the wall and stood tight.

The engine grew louder, its roar replaced by the squeal of heavy-duty brakes as the Sungri container truck pulled up. The assassin waited as the driver alighted from the truck's cab and walked around to the vehicle's rear. He climbed up onto the truck's deck and unlocked the large steel forty-foot container that dominated the space. As the door swung open, the assassin stepped out of the darkness, heading straight toward the opening. After raising himself up, he extended his closed palm toward the driver. Not a gesture of greeting. The American dollars passed cleanly from hand to hand. No words exchanged.

The man gestured toward the back of the empty container. The assassin stepped inside, seeing nothing but blank space. Edging quickly in front of him, the driver reached the rear wall before the assassin, bending down to release a catch secured almost invisibly in the partition just above the floor. A small hatch, about two feet square, opened. The driver delved into his pocket and produced a flashlight. He offered it to Byrn before gesturing toward the opening. Byrn took the light, crouched down, and climbed through.

As the clunk of the metal hatch echoed behind him, the assassin shined the flashlight's beam around the space. Taking up the width of one end of the container and about three feet in depth, the small room contained a mattress, a deck chair, an electric light connected to three car batteries, a crate of bottled water and canned juice, numerous cans of tinned food and a camp toilet in the far corner. Byrn knew that enough airs holes had been surreptitiously created to let an adequate amount of fresh air flow into the steel prison.

The assassin sat down on the mattress. Some clanging and banging resonated through the metal walls. The driver would be sealing any evident cracks around the hatch with an epoxy-type substance before touching up the paint to match the rest of the wall.

Fifteen minutes later, Byrn felt the lurch as the truck pulled out of the gas station. A short time after that, the vehicle lunged upward over some sort of curb before stopping. Suddenly, there was a great deal of commotion outside. Men were yelling and the vehicle's platform seemed to bounce around as if pounded by heavy weights.

The assassin remained unconcerned.

Once the truck was loaded and the internal wall fully concealed, the real journey would begin. After less than an hour, everything went quiet save for the revving of the truck's diesel. Another lurch and the vehicle shunted forward.

Byrn lay on the mattress and closed his eyes. He hadn't bothered to switch on the light. It would be many days before he would see daylight again. He may as well get used to the darkness. Countless hours by road to the North Korea port of Chongjin. The container would be loaded onto a ship that would cross the Sea of Japan, eventually making port in Yokohama. It would then be transferred to another, larger vessel before the seventeen-day voyage across the North Pacific Ocean to its final destination.

San Francisco, USA. The land of the free.

Byrn knew the journey well. He'd done it before. The assassin would have a lot of time alone in the darkness to come to grips with recent events.

One in particular bothered him.

Who the hell was Regan Dia?

Chapter 24

"You've disappointed me."

"I know."

"I expected more from you, or perhaps in this case I should say less."

"I understand, sir."

Dia's boss stood in front of the floor to ceiling window that towered above Central Park. Despite his lack of height, his presence commanded attention in any company. Dia had witnessed others deferring to him time and time again. He hadn't even bothered turning around as he spoke to her.

Conscious disrespect.

Despite not seeing his face, she appreciated his aged and crinkled skin would now be etched into a frown. If anything, she was glad to avoid his death-ray stare.

Until she wasn't. He turned to meet her gaze.

"Dia, had I not been specific in my instructions? Your role was to observe and not participate in any events that may take place. Is it that difficult for someone who used to be in the military to follow orders?"

Dia shifted uneasily on her feet. Not many people caused

her to do that.

"In my defense, sir, the first instance was not of my doing. I was attacked in an alley. Byrn attempted to come to my aid."

The old man frowned even more.

"Attempted?"

"His help wasn't required."

The smallest hint of a smile.

"And the second time?"

"For anyone in Byrn's profession, the odds will eventually catch up with you. That's why most assassins don't retire to a comfortable life. In this case, a random and unforeseeable element turned the situation against the man."

The old man continued his penetrating gaze. Dia wondered how many people had stood on this very spot while he stared through to their soul.

"He couldn't have recovered from the predicament unaided, as you did previously?"

"It was a completely different scenario, sir. A different caliber of opponent. There was a chance that Byrn could have turned things around, but given your interest in the man, I thought it best to intervene."

Dia's boss remained motionless; his eyes locked with hers. Behind them, she knew she was being judged.

Eventually.

"You're good with words Dia. You are trying hard to turn this situation around."

"I speak it as I see it, sir."

Another pause. Then the old man turned, circled his desk and sat down. He waved at the chair opposite.

"Sit down."

It appeared she still had a job, so she sat.

"So, tell me your impressions. What do you think of this man, Byrn?"

Dia considered her response.

"Without doubt, I consider him to be the most deadly and efficient killer I've ever witnessed in action, and I've seen a few. Lachlan Byrn is also smart. His intelligence is way beyond a normally well-trained operative. But..."

Dia's words trailed off as she weighed her next statement.

"But..." repeated the old man.

Dia sat up straight in her chair.

"But something is missing. Inside him, something is not quite right."

"A mental issue."

"Not in the conventional way, but he doesn't have the same thought process as you and I." Dia paused. "It's as though he regards death as a perpetual challenge. If I was a poet, which I'm clearly not, I'd say he treats death as his dance partner."

The old man smiled.

"You're smitten."

"No, sir. I'm perplexed. But I can tell you this. After seeing him in action, I can honestly say that if you or anyone else were seeking out a ruthless killer, Byrn is not only the best, but also the most strategic in his approach. Everything he does is planned and considered."

"Interesting." Dia's boss reclined in his chair, deep in contemplation, as he stroked his chin. She knew better than to interrupt the process.

"I want you to bring him to me," he said.

Involuntarily, she chuckled, then quickly gagged her reaction.

"I don't think I'll have to, sir."

"What do you mean by that?"

Once more, Dia hesitated. The information she was about to reveal could make or break the relationship with her boss, which in result could lead her to seek employment elsewhere. She didn't particularly want to leave his employ, yet she couldn't avoid facts that were staring her in the face.

"Byrn believed that I had betrayed him," she started. "He suggested that every time I was in the area, Zhen Su's people seemed to turn up out of the blue."

"Was that the case, Dia?"

Another pause.

"I think that you know it was, sir."

Dia briefly noticed a hint of hesitation in the old man's expression, a subtle widening of the eyes. Then it was gone.

"Explain yourself," he said curtly.

Dia took a deep breath.

"I didn't pass information on Byrn's whereabouts to anybody… except you, sir."

Stony silence.

"Are you inferring that I have some way of communicating with Chinese intelligence personnel and informed them of Lachlan Byrn's location, Dia?"

"Well, you are in the communications business," she responded.

"That is a very serious allegation."

"With respect, sir, this is a very serious business."

Dia sat upright in the chair, waiting to be dismissed by her soon to be former boss.

Surprisingly, a broad grin appeared on his face.

"Well, Regan. I can inform you that you are completely correct."

Dia was stunned. Even though she'd assumed her conclusion to be right, hearing the old man admit it openly was, at the least, surprising.

"May I ask why you passed on that intelligence, sir?"

The old man looked at her, his glazed eyes betraying wheels turning behind them.

"I needed to see how good Byrn really was. Assessing his performance under pressure was crucial, even if we had to create the pressure ourselves."

"Again, with respect, sir, there is no 'we' here. I knew he was good, and most certainly I would not have consciously contributed to placing someone in needless jeopardy."

The old man laughed.

"For God's sake, Dia. Get real. The man is a killer. We had to see him kill. It was imperative that we saw how he operated."

"You will have my resignation on your desk by the end of business today, sir."

The old man's face darkened.

"Again, Dia, get with the plan. Where else is someone with your special skills going to earn the money I pay you? I suggest you reconsider your position." Her superior's voice was jagged and hard.

Dia watched as his shoulders relaxed and he put both hands on the desk in front of him. A sign of reconciliation.

"I'll tell you what. How about I give you my word that any additional communication involving your operations will be run past you beforehand? That's the best I can do."

Compromise from a man who never compromised.

"I'll consider it, sir."

"Fair enough," he replied. "Now, back to your original point.

Why don't you think you'll need to bring Lachlan Byrn in to meet with me?"

Dia leaned forward.

"Number one, sir, I suspect nobody brings Lachlan Byrn anywhere he doesn't want to go. Number two, as I mentioned, Byrn is an extremely intelligent man. Because I saved his ass in Beijing, he will have doubts that I was acting the part of Judas. He will look elsewhere. And that road inevitably leads to you, sir."

The old man's skin suddenly paled.

"Did you tell him you worked for me?"

"Of course not."

"Then how will he find out?"

Dia decided to make the most out of the moment. She stood up and strolled over to the large window. The park below appeared stunning in the early evening light. She couldn't fathom the cost of having an office here, let alone owning the entire building. As she spoke, she looked out the window, not at the old man. A trick learned.

"Everything I've researched about this man tells me he's resourceful and thorough. If the rumors are correct, he's managed to take out both the US Secretary of Defense and the president of the Russian Federation with no significant backlash. My understanding is that if he's crossed, either by an enemy or a client, he responds with merciless retribution."

Dia continued to stare ahead. She didn't need to turn around to appreciate the impact of her words on her employer. The old man, who dedicated his life to controlling finances, information, business, and governments, was about to encounter an unprecedented threat. She carried on speaking.

"Sir, I will not only be unable to go and 'fetch' Byrn, but I won't need to. The glaringly obvious fact is that he is going to come after you."

Silence.

"Then you must stop him."

Dia pivoted to face her boss.

"Sir, once his mind is made up, I don't believe anyone is capable of stopping Lachlan Byrn."

The old man gazed up at his operative, the stare no longer death-ray.

"Damn it."

Chapter 25

LACHLAN BYRN

Byrn scrunched his eyes against the blinding Californian sunlight.

He stepped out of the empty container into the vast industrial yard. The steel metal box sat amongst dozens of others, well away from the main port area and the watchful gaze of US Customs and Border Protection.

Byrn liked San Francisco. He figured it had more character than most US cities, but it also had its fair share of violence and crime. The assassin didn't plan on hanging around for too long, but before continuing his journey, he needed to do some research. Byrn never acted without all the available intelligence at hand.

The immediate task was to create some distance between the container yard and himself. The assassin was under no illusion about the usual nature of the work undertaken by the crew who brought him here. People smuggling. It was a nasty business run by individuals with the ethics of an alley cat. Byrn had paid good money in advance for his extraction from China. He knew that the authorities would be looking for him and that conventional means of travel were out of the question. That said, he still held those responsible for getting him to the US in contempt and didn't trust them one bit. There were operators in his numerous networks around the globe on whom he could depend. Those who dealt in human trafficking were not on that list.

Once sufficiently distant from the area, he hailed a cab, instructing the driver to head toward the San Francisco Public Library in Mission Bay. It amazed Byrn that authorities continually looked for assassins and rogue operatives in all the wrong places. What better place to search for information and lose yourself in a crowd than in a public library?

Thirty minutes later, Byrn stood at the library's circular reception desk, presenting his false ID to gain internet access. The library receptionist was a tall young lady with long, dark hair and a welcoming smile. Byrn didn't shower on the way, so he wasn't surprised when, although still smiling, she stepped back from the counter when confronted by a bearded and smelly stranger.

"I do apologize, Narissa," said Byrn, glancing at the attendant's name tag. "I've just arrived after a long bus trip from the east coast and haven't been to my hotel to shower and change yet. My cell has run down, and I need some internet access before cleaning up.

Narissa grinned some more, placated by the explanation.

Seated a good distance from any onlookers, Byrn began his search. After a decent night's sleep in a comfortable bed, the assassin would restock the vital tools of his trade, including some burner phones. In the meantime, there was work to be done. Nearly three weeks of being out of touch with the world required some catching up.

First, he checked the Chinese news sites for any information regarding the missing Zhen Su. As expected, nothing. No intelligence agency likes to air their dirty laundry in public. Byrn relegated that mission as a job done before moving on.

Byrn had lied to the girl at the desk. His one remaining cell phone was still operational, he just wanted to keep its use to a minimum. Ensuring his back shielded the phone from the attendant, he turned it on and waited. He called up the photo he'd taken of Dia without her knowledge and uploaded it into his facial recognition app. The biometric tool was incredibly accurate. It quickly scanned several social media sites before moving onto the wider internet.

Within a minute, Byrn had confirmed that the woman he knew was really Regan Dia. Only one news article appeared in relation to her, but it provided all the evidence he required. It was a 'puff piece' from a military news outlet celebrating Dia's graduation from Ranger training and included a picture. It perplexed Byrn that in this day and age, women succeeding in traditionally men's professions was still a topic of discussion. Still, he supposed it *was* news to those thugs in the alley back in Xi'an. The assassin turned off his phone and began a traditional internet search for Dia's name using the library computer.

Several hits quickly appeared on the screen. The woman he spent time with was not the only Regan Dia, so the assassin started eliminating candidates based on nationality. Although Dia was of Asian heritage, she was definitely American. That narrowed the field.

First, Byrn attached the term US military to Dia's name. Nothing came up apart from the original article. It wasn't surprising. To Byrn's knowledge, there was no public database that could be used to find active-duty military personnel or retirees. Still, he had to try. The next step was to search common social media platforms using her name. Again, little of relevance turned up. Also, unsurprising. An operator of Dia's experience wouldn't plaster her identity all over the web.

With no useful information appearing, Byrn tried another tack.

He returned to his cell, this time expanding the facial recognition search to include background and distant shots. It would mean more mishits, but it could also bring further intelligence. Twenty minutes later, the assassin had two hits that piqued his curiosity. Dia appeared in the background of two photographs, but to Byrn, the point of interest was the figure in the foreground of both shots.

The face was iconically familiar.

Byrn shut off his cell and typed foreground man's name into a general internet search. The screen exploded with information.

Byrn sat back in his chair and considered the situation.

What on earth was an ex special operative doing in the company of Randal Byers, arguably the most powerful media magnate on the planet?

Byrn logged off the house computer, stood up, and strolled over to the reception desk. He logged out of the library using the same false name he'd signed in with.

An hour later, the assassin sat in a semi-comfortable chair in a small hotel room near the docks. The place had seen better days, as had the threadbare carpet beneath his feet. He stared into the exposed light bulb, which emanated the only brightness in the space.

His mind scrolled through the possibilities. Slowly, a plan emerged.

Byrn would rest now and catch American Airlines' 11.16 p.m. red eye out of San Francisco International. The flight should get him into JFK around 7.00 a.m.

For Lachlan Byrn, things had just got interesting. For Randal Byers, the assassin anticipated that life was about to become significantly more difficult.

Chapter 26

Byrn's eyes snapped awake. He glanced at his watch. 7 p.m. Three hours wasn't enough sleep, but the assassin understood the reason a full night's rest would elude him until the job was done. It was the smell of blood. Once it permeated his nostrils, Byrn would remain restless, unsatiated. A hunter's instinct.

The assassin was famished. With ample time to spare, he quickly rinsed his face, grabbed his wallet, and headed out the door. Any food he could find nearby would surpass the plastic garbage offered at the airport.

He made his way east down Cesar Chavez Street, toward Pier 80 and the central waterfront area. Byrn spotted a Mediterranean restaurant right before the interchange and was about to cross the road toward it when he heard raised voices. They seemed to be coming from behind some trees bordering a park on the far side of the intersection just ahead.

Not his problem.

Suddenly a kid, a boy, scrambled out of the shadows. Before the kid could find his feet and take off, a hefty sized man appeared behind him, grabbed the boy by his collar and hoisted him back behind the trees. The kid let out an almighty scream.

Not Byrn's problem.

Out of idle curiosity, Byrn peered toward the shadows. He could just make out the outline of a second man. He wasn't as massive as the first but seemed equally menacing. His silhouette revealed one hand thrust forward, holding some kind of blade.

Damn.

Byrn didn't need the complication, but he had been cooped up for some time, and needed some exercise. He crossed the road, striding purposefully toward the park. As his intentions became obvious, the men looked up. The larger man retained his hold on the kid.

"Is there a problem here?" asked Byrn, staring the big guy directly in the eye.

Byrn could see the child was only eleven or twelve, and his face was screwed up in terror.

"Please, mister…."

"Ain't no problem that concerns you, buddy," the man interrupted, dragging the kid with him so that they stood between Byrn and the guy with the knife. The kid yelped as the man's grip grew tighter.

"Best let the kid go," said Byrn.

"Go back to whatever fucking country you came from, and mind your own damn business," snarled the man.

Byrn smiled but didn't move an inch.

"Your powers of observation are impressive. Good job picking up my British accent. However, I won't be returning to my home country tonight."

The guy grunted.

"Your mistake, stranger. Take one more step closer to us and we'll take care of you and this little brat who lifted my wallet."

Byrn turned toward the kid.

"Is that true, son? Did you steal his wallet?"

The child hesitated. Byrn figured that from where he was standing, all he could see was trouble coming his way from every direction.

"But I gave it back," the kid replied.

"Yeah, sure you did, you little punk. Just as soon as we caught you with it."

The kid said nothing more. Smart.

Byrn turned in the direction of the man.

"Okay, you've proved your point. You've got your wallet back and scared the shit out of this kid. You and your mate aren't seriously going to cut him as well?"

"What we are or aren't going to do is none of your business, dickface." The man with the knife had now stepped out from behind his comrade. Even in the fading light, Byrn noted his dark, lifeless eyes and lips permanently set in a snarl. "So just keep on moving, or we'll share the joy with you, too."

He waved the knife in front of him.

Byrn sighed. He'd done his best. He looked toward the restaurant across the street, imagining himself settling into a tasty pasta. Sweet dreams.

He turned and took a step in the direction of the eatery and away from the men.

"Please, mister," the kid called out.

Byrn took another step.

"Smart call, asshole," shouted the big man.

Byrn stopped, inhaled deeply, and let his shoulders slump. Still facing along the road, he turned his head toward the man. The boy was visibly shaking, but the large man held him close.

"You know," the assassin began. "It's people like you, the scum of this planet, that actually make me feel like a moral individual, and that's pretty hard to do."

The big man's offsider, knife still in hand, appeared surprised at Byrn's words. He lifted his eyebrows and ever so tightly tilted his head. Confusion.

As he spoke Byrn let his right-hand slip down the side of his leg, retrieving his diving knife from its scabbard. A second later he hurled the blade across the space between them. It landed directly in the knifeman's throat. The man died with the same confused expression on his face.

As his victim lay on the sidewalk, gargling blood, Byrn closed the distance between himself and the larger man. As he charged ahead, he lowered his left shoulder, propelling himself straight into the guy's gut. As the man swayed backwards, Byrn grabbed one of his ankles and yanked it forward. The thug relinquished his grip on the child and crumpled to the ground with a thud.

"Get out of here, kid, and not a word to anyone," yelled the assassin.

"You got it, mister... and thanks."

The kid bolted down the road.

The big man had gone down, but he wasn't staying down.

"You asshole, you've killed Danny. You're gonna pay..."

Nothing further came from the man as Byrn stomped his foot down on his throat.

The thug exhaled a gurgling wheeze before rolling onto his side, gasping for clear air.

Byrn stood upright above him. The issue was what to do with this moron now. Whatever he did would have to be quick. Does he live or die? the assassin asked himself.

A second later, the big guy answered the question for him.

As he rolled onto his back, the man revealed a Colt .38 revolver at his waist, pointed directly at Byrn. The gun looked old, but Byrn knew that made it no less lethal.

"Looks like you're gonna get to apologize to Danny sooner than you figured, asshole."

Byrn raised his arms in surrender, staring darkly into the man's eyes. They were wide and round and filled with hatred. Yet Byrn detected no sign of panic behind them. This guy had killed before.

The situation had turned on a dime. Byrn bit into his bottom lip. How degrading would it be to die in a street fight? Damn.

"I'm afraid you'll have to deputize for me. I've no plans to meet your friend again any time soon," he said. Every second he bought created possibilities. "Besides, I suspect he'd enjoy your company…"

As he spoke, Byrn kicked his right foot forward, connecting deep into the man's groin. The man groaned in pain as he fired the colt at Byrn.

Only the assassin wasn't there.

As his foot connected, Byrn had dived right, landing on the ground right next to the big man. To get another shot off, the man would have to swing in an arc, which would take time. The moment he hit the ground, the assassin released two sharp punches, his balled fist obliterating his opponent's nose. Simultaneously, he hoisted his knee, sharply knocking the revolver out of the man's hand.

A level playing field.

Almost. Byrn's opponent was strong and remarkably quick.

Realizing he'd lost his weapon and although still gazing upward, the man launched a flurry of jabs with his elbow. Aiming at Byrn's head, he connected three times in rapid succession. The blows caught the assassin's cheek, sending his head snapping sideways. His vision temporarily blurred, Byrn sensed the guy begin to rise. That couldn't be allowed.

Byrn clasped his hands together and swung them hard into his opponent's gut. The thug, now on his knees and looming above the assassin, grunted, his head dropping forward. Byrn used the opportunity to raise his shoulders and headbutt him directly on his fractured nose. Suddenly, Byrn felt a heavy weight on his chest as the figure above him slumped down.

The assassin rolled him over, extricating himself in the process. He rose to his feet, breathing heavily.

The guy was conscious but groaning in pain. Byrn scrutinized the surrounding ground, searching for the gun. Nothing. As his victim attempted to get up, Byrn kicked him hard in the chest with the heel of his boot. They both heard the sound of ribs snapping before the man slumped back down.

"You know," Byrn began. "Where possible, I usually like to take a little time to make sure that the people I kill appreciate exactly why they're going to die. For me, it's a kind of professional obligation. But I've got to tell you that in this case, I'm certain that you're just too stupid to understand. Suffice to say that I think we both know that the world would simply have been a better place if you'd just never been born."

The situation needed to end quickly. Who knows what reaction the gun shot might have initiated.

Byrn took a moment to catch his breath before strolling around the thug's side and standing next to his head. What he intended would be quicker and more straight forward than retrieving his diver's knife from Danny's throat. He raised his right foot over the man's face.

Given his opponent's state of semi consciousness, Byrn was surprised when the man reached up, grabbed Byrn's ankle with both hands and twisted it. Byrn staggered to his right, attempting to regain his balance.

Shit. Lesson learned. Never underestimate the desperation of an amateur.

The assassin found his footing and prepared for the inevitable attack that would follow.

Only it didn't.

With surprising agility, the large man climbed to his feet before turning and bolting across the park, his receding silhouette highlighted by streetlights.

Byrn sighed. He didn't really want a foot chase, but he needed to put this guy down. As he leaned forward to take the first step, the assassin glanced downward. He stopped mid-action and smiled.

The thug had been lying on the gun.

Byrn reached down and grabbed the colt off the ground. He pushed the release catch and opened the cylinder, checking it was fully loaded minus the shot already fired. Satisfied, he clicked it back into place. The old revolver felt well balanced in his palm. The assassin wrapped his hand around the small western grip. Given that the conventional style of shooting was one handed when this gun was made long ago, Byrn decided to have some fun. He raised a single arm in front of him.

The thug was halfway across the open space now and moving at a fair clip. Byrn looked along the site to the blade at the end of the barrel. These weapons were well known to shoot high, so he aimed to the bottom of the sight.

It appeared the man was beginning to slow down. Desperate yet unfit. Or maybe he thought he'd made it.

Not today, motherfucker.

He squeezed the trigger three times, following the man's fall to the ground.

"Give my regards to Danny," Byrn said aloud to nobody at all.

Chapter 27

NEW YORK

The bench near The Pond in Central Park offered Byrn a clear view across West 59th Street and up 6th Avenue. It was mid-morning and the street leading to Midtown Manhattan was a hive of human activity. Nowhere in the world was busier than New York City.

The assassin felt quite secure, hiding in plain sight. The ever-changing camouflage of people going about their business provided all the concealment he required.

From where he sat, Byrn could clearly see the glass and metal facade of the Byer Corp headquarters. As the lunch hour neared, Byrn would increase his forays along 6th Avenue. He'd dedicated the day to observation. He wanted to check out Randal Byers in the flesh, get a sense of the man's disposition. Byrn's research suggested the man was in his building today. He thought there was a fair chance he would appear, if not at lunch, then by day's end.

The assassin spent a couple of hours researching the 'great man' online. Of course, there was a plethora of information about him, his company, and his successes. Byers owned newspapers, a television network, a movie studio, the world's largest streaming service and had more recently ventured into social media platforms. He may have begun life as a newspaperman, but he'd certainly adapted with the times. Now in his eighties, the media tycoon surpassed his contemporaries in a shifting communication industry and grew from strength to strength. From the data Byrn had acquired, the man rarely set a foot wrong, and when he did make a miscalculation, he remedied it with such speed and vigor that no one ever really dwelled on his error of judgement.

Randal Byers was brilliant. And ruthless.

His story was littered with competitors who had stumbled, enabling Byers to make the most of their misfortune. To the tycoon, it was just business. From what Byrn had read, to Randal Byers, life was just business.

The entrepreneur's personal story was reasonably well documented. He'd been married several times, always to younger women, and divorced the same number of times. He had two sons with his second wife, both of whom had gone into the family business. The eldest had died five years earlier from cancer. It seemed not even all the money in the world could ensure a long and happy life.

To Byrn, the second son sounded more interesting. In his late twenties, as a young man, Bradley Byers turned his back on the family company. Nothing was ever officially announced, but the rumors surrounding his departure suggested Bradley Byers grew weary of his father's flexible morality and unending pursuit of profit. He left Byer Corp in search of credibility.

Byrn figured that was easier to do when daddy was one of the richest men on the planet.

Strangely enough, the prodigal son returned to the fold a few years later. He rejoined the company in an upper management function, wielding influence over the complete suite of family entities. Byrn wondered what deal had been done to bring that about. Was it just too hard for the kid to make it on his own in the big, wide world? Or was there more to it? Did young Byers think he could do more to change the corporation's direction from the inside? Was Byer's senior prepared to compromise to bring his son back in from the cold? The commentators speculated, but no one really had all the answers.

Byrn glanced at his watch. 12.15 p.m. Still too early for a fat cat's lunch. Yet, for the sake of certainty, the assassin stood up, stretched his arms and legs, and sauntered across West 59th and up 6th Avenue. His New York Yankees baseball cap drawn down over his face, the assassin noted no unusual activity from the opposite side of the street as he passed the Byer Corp building. He decided to stroll further into the midtown area before returning to the bench in the park.

Two immediate issues puzzled Byrn. First, what was Regan Dia's relationship to Randal Byers? Was she in charge of his security detail? Possibly, but it seemed unlikely. Her skill set was way too specialized for a role like that. She'd need more of a challenge than babysitting a rich dude. Besides, when Byrn scrolled through the many online pictures of the media baron, Dia had only appeared in a small percentage of them, indicating that hers was a different function within the organization. Either way, simple observation could clarify the situation. If Dia stayed glued to Byers' side, despite Byrn's skepticism, that was probably her job. On the other hand, did Dia perform another, more covert role for Byers? That would tie in with her presence in Beijing.

Then there was the second question. Why was Randal Byers interested in Byrn? Had Byrn taken out a friend or colleague of his? Possibly, but the assassin didn't recall any job that had a link to Byers or his company. At least, not that he was aware of. Then there was the possibility that Byers needed the services of an assassin. The entrepreneur clearly seemed like a tough businessman, but was he that tough? The business of killing competitors takes things to a whole new level. In Byrn's experience, not many people had that in them. Sometimes they thought they did and then backed down at the last minute. Was this one of those cases?

Who knew?

Regan Dia did.

Dia would appreciate that eventually Byrn would figure out the connection between her and Byers. If she had discovered as much about him that she claimed to, she'd also understand that he'd come calling. The nature of the beast.

If Dia was part of some wall of protection around Byers, things could suddenly become very interesting. Byrn wondered which side she would ultimately choose. She may not even know the answer to that question yet.

Byrn stopped fifteen yards south of the Byer Corp edifice, feigning an interest in a delicatessen window. A couple of minutes later, there was some agitation in front of the building. Three men and a woman, all wearing dark suits, sunglasses and sporting large bulges in their jacket pockets, appeared on the sidewalk. They took up positions between the building's door and the black limousine, now pulling up next to the curb. Security.

The woman was not Regan Dia.

Byrn sauntered further down the sidewalk, intending to get a closer view without attracting the security detail's attention. He scanned purposefully across the street, as though looking for someone, before allowing his gaze to wander back to the Byer Corp front doors. On cue, the glass doors opened automatically and another man in a dark suit appeared. He looked up and down the avenue before turning behind him and saying something to a yet unseen person. Five seconds later, out walked the man himself.

It was the suit that Byrn noticed first. A deep navy blue, cut to within an inch of its life, the high-quality two-piece reeked of wealth. The assassin figured Byer may as well have strung together an array of tailored one-hundred-dollar bills to achieve the same effect. Abruptly, the man's face appeared in the direct sunlight. The entrepreneur looked every bit of his eighty something years, his skin etched in lines like a dry river delta.

Byers strode toward the limo, but his gait was deceiving. Although only a short distance, he moved with a purpose and vigor that belied his age. Interesting. The man still had commitment and energy.

As he reached the open limousine door, Randal Byers paused, raised his head, and glanced around. From the wide-eyed look of alarm on each of his security details' faces, the businessman was clearly not following the instructed procedure. Byrn wondered how many orders this man had ever followed in his life. The assassin searched the tycoon's eyes. Even in such a brief moment, Byrn saw aggression and confidence in the man's gaze. Yet Byrn was certain he'd also glimpsed an instant of hesitation, a tightening of the lips, perhaps even an extra unneeded blink.

Yes, there was something apart from business at play in the great man's mind. Byrn had seen the look many times before.

Fear.

Chapter 28

After observing three members of the security detail join Byers in the limo and the other three return inside the building, Byrn continued his casual stroll back to his park bench in the park. He had some thinking to do.

Lachlan Byrn was proud of the artistry involved in his profession. Any halfwit can look up information on the internet. But a true artist employed the powers of personal observation to learn about their target. Not just how they moved, but a multitude of intimate details that revealed themselves under a professional eye.

Byrn was pleased with his sojourn. He decided to wait a little longer in the park to process the intelligence he'd gained so far.

The assassin reflected on the information he'd picked up earlier in the day about the functioning of Byer Corp. It appeared that after Bradley Byers returned to the company, he'd settled down, finally in the position of influence he sought. His profile was prominently featured in the corporation's publicity as the 'face of the future'.

Then suddenly, the future didn't have a face. Bradley Byers disappeared from public view. Because Randal Byers controlled a significant portion of the media landscape, questions regarding the younger Byers' public absence were minimal. Those questions that did arise from competing media outlets were quickly shut down. Bradley's absence was explained as personal time. His father had arranged for a sprinkling of articles to appear in some of their lifestyle publications, suggesting his son had found love and was taking a pause to smell the roses out of the public eye.

Byrn did note that a couple of journalists from rival outlets had pushed the point and were writing investigative articles, probing deeper into the issue. Both journos ceased following the trail at approximately the same time. Further research indicated that one of the correspondents had been transferred to a post in Europe and allocated other stories. The second journalist now worked for Byer Corp in a substantially promoted position. Next level 'catch and kill' journalism.

Interesting. A clearer picture developed in Lachlan Byrn's mind.

Randal Byer's relationship with Regan Dia.

Byer's interest in Byrn.

Bradley Byer's maverick attitude and eventual disappearance.

Randal Byer's unusually heavy security entourage.

A man who should fear nothing, exhibiting an unmistakably micro expression of fear on his face.

Possibly, all these aspects were unrelated.

Probably not.

Either way, as he'd explained to several clients through the years, Byrn was not a detective, nor did he intend on becoming one. His role wasn't to explain problems, just to eliminate them.

Nothing he learned about this situation changed that. Once

Byrn had fulfilled his due diligence and evaluated the scenario as it reflected on him, he would act.

The shadows in the park grew longer. The end of the workday neared for those who closely monitored the clock, a minority in New York City's working population. Byrn gazed down West 59th Street as the sidewalks grew more frantic. The assassin was beginning to contemplate where he'd lay his head for the night when he sensed the hairs on the nape of his neck spike.

Professional intuition.

Experience told him not to ignore the feeling. Better to be wrong than caught wrongfooted.

Chapter 29

Dia was conflicted.

Lachlan Byrn was an impressive operator; she'd seen that firsthand. Yet the former ranger carried a sense of guilt that she'd been the unknowing catalyst for bringing needless trouble into Byrn's world. Although he didn't seem to care, Dia remained aware that if not for his extraordinary skills, any one of those situations in China could have ended Byrn's life.

Now she stood, two hundred yards further into Central Park than Byrn's current location, watching him. He seemed lost in thought. Without a doubt, Dia knew that Byrn's presence in New York indicated that he had plans. And those plans would impact her boss, Randal Byers.

That was the reason Dia was uncertain. Her relationship with Byers was complicated, but he had stood by her and provided her with opportunities that the military never did. On the other hand, his manipulation of the Byrn situation was unacceptable. You never placed a field operative in needless danger just to 'test their metal'.

So where did Dia's loyalties fall? Without intervention, she knew she would soon have to decide.

Without intervention.

Dia needed to talk with Byrn. But it was awkward. He'd warned her to stay out of his affairs. To inject herself into the situation now could bring an element of personal danger. Normally, that wouldn't bother her. She was trained to handle those situations. But Byrn was different. Dangerously different. Still, this opportunity may not present itself again. She didn't exactly have Byrn's contact details.

Dia decided to press forward and initiate a conversation, yet to be safe, she would control the interaction. She turned left and started walking in a large semi-circle a full two hundred yards behind the assassin. Reaching into her jacket pocket, she wrapped the fingers of her right hand around the grip of her Glock 19. She respected Byrn but didn't trust him. The gun would remain in position for the duration of their discussion.

Insurance.

Dia joined in behind a group of tourists that strolled a path from The Pond area toward West 59th. That got her to within fifty yards of the assassin's location on the bench. Perched with his back to her current position, his dark jacket and red New York Yankees cap made zeroing in on her target a reasonably straightforward operation.

Dia checked herself. She was going to a great deal of trouble for a simple conversation. Then she checked herself again. No, in this situation, all caution was required. She made a straight line for Byrn's position. Her tactic would be to announce herself just as she approached. Startling a man like Lachlan Byrn didn't seem like such a good idea.

Dia smiled nervously.

Five yards out, now confident in her strategy, she spoke.

"Good evening, Lachlan, my advice would be not to make any abrupt moves. I have a pistol pointed at the back of your head."

"My goodness, I wouldn't dream of it. But you really don't need a gun to have a chat with me, young lady."

Dia froze. The figure turned on the bench toward her. Neither the voice nor the face were Byrn's.

How in God's name had he done it to her again?

LACHLAN BYRN

Byrn stood on the corner of 59th and 6th, chuckling. From her posture, it was clear that Dia had some sort of weapon in her pocket and seemed keen on managing the interaction. For two hundred bucks and the loss of his cap and jacket, Byrn was satisfied he'd gotten his money's worth from the somewhat surprised but willing stranger on the pathway.

The assassin turned and strode northwest, vaguely in the direction of Hell's Kitchen.

'No Regan,' he thought to himself. 'No time for games today.'

Chapter 30

The waves rolled in like watery knights collapsing, fatigued from battle, onto the respite of the welcoming sand. Their arrival was constantly underscored by the deep roar of the relentless swell, never ending, never pausing for anyone or anything. Byrn found the inevitability of the ocean a rare panacea amidst his world of jagged violence and distrust. His background in the British Special Boat Service had almost provided him with a career that entwined his two passions, the sea and killing, until it didn't. It turned out that his nature wasn't specifically suited to taking orders, especially from those he held no regard for. His skills were embraced, his temperament not so much. Either way, that career path came to a brutal end when his superiors betrayed him, and he fell into the hands of the Chinese Intelligence Service.

Not to matter. Those in the SBS that had broken faith with him had met their just desserts, as had the politicians who commanded them. Like many of the narratives that compromised Byrn's angular existence, the final chapter had been bloodied and absolute.

The squawk of the protesting seagulls riding the offshore breeze distracted the assassin from his moment. Byrn rubbed his shoes in the sand and looked out over the North Atlantic.

Once again, his two pleasures entwined: the sanctity of the sea and the anticipation of death.

There was no way that he'd contemplate taking down Randal Byers in New York, either at work or in his sprawling penthouse on Park Avenue. The man's security was painfully tight, and the access was limited. Down here, in the Hamptons, where Byers maintained his weekend home was a different matter. There was space, there was cover and there would be opportunity.

Byrn just hoped that Regan Dia didn't get in the way. He had no specific desire to kill her, but he'd do whatever was dictated by the situation.

Social media reports on Byers' lifestyle had documented his frequent trips to his sprawling beachfront estate. It hadn't taken much digging for Byrn to find out the exact address in Medow Lane, Southampton. The neighborhood and the street itself reeked of wealth beyond imagination. Byer's property sat at the pinnacle of the local real estate tree.

Byrn figured he had at least twenty-four hours before the media magnate and his entourage would arrive. That would give the assassin an opportunity to scope out the estate and formulate his plan. There would be heavy security, but down here they would be spread more thinly. Byrn would use that to his advantage and minimize its effectiveness.

Once night had fallen, Byrn would examine the property both inside and out. Certainly, there would be staff permanently stationed on the estate. The assassin had to determine how many, and an optimal way to lessen his impact on them. Byrn didn't hesitate to take life when he had to, but he wasn't reckless when it came to collateral damage.

Reluctantly, Byrn climbed to his feet and yielded his spot

on the beach just down from Byers' compound. He'd return tonight. In the meantime, he had a connection to make midway back to New York. He needed to resupply himself with the appropriate armory. The arrangement had been made, it now awaited pickup. The weapons were coming from a source he'd used before and trusted. Byrn traipsed further along the sand toward the track that led back to the road where his rental car was parked. He pulled his new baseball cap down firmly on his forehead. The one thing this area didn't lack was security cameras.

It was after midnight when Byrn returned to his location on the beach. He steadily made his way along the foreshore until he was parallel with Byers' property. The night sea breeze was chilled, but not painfully so. It wasn't summer yet, the ambivalence of spring weather still hung in the air. The assassin opted to approach from the beach. He was acutely aware there would be high levels of electronic security in position, no matter how he approached his target.

Although Byer's compound had direct beach access, it was across a lengthy wooden boardwalk which traversed a small dune teeming with low growth plantation. The arrangement supplied the property with ample privacy. Byrn stood on the sand looking up at the outline of the long flat walkway. Somewhere along its length there would be motion sensors. The assassin decided the best way to circumvent them was to crawl directly under the boardwalk for its full length. The sensors would most likely be angled either out over the surrounding dunes or across the access itself, although he'd still have to be careful.

Twenty minutes later, caked in sand, he'd made it to the

edge of the property's garden. The assassin hauled himself up from the sandy soil onto the freshly cut lawn, his belly hugging the ground. Without doubt, there would be cameras covering the area. Byrn reached into his pocket and retrieved a small black box. He used the RF detector to scan the area, searching for radio frequency emissions. He identified three locations. Cameras. He then pulled out his cell phone and used its own camera to pinpoint the positions exactly. The phone's lens detected the three red dots, invisible to the naked eye, indicating the presence of infrared used by the cameras to enhance images in the dark. Now Byrn knew exactly where the surveillance cameras were. He had a choice to make. Originally, he planned to avoid their surveillance by maneuvering around behind them, but their coverage of the garden was so comprehensive that the assassin decided to instigate his Plan B. He called up the Wi-Fi blocker app on his phone and blocked internet access to the entire immediate area. The cameras would go down, as would every other internet-based security device in the house. Hopefully, any staff on the premises would be asleep and not notice. He'd deal with any insomniacs as the need arose.

Technology certainly did make some jobs easier.

Byrn surveyed the rear of the residence under the bright moonlight.

It towered like a palace amongst the dunes. The assassin figured that some people simply have too much money. Under the moonlight, the double story façade of shingles, typical of upmarket beach side architecture in days past, combined with regally high windows edged in glossy white frames, stood proud, almost like a setting for a movie. The second level featured a long white railed verandah while a sandstone patio on the ground level, surrounded an enormous swimming pool. At the extremities of the majestic home, bay windows protruded out toward the sea. Byrn decided that the property's price tag would run into the tens of millions. He also concluded that a man with such excessive wealth would be used to getting his own way.

Byrn had a decision to make. How far did he insert himself into the property for the sake of reconnaissance? It was a fine line between gathering much needed intelligence and risking needless exposure.

The assassin presumed that Byers would have some kind of study in the house. That would be the assassin's preferred place of contact with the man. Somewhere private, away from the rest of the household. Byrn had failed to locate any plans or substantial pictures of the building's interior online. He imagined Byers paid well for his privacy. So, would the tycoon's study be on the higher or lower floor? Byrn considered the man and the inevitable ego that would be embedded in his psyche. He decided that Byers would want his study in the most impressive location possible. That would mean upstairs, where the sea views would be extensive. There would also probably be less interruption from activity by the domestic staff up there, once the routine of bed making and cleaning was fulfilled each morning.

Yes, Byrn was almost certain the great man would have his private enclave upstairs. That made the assassin's job a little easier right now. Assuming any resident household staff had their rooms downstairs, Byrn decided to make straight for the upper level. Pausing to listen for any extraneous sounds coming from the building, he prepared to make his move. Satisfied that the pounding of the waves on the beach was all he could hear, Byrn stood up, closing the distance between himself and the house in a matter of seconds. He pressed himself into the shadows under the top verandah and waited.

Still no sound.

He stepped back into the moonlight, wrapped his arms around one of the wooden support columns, and began to climb. A minute and a half later, the assassin stood at the veranda's exterior door, jiggling the handle. Unsurprisingly, it was locked.

The problem was easily surmountable. Byrn retrieved a lock pick from his pocket and got to work. An age old yet useful skill that had enabled cat burglar's entry into untold properties for years.

Once inside, Byrn surveyed the space. It was clearly some kind of sunroom or lounge. Through the enormous windows, the moonlight revealed a layout of luxurious oversized couches and wing-backed chairs. Two large bookcases filled the walls at each end of the room. A door in the middle, adjacent to an entrance, led to a landing. That would be the access downstairs. To his left, Byrn noted another door in the middle of the bookcase. It remained closed. Byrn stole quietly over to it and twisted the handle.

The door opened. The assassin passed through the door-way.

The room he entered displayed equally large windows facing the sea. The space was significantly larger than any home study Byrn had ever seen. The right-hand wall contained a massive stone fireplace under a majestic wooden mantle. Shelves on either side were lined with ornaments and awards. On the far wall, another bookcase acted as a backdrop to an enormous oak desk, behind which sat a buttoned velvet green chair.

The king's throne.

Option confirmed. This location would be Byrn's preferred choice for the confrontation and its aftermath. The assassin turned and gazed across the white wave-tops glowing in the bright moonlight. A reasonably straight-forward escape route. Of course, the term 'reasonable' depended on who was chasing his tail at the time.

Byrn spent ten minutes exploring each room on the upper level, understanding their purpose and layout. He counted seven bedrooms, including a master suite bigger than most apartments. He also paid particular attention to the ceilings. Access points came in all shapes and sizes.

With his sortie complete, Byrn returned to the main room. With a final look around the room, he memorized the layout and silently headed toward the door he'd entered through. He'd made it halfway across the room when the shadows suddenly changed.

Byrn looked around.

Damn, somebody had flicked on a light downstairs and the glow permeated upward from the stairwell.

The assassin froze.

Within a second, he heard it. The creaking of floorboards as someone made their way up the stairs.

The last thing Byrn wanted was a confrontation now.

The assassin retraced his steps toward the study door, barely making it through the doorway as the light in the lounge was switched on. Behind the door, Byrn couldn't see, but sensed someone in the lounge. Would they find the unlocked door? That could be a problem.

More creaking. The footsteps grew closer to the study

door. Byrn looked around the room. There was nowhere obscure to hide. He tensed, ready to pounce. A second later, the footsteps paused, just on the other side of the door.

Then a thought occurred to the assassin. He bolted silently toward the fireplace, skirting the large chairs positioned near the desk, before climbing into the pit. He hoped like hell the chimney was functional. Byrn optimistically reached for the bricks that he anticipated would form a ledge leading upward to the main section. His fingers found what they were seeking. Within a moment, he was able to press against the walls of the chimney and crab crawl his way upward. There wasn't much space, but being such a majestic old house, everything was built to excess. He kept the pressure up, pushing his shoulders and knees outward. unsure how long he'd be capable of maintaining the convoluted position.

The door opened, more footsteps. If he had to come out fighting from this new position, things might not go his way. The footsteps seemed to circle the room before pausing… directly in front of the fireplace.

Byrn heard a jiggling sound. The person appeared to be fiddling with something on the shelf next to the fireplace. What the hell was it? Then it hit Byrn, a modem. Of course, he or she was making a futile attempt to reboot the internet. Byrn's shoulders ached. He pressed harder, knowing it was physically impossible for him to remain in this position much longer.

The intruder showed no sign of leaving.

"How's that?" A male voice suddenly called out. "I've turned it off and on."

"No, nothing." The response of a distant voice. A woman. Damn, this place was full of night owls.

"I'll try again." The man.

Byrn knew he'd have no luck. Equally, he knew that if the man tried a third time, Byrn would simply fall at his feet.

There was one chance. The assassin leaned over slightly to his left, enabling him to reach a hand into his pants pocket. With a little juggling, he was able to withdraw his cell phone. Before turning it on, he attempted to use his pocket to shield the light emitted from its screen, at least as much as possible. It was difficult. Every move in that confined space was challenging.

"How about now?" yelled the man.

"Wait a minute," the distant voice. "No, nothing."

"I'll give it one more try."

Shit.

Byrn flicked on his phone. If the man in front of the fireplace glanced down, the glare would be visible and Byrn would be finished.

If the assassin moved, soot or debris might fall into the pit. Once again, if the man noticed, Byrn would be exposed.

Craning his head to see the screen on his cell, Byrn quickly scrolled through to the Wi-Fi blocker app.

"Just about to give it a final go," yelled the man.

"If that doesn't work, screw it," said the distant voice, now clearly a woman. "We'll get someone in tomorrow before the boss gets down."

"Too freakin' right."

Byrn ran his finger down through the settings. He felt himself begin to slide downward.

"Anything now?" shouted the man.

Byrn slid the Wi-Fi setting to 'enable.'

"No, nothing," yelled the woman.

Byrn began to slide further. He pressed hard against the bricks with all the strength he could muster, but his muscles were giving out, refusing to yield to his control.

Why was this guy still there?

"I'll give it one last go; I really want to finish watching the replay."

Byrn's slide began to pick up momentum. He braced himself for the fall and readied himself to engage. If his cramped body would follow orders.

"All right, one last… oh… hang on, it's working," came the distant voice.

"Okay, I'll come down."

The man's footsteps padded across the room. Byrn heard the study door click shut just as he thudded down into the fireplace, his muscles spasming with painful cramps.

Mental note. Next time, just stand behind the door and shoot the bastard.

Fifteen minutes later, after cleaning up the mess around the fireplace and retracing his tracks out of the property, Byrn jogged along the beach. He'd disabled the Wi-Fi one more time as he made his way across the lawn, turning it back on when he reached the sand.

It had been an inelegant insertion, yet Byrn now had the required intel to move forward.

For certain, Randal Byers was going to have a very bad weekend.

Chapter 31

Late on the Friday afternoon, Byrn was once again perched on the beach, a short distance from Randal Byers' extravagant beach house. This time, he sat a little further back into the windswept bushes scattered amongst the low-lying dunes. He stared through his pocket size binoculars toward the sea. The deep gray of the ocean matched the cloudy sky, yet the temperature remained warm enough for a smattering of people to be sitting or walking on the sand. The assassin swung the binoculars in an arc, leaving the sea and focusing on the shoreline. The beach in front of Byers' home appeared clearly visible, but Byrn didn't want to linger on it too long lest anyone become suspicious. He kept swinging the glasses in a series of intermittent slow arcs and waited.

In the end, his patience paid off. Out of place on the beach, two men in dark suits suddenly materialized in front of Byers's residence. After checking the shoreline, they nodded in the direction they came from. A minute later, wearing casual pants and an open-necked shirt, Randal Byers appeared. The tycoon's shoulders exhibited a slight forward hunch, indicating some level of tension. Perhaps his presence by the seaside was intended to relieve some of that stress.

Byers stood, hands in pockets, staring out to sea, his wispy gray hair blowing in the breeze. A man lost in thought. A couple of minutes later, he turned and spoke to someone back toward the house. Byrn couldn't see who because of the trees, but the set of the great man's jaw suggested the conversation was intense.

Had the job been a straightforward assassination, Byrn would be done and gone by now. He could have easily taken Byers out with a medium-range rifle shot from his current location and be gone before anyone realized what had happened. The trouble was, Byrn wanted to understand Byers' motive for involving the Chinese. If there was more at stake here, the assassin had to determine what it was before Byers died.

Byrn dropped the binoculars around his neck. He'd seen all he needed to.

Another complication arose. Byers had brought a stronger security contingent than Byrn had expected. Seven men in two cars, in addition to anyone already inside the residence. The assassin had watched them arrive. Then, seeing the businessman accompanied onto the beach by some of his detail excluded the opportunity of an easy approach by the water. Byrn would be forced to revert to his original plan of another foray into the house at night.

With seven-plus professional security operatives present, that task would probably be more difficult than anticipated. Byrn held no doubt that he could take out all the men, but the speed and sheer amount of people would require some of them to be permanently put down. He wouldn't have time for subtlety. The assassin obviously had no compunction in taking lives, but until Byers' motives were resolved in Byrn's mind, he would prefer to remain focused on his main target.

Byrn would have to think outside of the square.

It was clear that Byers looked troubled about something. Surely surrounding himself with such a high level of security at the beach house wasn't his typical practice. Was Byrn the reason for it? Was the purpose of this show to frighten the assassin away? Perhaps, but it would take a stronger display of force than that to stop Byrn from doing his job. Was there something more? Maybe another factor at play that Byers found threatening. Whatever it was, Byers seemed to be under some form of pressure.

Interesting.

Byrn traipsed back further along the beach, across the dunes and up a small track to reach his rental. It was time for sustenance and thought. He'd be back on the beach by midnight. Already, a variation to his original plan had begun to form in his mind.

Chapter 32

Just before 1 a.m. Byrn made a move.

With his original plan on ice, the assassin decided to make the most of his misadventure the previous evening and lean into the situation. As he had the night before, Byrn began crawling along the sand underneath the boardwalk. This time the task was trickier as he was loaded up with weaponry, including two knives, two pistols and some flash bangs. When he made it to the grassy verge at the end of the garden, he stopped. Once more, he reached into his pocket, retrieved his Wi-Fi blocker and disabled the internet connection to the property.

Then he waited.

In his mind, Byrn could see what was probably happening in the house. For certain, there would be at least one man on overnight duty. Most likely they would be either monitoring the security cameras or whiling away their time on some online device. When internet access disappeared, they'd be pissed and if they were professional, they'd be suspicious.

Right on cue, one of the downstairs lights turned on.

The first thing they would do would be to wake up some of the remaining security detail. The cause of the Wi-Fi blackout would have to be explored.

Two more lights switched on.

Then the most likely course of action would be to check with one of the permanent staff regarding the location of the modem or modems and enquire if the internet here was reliable.

Another light.

The security people would be told that there had been some reliability issues regarding the signal, but they thought they'd been resolved.

Byrn expected the security team to be alert and diligent, but not overly concerned due to unreliable internet service.

The assassin lay low, with only his eyes and forehead protruding above the level of the lawn. Covered with a full balaclava, he would be difficult to spot.

Expectantly, he watched the events unfold.

The outside lights flicked on, and two patio doors opened. Two operatives came through the left door, one through the right. They quickly strode past the pool and across the grass. Byrn was certain the same procedure would be duplicated at the front of the property.

The assassin pressed himself harder into his small hide.

After five minutes roaming the garden, Byrn heard the men one by one shouting 'clear'.

Everything revolved around what happened next.

As the operatives headed toward the wooden walkway that led to the beach, Byrn relinquished his hide and slid directly under the structure. Within seconds, all three men gathered almost directly over his position.

Slowly, the three of them marched in line down the walkway. The first man cast his flashlight directly ahead, the second man to the left, and the third to the right. It was an adequate and professional sweep of the area, but certainly these guys were not working on a razor's edge.

Byrn figured he had around two minutes to complete his move.

He rolled out from under the boardwalk and stood up, careful not to make a sound. He then bolted across the grass to his previous position at the column leading to the top verandah. Anyone watching from inside the house would spot him easily. Byrn was counting on the rest of the security detail being occupied at the front of the property. If he was in charge, he would have instructed non-essential personnel to remain in their rooms.

He made it.

A minute later, breathing hard, his feet landed quietly on the wooden deck.

He was three quarters of the way toward the door he'd used the night before when the handle turned, and the door swung open.

Man number seven.

They saw each other at the exact same moment. The guy reached into his jacket, Byrn leaped toward him.

The assassin rammed the security operative's throat with his shoulder, rendering him mute. Simultaneously, he grabbed the man's wrist, blocking his hand under the jacket. Byrn then jerked his head backward before head-butting the guy hard in the forehead.

The operative stumbled backward, but Byrn still had hold of his wrist. If his opponent pulled a knife, it would be an inconvenience. If he drew a gun and got a shot off, all hell would break loose. And not the kind of hell Byrn had in mind.

As he attempted to gain his footing, the security guy managed to strike the side of Byrn's head with two quick jabs. From the snap in his neck and the sudden bolt of pain running down his temple, Byrn realized the man packed some power.

This would need to end quickly.

Byrn slid to the right, dodging the third punch, and swiftly grabbed the man's empty hand from under his coat. In a second, the assassin forced the guy's forearm high behind his back. His opponent began to cry out. Discomfort… warning… whatever. Byrn couldn't allow it.

The assassin reached around the man's throat with his left forearm and squeezed hard. A moment later, his victim's body went limp.

Byrn lowered him to the deck before pressing himself against a wall, out of sight from the ground below. He knew the security guy wouldn't be out for long, but his silence needed to be ensured. The assassin dug into his pocket and retrieved a small leather case. He opened it, took out the needle inside, flicked the protector off the tip and inserted it into a vein on the man's neck.

The dose of ketamine would keep him out for some time.

Byrn dragged the operative's comatose body across the deck. At the far end was a large, molded plastic box for shielding outdoor cushions from the weather. He lifted the lid and heaved the man inside, pressing him down amongst the cushions. The assassin then returned to the opened doorway and entered, locking the door behind him.

Step one complete.

Byrn's next move would be dictated by the evidence at hand. Byers would either be in his master suite, or, if awakened, would likely have moved to his study. It made sense. If under any sort of threat, a leader would get himself to a location where he can control things. Headquarters.

Byrn stepped around one of the couches and noted the thin strip of light under the door that led to Byer's study.

Bingo.

Byrn withdrew his SIG Sauer from its holster before padding lightly across the floor toward the door. He twisted the knob in small gradations. When he felt the latch release, he shoved the heavy wooden door open. The great man sat behind his desk, jabbing at the keypad on his computer.

He looked up.

"Good evening Mr. Byers. My name is Lachlan Byrn, and to be honest, I'm quite pissed at you."

Chapter 33

The media tycoon glared back at the assassin. Byrn caught another fleeting micro expression on the man's face. Eyes wide; lips drawn tight. Alarm. And then it was gone.

"Well, Mr. Byrn. It's a pleasure to meet you finally, although not under these circumstances."

Cool under pressure.

"Before we go any further, I need you to pick up your phone and call your security chief. Tell them you don't want to be disturbed. Also tell them that the big guy with the red hair, I think his wallet said Hemmings, is here with you."

Byers smiled. "I'm afraid Hemmings is my Head of Security, or should I saw was? Is he still alive?"

"Just having a good sleep," replied Byrn.

Byers nodded, showing no signs of being bothered by the situation.

"I'll call one of the others."

"And please don't try to send any signals. A prolonged confrontation would only involve lives being lost unnecessarily."

Byers nodded again.

"There's really no need to make that call, sir."

Byrn whipped around. Regan Dia had been behind the door the whole time. She now stood with a pistol pointed at the assassin's gut.

"Hello, Dia."

"Lachlan."

"I still think there are some aspects in the Ranger's training program that are lacking," said the assassin.

As he finished his last word, Byrn kicked up his right foot, smashing into Dia's gun arm. The weapon flew into the air, but the operative responded with a sharp kick aimed at Byrn's knees. He stepped backward, grabbed her weaponized leg with his remaining hand, and yanked it forward. She lurched toward the desk.

By the time she'd found her footing, Byrn had his SIG targeted at her chest.

"Two points to make here, Dia," Byrn began. "First, to cover me, you should have moved closer to the corner where I couldn't reach you. Second. In my trade, we tend to stand behind the door and simply shoot. I've recently been reminded of the value of that approach myself."

Dia appeared angry. Her jaw was tight and her wrists tense. She'd been humiliated in front of her boss.

Byrn turned to the tycoon.

"Don't be too disappointed in her, Mr. Byers. I've seen Ms. Dia in action. She's actually incredibly effective."

"I don't doubt that for a second," Byers responded. Despite being in a vulnerable position, he remained calm.

"Now, the phone call, please, sir."

The businessman did as instructed, speaking softly but audibly into the phone.

With his pistol, Byrn motioned to Dia and then a comfortable chair beside the desk.

"There," he commanded.

"I'd rather stand."

"I'm sure you would. There," he motioned again.

"Do as he says, Regan. Mr. Byrn has gone to a great deal of trouble to call on us today," said Byers.

"Yes, sir," she responded, almost sulkily.

Still keeping his weapon arcing between Byers and Dia, Byrn reached behind his back and latched the door. He then strolled across the room to retrieve Dia's gun before returning to a position to the right of the door. If anyone kicked it open, he'd be concealed.

The assassin stared at the old man behind the desk. Up close, he looked every bit the octogenarian. His skin was covered in the crinkly lines Byrn had noticed in New York. But here, the elderly man's eyes appeared more deeply set back into their sockets than he'd remembered. His irises were no longer the piercing blue that appeared in earlier photos. Now they seemed dull and lifeless. Yet behind them, Byrn knew the man's brain was as sharp as ever.

"So," said Byrn. "I have a couple of questions. The answers that you provide will dictate whether you live or die. To be honest, I'd only give survival a three percent chance in this instance. And by the way, if you've somehow signaled your team downstairs, that turns into zero percent."

Byers nodded. "Message understood. Your instructions were followed to a tee."

Byrn paused for a moment's thought. He searched the old man's expression for any sign of betrayal.

"Okay. First, what is your interest in me? Second, why did you disclose my whereabouts to Zhen Su in Beijing and then again in Xi'an?"

"They are fair questions, Mr. Byrn. They are also the issues

I would expect you to address."

Byers then took a moment.

"If I'm correct, you expect nothing less than total honesty from me. If I fail to satisfy your curiosity, I have no doubt you'll act decisively."

The assassin nodded before saying. "Honest responses alone may not be sufficient to save you, just to clarify."

"Everything is black and white to you, isn't it, Byrn? Perhaps when you understand the full scenario at play here, you may appreciate the nuances of the situation. The grays, if you like."

Byrn pursed his lips.

"My advice would be to stick to black and white."

Byers nodded again. Dia remained silent.

"Very well," began Byers, his tone confident. "My interest in you is professional. I have some work that I believe would suit a man of your skill set. The reason I utilized my network to inform Zhen Su of your location in those two instances was that I needed Regan to see you in action. It is important to me that I hire the best. As it transpires, from what Regan has reported, when placed under extraordinary pressure, you performed admirably. Apparently, it turns out that you are the best. Well done."

Byrn felt the anger stir within, but he placed it to one side. His choice to respond aggressively to the businessman was calculated.

"Well fucking done? You're playing with people's lives here, Byers. Are you so removed from reality that you don't understand the ramifications of your little games?"

Byers looked Byrn square in the eye.

"I can assure you, Mr. Byrn, I am well acquainted with the

ongoing fragility of mortality. Like you, I have seen it in a very personal way."

There was a tiny tremor in the old man's fingers as he spoke.

"No, not like me," stated Byrn bluntly.

Byers shrugged his shoulders.

"Please forgive my error."

The assassin didn't respond. His gaze alternated between Byers and Dia. What was going on here? What was their relationship?

Time was control.

"After what you did, what on God's earth made you think I would work for you?"

"Yes, that was an unusual conundrum. I appreciated that if you figured out that I was the one behind Zhen's information, you probably wouldn't want to work for me. Conversely, if you didn't figure it out, you weren't the man I needed," Byers responded.

Byrn glanced at Dia. Her eyebrows raised, surprised by her boss's response.

"I won't be working for you." Byrn stopped moving the gun around and pointed it directly at Byers' forehead.

"Before rushing into any rash decision, let's talk about compensation." Byers leaned over the desk, writing something down on a notepad. He pushed the pad across the surface toward Byrn. The assassin edged forward and glanced down before returning to his station.

"That's a lot of money."

"I can afford it."

"I'm sure you can," Byrn responded. In fact, it was double any amount Byrn had been paid before, and he'd earned some generous commissions for his work.

Byers sat forward in his chair, hopeful.

"No," replied Byrn.

"Triple it," said the entrepreneur.

Byrn was acutely aware that Byers was not only bidding for the assassin's services but also for his own life.

"No."

"Name your figure."

"There is no figure."

Byers smiled. To Byrn, he resembled a snarling cat, not a world-weary old man facing his demise.

"Black and white, Mr. Byrn?"

"Life is simpler that way."

The old man sat back in his chair.

"Very well, before you do what you need to, please allow me to provide you with the full picture. I understand you have a habit of doing due diligence on all your operations."

"Go ahead, you have two minutes."

Dia grew edgy, fidgeting with her fingers, twitching restlessly in her chair. Byrn didn't want her to make a futile attempt at saving her boss.

"Thank you," Byers responded. "Let me say I'm not afraid to die. I've lived a fulfilling life and reaped the benefits of a lifetime of hard work. If today is the day, so be it."

Byrn tilted his head, surprised the old man's fatalistic attitude wasn't dissimilar to his own.

"I wouldn't spend too much time reflecting on the 'honest hard-working man' bit Byers. From what I understand, you've stepped over many broken corpses to get to where you are."

"Fair point," the tycoon responded. "I am a businessman."

"'Business', yes," responded Byrn. "It remains to be seen

how much of a 'man' you really are."

"May I continue?"

The assassin nodded.

"I'll put this simply, as you would like it. Two months ago, my son Bradley was kidnapped. His abductors attempted to ransom his life to me. I was willing to pay without hesitation."

The tycoon gazed at Byrn.

"Were the police involved?" asked the assassin, his interest marginally piqued.

"No. I wanted to prevent them from mishandling the situation and risking escalation. I employed a top-level negotiating team to bring my boy home."

Byers paused, his breathing slightly labored, before continuing.

"The team failed completely. My boy was killed. Now, I want justice."

Byers hesitated again. To catch his breath, or for effect, Byrn wasn't sure.

"I know the identity of the person who killed my son and the negotiator who turned a blind eye. I'm assuming he was paid off. Bottom line here, Byrn. I require you to eliminate those two men."

Byrn considered what he'd just been told. The scenario would explain the missing heir that he'd read about. It was his kind of job, but that didn't absolve Byers of playing him like some sort of pawn.

Finally.

"It's not enough," Byrn exclaimed. "You play games with a man like me; you'll find there is a cost beyond money."

He began to squeeze the SIG's trigger.

"One more thing," Byers quickly added.

"What?" asked Byrn, pausing his movement.

Surprisingly, Byers turned to Dia and nodded.

"You may have wondered about my role in this, Lachlan," she said.

Byrn glanced at her.

"It had crossed my mind."

"You should know that Brad Byers is, or rather was, my husband. Asleep in my room downstairs is our twelve-month-old daughter, Clementine."

Lachlan Byrn saw most things that came at him well in advance. But he hadn't seen that.

Chapter 34

"Explain."

Byrn lowered his weapon temporarily.

Dia continued speaking.

"I started at Byer Corp two and a half years ago. The situation was exactly as I had explained to you. The military was stifling me. I wanted to do more with my life, but as you well understand, Lachlan, people with skill sets such as you and I have limited career opportunities in the civilian world. Turning mercenary just wasn't my thing, neither was your line of work."

Byrn smiled, amused.

"Our family has always had an interest in weaponry," added Byers. "It probably comes from our confederate background. Bradley and I were attending a gun show together, as the guests of the chief executive of the company that made the pistol you hold in your hand. My son was introduced to Regan by a common military contact. They connected immediately."

"I won't bore you with all the details. To be honest, at the time, I knew that the Byers name was a big thing, but I didn't realize how big. Mr. Byers ended up offering me a job, and that was it," said Dia.

"What sort of job?" asked Byrn.

"I oversee his personal protection detail, but from a distance. I'm not a 'by your side' type of bodyguard. I also perform research duties. Any interaction with operators from our, or any other country's military industry gets investigated by me. There are a lot of shady operators out there."

"Byers, why would your corporation engage with the military? Isn't media communication your strong suit?" asked Byrn, feigning ignorance.

"Correct," Byers responded. "But what sells more papers, generates more clicks or creates more interest than anything else? War. Wars make me money and wars need the military to flourish."

"How Machiavellian of you," said Byrn, the sarcasm in his voice evident. He turned to Dia. "And you were comfortable operating in this environment?"

"Yes," she replied, "at first. Although, to be honest, after a few months of working for Byer Corp, I began to have my doubts. It's one thing to report a war, it's something else to finance one."

Byrn glared at Byers.

"The bottom line is that I'm an old-style newspaper man at heart," he replied. "I do whatever it takes to sell the news. There are times I use any possible influence I might have to affect certain outcomes." Byers shifted his gaze to Dia. "I don't believe there's a need to air any further dirty linen here, Regan."

Every part of Dia's body tensed, Byrn noted her fists squeezed tight.

"If we are to deal with Brad's killer, Lachlan needs to

know everything," she replied. "And to finish answering your question, Lachlan, I expressed my discomfort to Brad, and told him I planned to leave the company. He had frequently been at loggerheads with his father regarding the way the corporation functioned. He implored me to see it out. He said changes were coming and that he'd ensure the company raised its ethical standards. He told me he'd already put some things in place. Are you aware that he even left Byer Corp at one point, such was his frustration?"

"But he came back," interjected Byers.

Byrn needed more information, despite his annoyance with Randal Byers increasing by the second.

"If you are this woman's father-in-law, what's with all the sir, Mr. Byers and Ms. Dia shit?"

"Ms. Dia was employed as a professional. That is our primary relationship."

"You are some piece of work," replied Byrn. "My inclination is to put a bullet in your 'newspaperman's heart' right now."

"But you haven't, and I don't think you will, at least not yet. You don't get to my position in life without being able to read people and predict their behaviors," Byers responded.

"I suspect you have several skills that have got you to your 'position in life', most of which even I would find distasteful. But for now, carry on. You say your son is dead and you want me to take care of his killers? Elaborate," ordered Byrn. "You've already exceeded your allotted two minutes, so be quick."

Byers leaned forward, placing his forearms on the desk, his meaningful sincere pose.

"Brad shunned much of the attention that comes our way. He always preferred to live a quieter life out of the spotlight.

When he did return to the company, he was extremely clear that he wanted greater input into the corporation's direction. He also said that he would sacrifice some of his anonymity to lead that process."

"What was your response to that?" interjected Byrn.

Byers grinned.

"Surprisingly, I was fine with the idea. You may have noticed that I'm not getting any younger. Every successful company, and government for that matter, requires generational change."

Byrn could also read a person like a book. Everything in Byers' tone and manner indicated that the tycoon was telling the truth, yet an uneasiness permeated the air.

"So, his disappearance?" asked the assassin.

Dia spoke.

"It was a Friday afternoon. Brad rang me from the office to say he was on his way down here. I'd already arrived in the morning with Clementine. Brad often drove himself; he said it was good therapy. He never arrived."

"Our security cameras picked him up, leaving our building. After that, he simply disappeared," added Byers.

Byrn considered the statement. It was rare that someone would or could 'simply disappear'.

"Ransom?" he asked.

Byers returned Byrn's penetrating stare.

"One hundred million dollars," he replied.

"And you agreed to pay?"

"Of course. I can afford it, but I did tell them it would take a few days to convert assets into that much cash.

"How did they contact you?" asked Byrn.

"Encrypted email. I had my tech people, at least one that

I trusted, attempt to trace the source. He came back saying it was an impossible task. The originator of the email was a professional, and the trail was too convoluted."

"Yet with no digital trace to follow, you still didn't alert the authorities?" asked the assassin.

Silence.

Dia looked over toward Byers, her eyes narrowed and intense.

"Go on, tell him. Tell him how you tripped over your own ego and now my husband is dead."

For the first time, the old man appeared uneasy. He cleared his throat and shifted in his chair.

"It confirmed my decision," he began. "If these people were that professional, the police simply would not have the resources or the expertise to track them down. I have my own network. I decided to utilize their services. I was recommended to a company that specializes in hostage negotiation. They are the best of the best."

"Apparently not," said Byrn.

"Working privately also meant no publicity," added Dia, her voice riddled with contempt.

"That factor was of no consequence," said Byers. "I simply wanted the optimal chance of getting my son back." He turned to Dia. "You seem to have suddenly found a new level of confidence in criticizing my actions, Regan."

Dia sat bolt upright.

"No. It's just after seeing Lachlan operate, I believe that we need to place our faith in a real professional, not your ass licking corporate 'wannabes'."

Byers had the grace and sense not to respond.

"I employed Seaton and Associates. I was told by a trusted

source that Jason Seaton and his team had a successful track record in high-level hostage negotiation. I saw no reason to believe the outcome in this case would be any different."

"How transactional," Byrn responded. "But it was different. What went wrong?"

"I passed the money on to Jason. It was like a Hollywood movie. Used unmarked bills of varying denominations in a couple of suitcases. I sourced the cash from a variety of financial institutions to avoid arousing suspicion."

"And publicity," said Dia.

Byers ignored her, focusing his attention on Byrn.

"Jason Seaton's team delivered the money as instructed and left the drop off point."

"Did they pull back and surveil the area?" asked Byrn.

"No. Our instructions were to vacate the vicinity completely. We were told that to do otherwise would be to forfeit Brad's life," Byers responded.

Byrn leaned forward.

"And you didn't do a side deal with your man Seaton, maybe leave one man behind to see if they could follow the money."

"No. Of course not."

Byrn stared at the old man, letting the silence work its magic.

"Mr. Byrn, I can assure you, one hundred million dollars is not a lot of money to me."

There it was again. The lie.

"So, all communication with the kidnappers came through the encrypted emails?"

"Yes."

"After Seaton's team paid the cash, what happened?" asked Byrn.

"Nothing, at least not for a few days. We were growing worried, but Jason assured us this wasn't an unusual practice."

"Then?"

Byers began to speak, falteringly. He took a moment before continuing.

"On day four, I received an email. It stated we had been warned about the consequences of failing to fully comply with their demands. Accordingly, they informed me that Bradley was dead. They also sent a photograph of his bloodied body as proof."

Dia interrupted.

"It looked like my husband had been shot several times and had his throat slit." She spoke like a machine. Devoid of emotion.

Byrn considered all that he'd heard. There were truths and there were lies. The hard part was telling the difference between the two.

Eventually.

"Do you have Bradley's body?"

"No," Byers shifted uncomfortably as he talked. His forehead scrunched and his eyes cast downward. "But they sent us all ten of his fingers, which we've since verified. There is no chance that they just lopped off a finger but kept my son alive."

"At the beginning of this story, you mentioned that you hold two people responsibly for Bradley's death. Who and why?" asked Byrn.

"Karl Brill was the operative leading Jason Seaton's team. Two weeks after the failed ransom drop, he resigned by email from Seaton and Associates and disappeared. Jason Seaton has attempted to locate him, without success," replied Byers.

"And the second person?"

"Dominic Nazar."

"And who the hell is Dominic Nazar?" inquired Byrn.

"The man's name was found buried deep in some files that Karl Brill had saved to the cloud. The man's significance lies in his leadership of a small yet effective terrorist group in Southern Sudan," Byers replied.

"Why is that relevant?" asked Byrn.

Byers inhaled deeply.

"It may or may not be the case that I was able to influence, in my own minor way, the Sudanese government's crackdown on Nazar's group nearly a year ago. They were all but routed."

"Because you thought that was the proper and humanitarian thing to do?"

"Please Byrn, don't be so pious. You're a paid killer and a mercenary. You have no right to cast judgment on me."

Byrn chuckled.

"Yet I'm the one with the gun. I'll judge whoever I fucking want."

The old man hesitated. Byrn wondered if he worried that he'd gone too far.

"I refer you to my earlier comments. I'm a businessman. The story was of interest because it was a local battle between Christians and Muslims. War and religion, our two biggest sellers."

Byrn stepped forward, three paces to the desk, his anger rising. He leaned over and pistol-whipped Byers hard across his face. The tycoon recoiled in shock, blood dripping from his nose and mouth.

The assassin looked down at the shocked businessman.

"Death and violence, *my* biggest sellers," he spat. "I'll do your job, old man, but I'm doing it for her, not for you." He gestured to Dia, who sat mouth agape in her chair. "Then I'll decide whether we have further business."

From the look on Byers' face, he clearly understood that any further business with Lachlan Byrn would not be to his advantage.

Chapter 35

Someone had to die.

Byrn had sensed his anger rising with each minute he spent in Randal Byers' company. The man was a self-centered manipulator whose own ego colored every relationship and situation he encountered. He stood for everything Byrn loathed.

The assassin pushed his rental hard as he chewed through the miles heading west along the Long Island Expressway.

Regan Dia was a different kind of beast. Although not totally convinced where Dia's cards would fall when the shit hit the fan, her frustration with her father-in-law was palpable. Byrn supposed that with the loss of her husband and a young child in tow, she felt a certain vulnerability. That said, watching her in action in the back streets of Xi'an and then again in Beijing, she'd acted confidently and assertively.

Byrn fleetingly wondered why he was here at all. Dia appeared more than capable of handling the situation, but again, there was the kid. The child had already lost one parent, and Dia was probably sickened by the possibility of her losing another. Or was she more disgusted by the thought of her daughter growing up exclusively under the care of her grandfather?

She'd want for nothing... except perhaps a moral compass.

Byrn grimaced before pressing the gas pedal down harder. Byers was right. Who was he to point the morality bone?

Before leaving the house in the Hamptons, Byrn sat down with Dia to go over some of the details. If he'd stayed in that room with Byers much longer, things wouldn't have gone well for the smug bastard. The tycoon's security staff had been taken aback by Byrn's sudden appearance and even more startled by the state of Randal Byers' face. But the old man had waved them off. Hemmings, the lead guy, was still wobbly on his feet. He seemed ready to tear Byrn apart limb by limb, but he reluctantly followed his boss's orders to restrain himself. Byrn knew the type. He'd be hoping for an opportunity to retrieve his dignity and take Byrn down at some point. Of course, that would never happen.

As he drove, the assassin began to piece together an agenda. He wasn't the kind to make appointments at the office, yet he had several meetings to line up... on his terms.

The first was with Jason Seaton. He and his organization seemed to be at the heart of the scenario. Byrn needed to find out more about Karl Brill, Seaton's former employee. He also wanted another perspective on how the whole kidnap-ransom bit had gone down. The assassin had little faith in Randal Byers' recollection of events.

Byrn had an address in his pocket, and that's where he headed now.

Just after midday, Byrn pulled up at the upmarket two-story home in New Rochelle, Westchester County. From across the street, the assassin noted the fastidiously kept front garden and Mercedes-Maybach S-Class parked in the driveway.

There wouldn't be much, if any, change from two hundred thousand dollars for the vehicle. Jason Seaton must be doing okay for himself.

Byrn didn't want to waste time. He had a lot of information to gather if he was to track down and eliminate the two men Bradley Byers' father held responsible for his son's murder. Jason Seaton wasn't a target, just a potential source of information. The assassin looked at his map app. Seaton's house backed onto a wooded area. That made the approach a little easier. Byrn glanced at the driveway again. He hadn't noticed it the first time, but a small bicycle lay on the drive just in front of the Mercedes. Kids. That made things more difficult.

Byrn hoped that Jason Seaton would be in a cooperative mood.

Twenty minutes later, Byrn stood in the shadow of the tall maples and oaks behind Seaton's house. If the man didn't show up in his backyard within two hours, the assassin would breach the home, but it was better to wait for his subject to emerge on his own. Fewer complications.

Forty minutes later, fortune smiled on the assassin. A tall man with broad shoulders stepped out of the back door. Byrn recognized him as Seaton from the photo on his company's website. While the man appeared quite fit, there were some telltale signs to the contrary. The beginnings of a slight pot belly and his complete lack of surveillance of the area, even if it was his own backyard. Rusty fieldcraft. The assassin waited. Seaton strolled over to a small shed behind the garage. He disappeared through the door, coming out a moment later with a plastic rake. From Byrn's point of view, that was better than a metal one.

Byrn gave Seaton ten minutes to focus on his task at hand before making his way through the woods to the property's rear fence. Although there was a gate that led out to the wooded area, Byrn didn't open it. He slid over the fence and moved immediately to the east of the garden, ensuring he remained out of Seaton's peripheral vision. Five yards from the man's back, Byrn slipped on his balaclava. He also withdrew his SIG.

Four more steps.

Seaton began to turn around.

"Don't," said the assassin. "Keep raking. If the rake leaves the ground, the bullet leaves the gun."

Seaton grunted.

"Just so you can do a quick threat assessment, you'll have every opportunity to live through this interaction if you do exactly as I say. If you don't, I withdraw my guarantee."

"Listen fella," Seaton began. "You've picked the wrong back yard. You're dealing with a professional here. Unless you go now, I would give you jack all chance of making it out of here intact. Why don't you do us both a favor and just piss off?"

Byrn glanced up at the house. They were out of view of any windows. He raised his right foot and jabbed hard at the back of Seaton's left knee. The man buckled.

"That was the one favor I'll do you today, Seaton. I appreciate exactly who I'm dealing with. A pussy cat. An overweight office boy who's grown out of touch with the world in which he professes expertise."

Seaton climbed to his feet and swung around. Byrn balled his fist and pounded the man hard on the side of his face. Seaton returned to his former position with a grunt and a thud.

"Geez. I must be in a good mood today," Byrn began. "That's two favors I've done you. Now get back on your feet and make your way directly to the rear gate. If you behave, you'll be reunited with your family in time for dinner. If you don't, well, as I mentioned, I offer no guarantees."

Seaton climbed back to his feet without looking around. Sluggishly, he stepped forward toward the rear fence.

Byrn didn't speak until they were well into the woods.

"Stop here. You can turn around."

Seaton turned abruptly, still nursing his damaged face. His eyes widened in surprise when he saw the balaclava.

"Yes, you're probably smart enough to appreciate that if I'm wearing the mask, then there is a strong chance this won't be your last day on the planet. I emphasize the word chance."

"Point acknowledged," Seaton replied.

Byrn continued. "We need to talk business. I need to understand as much as I can regarding the failed ransom and negotiation in the Bradley Byers' case."

Seaton's eyebrows rose.

"Well, judging by your manner and that mask you're wearing, I'm thinking you're not a cop. Only conclusion I can make is that Randal Byers has hired you to finalize some issues regarding this matter."

Byrn didn't respond.

"Why the hell didn't you just schedule an appointment with my secretary?"

"Not my style," Byrn replied. "Besides, I'm thinking not much goes on in your office that isn't recorded."

"Fair point. What do you want to know?"

"Karl Brill?"

"Yeah, that one surprised me. Karl had been with the

company for about five years. He was a good operator, otherwise I wouldn't have put him onto the Byers job."

"Why didn't you deal with it yourself? Byers must be a lucrative client."

Seaton smiled.

"You kind of made the observation yourself. I've spent most of the last few years behind a desk. Don't get me wrong, I can handle myself. If you hadn't got the drop on me, this would have been a very different conversation. Anyway, Karl was young, fit, and on point. If shit went down, I needed a man like that leading the team in the field."

Byrn smiled through the balaclava.

"Point one. If you'd been in professional shape, I wouldn't have got the drop on you. Point two. Did Brill have the brains to read the situation?"

"He didn't have to," Seaton responded. "I was on the phone the whole time calling the shots."

"So, what went wrong?"

"Nothing. Well, not at first. Karl delivered the cash and exited the zone, just as planned."

"Was he alone when he made the drop?"

"Yup, that was the instruction."

Byrn pondered the point.

"So, Brill had an opportunity to dispose of the cash, perhaps somewhere safe until he could get back to claim it?"

"Possibly, but unlikely."

"Why?"

"The rest of the team were out of the zone, but not far away. We didn't know where the drop off would happen until minutes before it did. Karl would have had no time to prepare."

"Where was the drop off?" asked Byrn.

"Out of town. An old farm in Bedford. Literally at the front gate. Easy access in and out. Quiet road. Good visuals to catch any observers. The location was well thought through."

"Did you trust Brill?"

"I wouldn't have sent him if I didn't. Although…"

Seaton stopped mid-sentence.

"Although what?" prompted Byrn.

Seaton hesitated for a moment.

"What the hell. I guess it makes no difference now. You're gonna do whatever you're gonna do. It didn't occur to me until afterwards, after Karl disappeared. The man lived luxuriously, almost beyond his means. We're well paid for our work, but he always wanted the latest car, a bigger boat. You know the routine. I did wonder if temptation had gotten the better of him."

"Did you share your doubts with Randal Byers?"

"Are you kidding? That would have reflected badly on the company and me."

"Do you still do work for Byers?"

"No."

"Bad blood?"

"Yeah, that's why I was surprised to see you in that mask. I thought Byers may have sent you after me. Nothing that went wrong was my fault, but with an arrogant prick like that, you just never know."

Byrn remained silent. Seaton stared at him, as though trying to come to a decision.

"So, assuming you're a hit man of some sort, and Byers is the one who hired you. Who are you after?"

Byrn stared right back.

"Sorry, need to know. And by the way, I prefer other descriptions to my role."

"Like what?"

"I'll leave that to your imagination."

Byrn was about to go when Seaton decided to make a point.

"Now listen here, tough guy. I've been mighty cooperative with you, but you've got to understand, a man in my position, well, you don't get to clobber me without some sort of retribution. I really have to teach you a lesson."

Byrn inhaled deeply and tilted his head to one side.

"I wouldn't go down that path."

"Too late, my friend. Personal alarm. Clicked it when you first opened your mouth. Isn't technology wonderful?"

Byrn paused. Listening to the almost silence of the woods.

"If you mean those two goons you've got coming up behind me, you'll be disappointed."

It didn't take long.

Byrn heard the first man advancing toward him over his right shoulder. He waited until his footfall was close, then pivoted, kicking the man in his gut. The man doubled forward. With synchronized precision, Byrn swiftly backhanded the man approaching to his left. The thug was huge, the blow barely slowing him. Byrn replicated the kick that he'd used on the first man, achieving exactly the same effect. The assassin figured he'd have less than five seconds before both men recovered enough to resume their assault.

Then there was Seaton to consider. Byrn sensed rather than saw him approach. Byrn stepped back, arcing the SIG between all three men.

"You're not going to shoot all of us before one takes you down," said Seaton.

"Maybe not, but you'll get to go first, Seaton."

Hesitation.

The security man pushed his palms up, signaling his men to stop. One of them didn't get the message. The guy on the right was two feet from Byrn when the assassin retrieved a PR-24 nightstick from under his jacket and brought it down viciously across his assailant's jaw. Without changing the direction of the blow, he swung around and brought the stick up under the second man's chin.

With half of their facial bones broken, they both crumpled to the forest floor.

Seaton stood dead still.

"Big mistake," said Byrn.

"Now, don't do anything rash…"

Byrn raised his pistol, took aim and shot Jason Seaton in the right ankle. He fell to the ground, moaning.

"Must be your lucky day, Seaton. Three favors in one day. I don't recommend you push for a fourth."

The assassin disappeared into the woods.

Chapter 36

Lachlan Byrn was frustrated.

Why did some people virtually beg him to shoot them? That situation could've had a simple resolution, but Jason Seaton opted for a different path. It turned out to be a foolish choice.

Good operators don't usually make foolish choices. If Seaton's mob were top level, they would have known better. If they were not highly skilled, why did Randal Byers recruit them for such a crucial situation? He should have known better.

Either way, Byrn had gained a vast amount of intel from the interaction.

At this point, he was certain of one fact. There would be no need to search for Karl Brill. The man had played out of his league and all the indicators suggested he would have paid with his life for that miscalculation.

His next task would be harder. It was essential he learned more about Dominic Nazar. Byrn figured the best place to start would be the Byer Corp publications. He needed to understand Nazar, in addition to Byers' published interpretation of the terrorist's role in Sudan. The way in which the situation had been reported may reveal a great deal.

Byrn reached into his pocket and retrieved the mandatory pills. The assassin faced a significant amount of ground to cover, and he wanted to stay one step ahead.

It was going to be a long night.

Chapter 37

REGAN DIA

Dia was no longer just conflicted. She was tearing herself apart.

At first, working for Randal Byers seemed like the challenge she'd sought. The work was engaging, diverse, and not solely physical. When the doubts about her boss's morality began gnawing at her, she attempted to cast them aside. As the relationship with Bradley developed, that became easier to do.

The fairytale romance led to the gift of their wonderful daughter. Clementine's birth changed Dia forever. She supposed every mother thought that way. As she and Brad agreed more and more regarding his father's unacceptable business strategies, it was easy to be comforted by the fact her husband had a plan. He appeared self-assured in his ability to steer the ship on a new course yet didn't disclose the details of his strategy.

Despite her desire to quit working, Brad insisted on her continuing. It wasn't as though they needed the money, but Brad wished for her to remain within his father's circle of confidence.

Strange, yet she trusted her husband completely.

Then the unthinkable happened. Brad was kidnapped.

Initially, it all seemed like a bad dream. Dia, however, remained confident in her father-in-law's willingness to dedicate every resource to the situation. She didn't know much about Seaton and Associates, although she'd heard their name around town. Randal said they were highly recommended specialists. It was no surprise that Byer Corp hadn't used them before. They'd never experienced a kidnapping before.

When Bradley was killed and the gruesome proof of death arrived, Dia's nightmare turned into a dark reality. She wanted to take Clementine and leave, but she knew her daughter would be safer under her grandfather's roof.

The night her father-in-law met with her in his study to request that she research and eventually observe Lachlan Byrn, Dia had been stunned. Although he didn't explain the purpose of the assignment, she had a fair idea of the old man's intentions. He seemed gutted by his son's death.

It was astounding that Randal even knew Byrn existed. The assassin didn't exactly advertise his services. It took her two months to even get the whiff of a trail. Even then it only occurred because Dia had been informed by the security people at Byer Corp's Beijing office that something unusual was taking place within the higher levels of the Chinese Security Service and it implicated an external threat from a lone killer, prompting her to make connections. That day at Beijing Capital International Airport, for the first time since beginning her search, two and two actually equaled four.

Dia sat in the downstairs lounge at the Medow Lane residence, looking out over the gray waves. Clementine slept peacefully in her room, thankfully oblivious to the turmoil surrounding her mother.

The question remained, what to do next? Dia could wait and let Byrn do what he had to do. After watching him operate, she had no doubt he would succeed. But would that bring an end to it all? Could she just get on with her grieving and begin to build a new life for her daughter and herself?

Dia shuffled restlessly in her chair, her mood as broody as the darkening clouds hovering over the ocean outside.

If she could rebuild, where did that leave her relationship with Randal Byers? His wealth provided security for Clementine. But was it enough? More and more, she felt like a prisoner in the old man's world, yet she had a certain obligation to him. Despite her skepticism regarding his ruthlessness in business, he'd been good to her. She owed him for that. And after all, he was her deceased husband's father.

Outside, the storm clouds suddenly opened up. A raucous thunder echoed through the almost empty house as torrents of rain pelted down across the garden.

Dia sipped her coffee.

Something consumed her internally, and despite her profound longing for her husband, it wasn't solely grief. It was as though an unidentified voice haunted her in the darkness.

So, what in God's name was it trying to tell her?

Chapter 38

LACHLAN BYRN

Lachlan Byrn knew a lot of people.

Many of them weren't nice people, but in his line of work, you didn't always get to choose the character traits of those you worked with. Most of his connections didn't know his name or what he looked like. Nevertheless, the relationships were firm, and money and information changed hands as required.

Again, Byrn waited. Two days had passed since he'd begun his search for Dominic Nazar, and the initial results were starting to come in.

Holed up in a small hotel in upstate New York, Byrn examined the evidence before him. Nazar had been reported in three separate locations. The first, logically enough, was Khartoum, in Sudan. If the assassin was required to travel there, so be it, but he placed the location third on his list. Besides, the information came from B grade sources.

The other two locations were Concord, New Hampshire, and Des Moines in Iowa. Of course they were in different directions. Byrn examined the quality of the intel and the reliability of the sources. Both came up as likely possibilities.

It came down to logistics and probabilities. Des Moines had a large Sudanese population, so Nazar may have reason to visit there and perhaps find easy sanctuary amongst like minds within the Sudanese community. On the other hand, New Hampshire was closer, and the intel was just as reliable.

Logistics won. Two hours later, the assassin having swapped his rental car over, headed north down the New York State Thruway. The road didn't demand much of Byrn's attention, so he revisited the information he'd uncovered about Dominic Nazar.

The man was a terrorist, there was no two ways about it. He wasn't a terrorist because he was Islamic or because he was Sudanese. Nazar was a terrorist because he killed guiltless people in the name of his cause. Byrn had known terrorists from numerous backgrounds, including Islamic, Christian, and non-religious Americans. It appeared to the assassin that they all shared a singular common trait. They felt part of a marginalized minority and any sacrifice of innocent life in promoting their cause was deemed inconsequential.

Several had died at the end of Byrn's gun.

Oddly enough, Nazar began life as a Christian and then converted to Islam. Southern Sudan seemed a perpetual battleground between the two forces. The assassin wondered why Nazar made the switch. Was it conviction? Was it convenience? Did one group satiate his ego more than the other? For sure, the man would have a huge sense of self-belief. Most killers did.

Byrn didn't really care for or about religion one way or another. He knew people found security in belonging. History told the story of individuals and armies fighting and dying for their beliefs. Byrn sometimes wondered if religious conflicts were just exaggerated gang wars. Still, it wasn't his place to judge. The assassin was agnostic. He'd decided quite simply that nobody who'd lived through the trauma of his past could believe in the existence of a higher spirit watching over them. His sole semi-religious thought was that religion may have been crafted by the devil to fuel factional wars and nourish evil.

Enough philosophy.

Nazar.

The man had developed a reputation as a brutal campaigner. His initially small band of followers grew as he led them into more violent activity. They'd kidnapped government officials and held them for ransom to boost their resources. Sometimes their captors were released, sometimes not. That went to prior experience when it came to the Byers situation. The group was known as *Ar-Ra'd*, The Thunder.

Good handle, bad people.

They'd raided churches, killing the men and leaving the women and children to tell of *Ar-Ra'd's* fury. They'd blown up two buses of Christian church groups spreading the Lord's word. The group had also placed bombs in village markets where the communities concerned seemed to waver between Christian and Islamic dominance. If Muslims were killed along the way, Nazar didn't seem to care. It was all for the greater good.

At the end of the day, Dominic Nazar was a brutal killer and sadist who, like all of his kind, brought many of the good people who shared his religious beliefs into disrepute. That is, *if* Nazar held genuine beliefs.

Byrn hated opportunists.

The motivation for Nazar's involvement in the Bradley

Byers kidnapping was straight forward. One hundred million dollars bought you a great deal of terror. Bruised ego was also an aspect. If Randal Byers was behind the public pressure that brought the Sudanese government down on Nazar's group, then the revenge of extracting money from the media magnate would have been a sweetener. From what Byrn could make out from the Byer Corp media coverage, Byers certainly had some impact on swaying public opinion against the group.

The rain poured down steadily by the time Byrn reached the outskirts of Concord, the state's capital. The assassin's information suggested Nazar and a couple of his henchmen were staying above an African restaurant on North Main Street in the heart of Concord. Byrn pulled off the interstate and drove directly there.

After finding an angle park in view of the restaurant, Byrn dug in and waited. The rain eased. He'd moved the car three times before his patience was finally rewarded. In the fading afternoon shadows, a tall, well-built man of African descent emerged from a side door near the eatery. Two men followed him. They wore western clothes, but their tops were colorful and eye-catching. The lead guy resembled Dominic Nazar, but Byrn couldn't confirm the ID from afar.

The assassin got out of his car, crossed the street, and strolled toward the men so he'd come up directly opposite them. They stood in front of the restaurant, talking. Their conversation appeared intense. Byrn felt his adrenaline build. Equally, a calm coolness enveloped him as the prospect of a kill loomed. If the men turned left and headed toward him, Byrn could make an ID. If they turned right, there would be a problem.

They turned right.

Byrn faced two choices. He could backtrack to his car, move it closer to the restaurant, and wait for the men to return, or he could follow on foot, and try to overtake them. He chose the latter.

Byrn strode quickly up the road on the opposite side to his potential quarry. He gained on them steadily. When they turned right at the next intersection, he lost ground, having to take a longer route on the far side. Once again, traveling parallel, but behind them, Byrn broke into a semi-jog. If any of the men glanced across and to the rear, they'd only see a man running late, perhaps scurrying for a dinner appointment. Byrn kept glancing at his watch, completing the picture. When he drew even with his targets, the assassin slowed to a fast walk. He still couldn't confirm that the big guy was Nazar. He pulled out his cell and checked Nazar's photo.

He then resumed his stride. Five minutes later, he was well past the three men who now seemed to be dawdling. Byrn crossed the road, reversed direction, and marched directly toward them. One close look would be all he needed.

With less than fifty yards separating them, Byrn stared straight ahead, as though looking past the men toward his fictitious destination.

Thirty yards. Height and physique confirmed.

Twenty yards. The center man looked to be in the right age range.

Five yards. A single careful observation, not overly pro-longed.

Everything checked.

Except it wasn't Dominic Nazar.

Byrn had just wasted twenty-four hours.

The assassin returned to his car and drove toward Manchester Boston Regional Airport. Thirty minutes later, he'd purchased a cash ticket for the 6.03 am. American Airlines flight to Des Moines, Iowa.

An hour after that, Byrn lay his head down on a pillow at the nearby Homewood Suites Hotel. He wouldn't sleep, but he would rest. Despite the inconvenient diversion of the New Hampshire experience, Byrn remained optimistic. Certainly, he wanted this job out of the way. It had become needlessly complicated and time consuming, yet the assassin wouldn't rush to its conclusion. Lachlan Byrn never rushed. He would locate, identify and then remove Dominic Nazar from the planet in an orderly and well-planned manner.

In Byrn's mind, Nazar was as good as dead.

Chapter 39

Enough with the internal warfare.

Dia had been trained to perform decisively. The 'mourning widow' thing just wasn't her. The only factor holding her back was the thought of her beautiful daughter growing up parentless. Yet would that be any worse than living with a mother who lived her whole life in regret because she didn't act when she could have?

Dia reviewed the facts once more.

What exactly could she do? Byrn was out searching for Karl Brill and Dominic Nazar. She didn't doubt that he'd find them, but was this really his fight? That said, Byrn was a paid assassin. No fight was his fight, and all fights were his fights. The man was a walking conundrum.

The problem was that Dia had no idea where either Brill or Nazar were.

She figured Byrn would start with Jason Seaton. If Dia adopted the same strategy, it would mean she was always one step behind the assassin. She needed to get out in front of this.

Assuming Seaton may lead to Brill, who might connect

Byrn to Nazar, Byrn's approach would have to be slow and methodical.

Again, what could she do?

Randal.

Did he know more than he was letting on? He'd drip fed information before, always manipulating the flow of intelligence to his own advantage. Maybe he was doing it now. Was her father-in-law/boss aware of Dominic Nazar's whereabouts, or if he was even in the country?

Unlikely?

Possible?

It was the only possible lead Dia had.

So, if Randal had that knowledge, and that was an enormous sized 'if', how would Dia get her hands on it?

Dia decided she'd stared at enough waves to sail around the world. She got up from her chair and headed to Clementine's nursery. She eased the nursery door open gently. The gorgeous child lay on her back, sound asleep. The nanny, an advantage of wealth, slept in the next room. Both rooms were linked by a baby monitor.

All right. This was it. To Dia's knowledge, she was the only person in the house awake, apart from the overnight guard stationed in the front foyer. She purposefully strolled past him.

"How are you traveling, Jake? Still awake?"

The young security guard slouched in a chair by the front door, watching something on his phone. He sat bolt upright when he saw Regan.

"Yes, fine thanks, Ms. Dia," he replied, slipping his phone into his pocket.

"I had to get up to attend Clementine, but experience tells

me I won't be able to go back to sleep for a while. Can I fetch you a coffee?"

"No thanks, ma'am. But it's very kind of you to offer."

"Not a problem, Jake. But if you hear someone fluttering around, don't call in the troops, it's just me."

"Very good, Ms. Dia."

Point made. Dia wandered off and up the stairs.

Toward Randal Byers' study.

The advantages of being family. Dia knew exactly where the independent alarm pad was for the study. Her fingers traced the architrave, finding the switch. She clicked it upward.

Passing through the doorway, Dia was surprised how much moonlight lit the room. It was her first time here with the lights off. She'd brought a pocket flashlight from her nightstand but didn't bother turning it on. If she discovered something of interest, she might use it.

Dia began with the desk drawers before moving onto to the credenza. These days, way less paperwork cluttered up workspaces. It didn't take her long to eliminate every document she encountered as irrelevant.

As expected, it came down to the computer. It troubled her that any foray into Randal's personal files would leave a digital footprint if someone chose to search for it. She decided it was a risk worth taking.

The password.

This was her most likely point of failure. How many attempts would she be allowed before the system closed down? What chance would she really have?

Common sense told her to exit the room, turn the alarm back on, and go to bed. Byrn would handle his end, and the job would be done. Instead, common sense exited the room. Dia was determined, angry, and set on revenge.

She held down the power button, and the screen lit up. Carefully, she typed in Bradley's name.

Password incorrect.

She tried Bradley's deceased brother's name.

Incorrect.

Her father-in-law's yacht's name.

Same result.

Then she had an idea. It probably should have been the first name she tried.

Clementine.

The light on the screen flickered.

Incorrect.

Shit.

Dia sat back in the chair. She'd exhausted every known family name, her only remaining options. Beyond those, the damn password could literally be anything.

Okay, that was it then. Dia stood up, reached over and moved the mouse to click on the 'turn off' setting.

Then she paused. There was one family name she hadn't attempted. She sat down and typed in five letters.

R -E -G -A -N

The screen sprang to life. Well, how about that?

Forty minutes later, her excitement had evaporated. Randal's filing system appeared complicated and, to some extent, haphazard. She'd discovered a great deal of extraneous information regarding how the man ran his corporation, but nothing specifically relevant to the kidnapping, Bradley's death, or either Karl Brill or Dominic Nazar.

Dia had simply run out of places to look.

Then she had a thought.

She backtracked to the security folder and searched 'tracking'. A lot of useless information that pertained to the physical transfer of company documents appeared. Irrelevant, again. Dia stayed withing the tracking file but drilled deeper. Within the original file was another marked 'personal'.

She clicked on the icon.

The folder had fewer documents, yet none seemed linked to recent events. There was some shifting of mortgage records on Randal Byers' various houses, all electronically tracked. He was clearly a careful man. She clicked on a file that had Randal's first wife's name: Jennifer. Surprisingly, she found some IVF related documents. She followed their tracking to a point in time where they were destroyed. Dia briefly wondered what she may be able to read into that situation.

There was nothing else in the personal tracking file that caught her interest. She clicked on each icon one more time, this time being increasingly open to anything she didn't understand.

She paid specific attention to Brad's file, but again came up with nothing. She was about to click away when she saw a folder marked Clementine. What could possibly be in there?

Dia felt her fury rise as she discovered documents pertaining to education. The child was barely twelve-months old, and the old man had already enrolled her in a swank private elementary school without her and, she assumed, Brad's knowledge. What a manipulating prick. Angry, her finger rested on the mouse, ready to click away when she noted another file.

'CF'.

Dia looked at it. No family member had initials 'CF'. She

stared at the screen.

'CF'. What the hell?

Then it hit her. CF, an accountant's slang for cash flow. She clicked on the icon.

There it was. The initials CF and a series of coordinates. She copied the first numbers and put them through an internet search. Randal's office location.

She repeated the action for the second set. The farmhouse that was the arranged drop point for the ransom money appeared.

Dia cast her eyes to the final set of coordinates on the list. She copied those figures and pasted them into the search engine.

She flipped to a satellite image and zoomed in.

What a bastard. Deep down, Dia knew it would be almost impossible for a man like Randal Byers to abandon one hundred million dollars. He'd tracked the cash the whole way.

Yet he seemed to have less difficulty abandoning his own son.

Dia closed down the computer, relocked the study, and made her way downstairs.

After grabbing her credit cards and purse from her room, she headed toward the foyer.

Once again, the guard snapped himself upright.

"I really can't sleep, Jake. I'm going for a stroll along the beach."

"Do you want me to wake up one of the other guys to go with you, Ms. Dia?"

"No need, Jake. I'll be fine. I just need some fresh air."

"Sure thing, ma'am."

Dia turned and exited the house through the main lounge and onto the patio. Once she'd crossed the boardwalk, she headed up the beach until she found the path that led to the road. Then she called a cab.

By the time the sun rose, she was reclining in her seat on a Delta flight out of JFK heading toward Des Moines, Iowa, specifically an abandoned railway yard near Gray's Lake.

Chapter 40

RANDAL BYERS

The vibrating alarm on Byers' wristwatch woke him. The old man glanced at the time. It was 3.10 a.m., long before the timer was due to go off. Clearly, something unexpected triggered it.

The old man rubbed his eyes before scrolling down.

The study computer.

Byers reached over to his nightstand and grabbed his laptop. He typed in his password, and the screen immediately mirrored the screen on the study computer.

Well, fancy that. Byers grinned.

He held no doubt as to who'd accessed the device. Only one person in the house would even consider interrogating his private files.

The tycoon watched and followed Dia's journey through the documents. It took a while, but in the end she got there.

Byers smiled again. So, it turned out the woman had balls of steel, after all.

He then closed down the laptop, rolled over, and went back to sleep.

Four hours later, Byers sat at the desk in his private study, examining in detail the files that had been accessed by Regan Dia the night before. There was nothing of great consequence apart, of course, from the data outlining the tracking of the one hundred million dollars ransom money.

It was always a risk to plant the GPS tracking mechanism amongst the cash, but the device was so thin it slipped easily within two bills in a stack and added no detectable extra weight. Despite what he'd told Byrn, one hundred million dollars was a substantial sum to lose for no reason. Besides, it assisted Byers in overseeing the big picture. Perspective.

A brief knock on the door disrupted the tycoon's train of thought. He looked up from the screen.

"Hemmings?"

"Sorry to intrude, sir, but this envelope just arrived by secure courier. I thought you'd want to see it immediately."

Byers' chief of security strode across the room and handed the package to his boss. He remained standing on the other side of the desk, awaiting further instructions.

"Thank you."

Byers took the sealed envelope and slit it open with a metal letter opener. He withdrew the enclosed papers and unfolded them.

The businessman sensed the smile crease his face as he read through the document.

Under the letterhead of the Federal Bureau of Investigation – Criminal Investigation Division, the letter was addressed to Byer's chief legal counsel, Steven Prince.

Dear Mr. Prince,

I am writing to inform you that the investigation into your clients, specifically Byer Corp and its chairman Mr. Randal Byers, in relation to allegations of corporate fraud, the falsification of financial information, securities and commodities fraud and the potential funding of terrorism has been permanently suspended.

This decision has been taken based on the following factors:

- *Lack of substantiated evidence*
- *Unavailability of appropriate witnesses*

We thank you for your cooperation with our investigators over the last twelve months.

You, Mr. Byers, or any of the companies outlined in our initial communication will not hear from our organization again with regard to the above matters unless new evidence comes to our attention.

Sincerely,
Walter J Ross
Executive Assistant Director

"Thank you, Hemmings. There will be nothing further."

The security chief nodded and left the room.

Randal Byers leaned back in his chair and swiveled toward the large window overlooking the sea.

It was almost over.

Byers had been through a lot over the decades. He'd made money, he'd lost money, he'd built, he'd destroyed, and all along the way he'd consciously remained aloof from personal connections. That was his magic, his secret ingredient. It was a transactional world, so he'd sought nothing more than transactional relationships. He surrounded himself with useful people and discarded the rest.

He wondered if some would call him a sociopath.

The entrepreneur regarded himself as an astute strategist.

The last couple of years had been his most challenging. His whole corporate world, which in effect meant his world, had nearly come crashing down. The worst part was that the betrayal came from within.

Now that this particular battle had been won, he'd keep going. Why would he stop? Byers had hoped to pass the business on to the next generation so it could continue to flourish and embed the name Byers in American corporate history, along with the Rockefellers and Fords.

But it wasn't to be. His eldest son, Jonathan, would have taken the reins and charged forward, allowing no one to stand in his way. Sadly, that damn disease had claimed the young man before he'd really gotten started.

As for Bradly. He just never had it in him. The signs were there from the beginning.

Weakness.

Fragility.

At one point, the tycoon had hopes for him. When Bradley returned to the company so eagerly, it seemed there was a chance.

Then the hope died.

Chapter 41

LACHLAN BYRN

Byrn strode through the terminal at Des Moines International Airport just after midday.

A quick check of the encrypted page where the assassin gathered vital 'real time 'information revealed that his Iowa contact had sighted Nazar. The source suggested Dominic Nazar's presence in Des Moines was now virtually confirmed. The informant stated that he'd personally sighted the terrorist and had verified his identity in comparison with a recent picture. The contact had also warned that Nazar had a team with him and recommended due care.

Good service. A considerable amount of money would be changing hands shortly.

Byrn dashed out of the terminal to his pre-booked rental. His false identification for the booking was totally untraceable. Once he climbed into the almost new Nissan, he set the map app to the abandoned railway yard on the south side of Gray's Lake, the location his man in the field had indicated.

The traffic was reasonably light, and Byrn made it there within the hour. After a brief drive past revealed nothing, the assassin parked the vehicle half a mile away and jogged back to the yard.

When he neared the fenced perimeter, he slowed to a walk. The chain wire fence allowed a good view into the yard. Byrn ducked down, as though adjusting a shoelace, and studied the layout.

The desolate area covered around two acres and consisted of a couple of abandoned freight cars in poor order, and in the distance, three dilapidated sheds. At first glance, no recent activity was apparent.

Byrn kept looking.

He was about to relocate to find a different viewing angle when he saw it. At the base behind one of the freight car's wheels, there was a boot and the lower leg of a pair of jeans. But the boot pointed upward to the sky.

Instead of risking exposure along the length of the fence line, the assassin climbed over the wire and descended to the other side. As he approached the freight car, he tried to keep its bulk between him and the sheds. When he reached the car, Byrn flattened himself against it and listened.

Nothing.

The assassin dropped down and rolled under the car.

Now in view, the man appeared tall, well built and totally unconscious. A Glock G19 lay inches from his open palm. Byrn confiscated the weapon and some extra ammunition from the man's jacket pocket.

The assassin surveyed the area beyond the freight car. At first, nothing significant caught his attention. But then, on his second inspection, Byrn spotted what appeared to be an elbow protruding from the far wall of the closest shed. He checked that the Glock functioned correctly before repeating his previous exercise. Keeping well out of view of anyone on the far side of the shed, Byrn jogged silently over to the near wall before inching himself carefully down the side. As he closed in on the corner, the assassin confirmed that his initial observation had been correct. The protruding offender was an elbow, yet it didn't appear to be moving at all.

That meant little.

Byrn was five feet from the corner when the elbow suddenly shifted. Its owner had obviously heard him. The assassin sprang forward, his finger ready on the Glock's trigger. As he did so, a male body slumped sideways down onto Byrn's boots. The assassin gazed downward at the prone shape. The man's throat had been slit clean across.

Byrn looked up, searching for the assailant.

Nothing.

What was going on here? Should he retreat and regroup, or proceed?

Byrn rarely retreated.

The assassin stepped forward, moving briskly in the direction of the next shed. It was larger than the structure he'd just left and appeared to have a large sliding door midway down its length. Byrn neared the building's corner, ready to move toward the door, when he heard footsteps. He immediately retreated behind the corner.

He needed to understand the situation before proceeding. The footsteps grew louder.

Byrn dropped to the ground and poked an eye around the end of the structure.

What the hell?

Amongst a flurry of long, dark hair, Byrn could just make out Regan Dia's face as she entered the building through the sliding door.

This couldn't be good.

Chapter 42

DOMINIC NAZAR

Nazar sat at the old wooden table, staring out the window. The shed was dark and cold, yet the weather outside was worse. He missed his beloved Sudan, its warmth, its culture, even his political foes. Nazar loved a good fight. Shortly, when he returned to his home country, those in opposition would see what a good fight he would bring.

They called him a terrorist. He thought himself a freedom fighter. What were words anyway? Nazar had always fought for what he believed was right, as far as it aligned with what would benefit him personally. Recently, all his planets seemed to align perfectly.

The hundred million dollars would greatly assist his people, as well as fund his new coastal residence on the Red Sea. The plan had run flawlessly. Kidnapping Randal Byers' son had been like taking candy from the proverbial baby. Nazar was a thorough strategist. Where he observed weakness, he built strength. That idiot Karl Brill was his insurance, just in case there were any unforeseen hiccups or misalignments in the process. Like so many westerners, Brill was perpetually greedy, consistently living just beyond his means. Allah certainly didn't share the purity of the satisfaction of a humble lifestyle with these barbarians. There was always something more. A new toy, a more prestigious symbol of grandeur.

Pathetic.

Brill was in debt, so the offer of ten million dollars to guarantee a seamless delivery of Byers' one hundred million had been too good an opportunity for him to refuse. The fool had actually thought he'd live to spend the money. Naivete personified. Within twenty-four hours of the transfer of the cash, Karl Brill was dead and the outstanding ten million dollars returned to Nazar.

The terrorist's group, *Ar-Ra'd,* had taken some hits over the last couple of years, but that no longer worried Nazar. This money would ensure that, although the thunder may have diminished, a hurricane of hatred was about to descend on his enemies.

There are no innocents in war.

"Dominic, we'll be set to leave in sixty minutes."

The terrorist turned around. He hadn't even heard Azim enter. His offsider was extraordinarily stealthy.

"I will be ready," he replied.

"We'll be home soon, Dominic. We left as paupers. We'll return as kings," Azim smiled.

"Yes, my old friend, we surely will. Yet again Allah has blessed us."

Azim nodded and walked off.

Nazar scratched his chin, leaned back in his chair and returned his gaze to the window. Not all the credit could go to Allah. 'My intelligence and forethought have also blessed us', he decided. Of course, those thoughts would never be spoken aloud.

Nazar had stayed in the US long enough to shore up local support and the appropriate networks that would ensure victory back in South Sudan. Wars were won as equally in the corridors of influence as they were on the battlefield. Here in Des Moines, Iowa, the Sudanese community was strong. Sadly, the majority of the African population would have nothing to do with Nazar. They regarded him as a violent radical, bringing their belief system into disrepute.

Fools.

They didn't see that he was going to be the one to save them. Their freedom would be gained standing upon his shoulders.

Despite his alienation amongst his countrymen, there was enough extreme support in fringe groups here and elsewhere in American African communities to provide him with what he needed.

People would die, but the cause, not to mention his own prestige, would grow. Then they would either become believers or be forced to submit.

Regardless, Dominic Nazar would come out on top.

The terrorist briefly considered the other western fool who played a crucial role in his plans. Bradley Byers. The man's death was inevitable. Events could progress no other way. Young Byers' family could grieve while Nazar rejoiced.

To the winners go the spoils.

Nazar glanced around the old railway shed. The location was perfect for them. Isolated, yet close enough to the community to do business. He'd only brought a handful of men with him, but they were professionals. The disused railway yard provided ample sightlines and man-made canyons to ensure their security. His team had seen to the task admirably. Victory was in the details.

Dominic Nazar continued to peer out to the dreary day. He and his soldiers would be home soon, and as Azim had said, they would return as kings.

Perfect.

Just over sixty minutes later, Nazar glanced at his watch. Azim would be coming for him at any time. Their journey home would shortly commence.

Ten minutes after that, the terrorist wondered why he hadn't been called.

"Azim, are you there? When do we leave?" he shouted toward the shed door.

No response.

"Azim?"

Nothing.

Nazar picked his phone up from the table and pressed a contact on speed dial.

No reply.

He left a message.

"Azim, I am beginning to grow concerned. Please call or come." He hung up.

Dominic Nazar had not survived this long by taking anything for granted. It could be nothing, but better to be certain. He leaned forward to where his automatic pistol lay on the table. As his finger touched the grip he noted a shuffling sound behind him. Footsteps.

"Ah, Azim, where have you…."

Nazar momentarily hesitated. No, of course not. It couldn't be Azim, because Nazar had heard the footsteps. The terrorist lunged for his weapon.

"No, not an inch further, or you will die with your face flat on the table."

The terrorist froze.

"Now turn toward me, slowly."

Nazar followed the instruction, rotating gradually in his chair.

The intruder stepped out of the shadows; a pistol pointed at Nazar's heart.

"I knew they would send someone after me," he began, "but to be honest, I'd considered all eventualities covered."

"You were wrong."

"Evidently so," Nazar responded. "But again, to be honest, I'm also surprised. It was not you that I expected."

"Life is full of surprises. So is death."

"I have resources. Is there a possibility of negotiation?" the terrorist suggested.

"No."

"I thought not when I saw your face. Do you seek information before I die?" Nazar was stalling, hoping a plan or some avenue of escape would appear.

"No, not information. Only retribution."

Shit. The terrorist saw no possible pathway of retreat. He shrugged his shoulders in reluctant acceptance.

"It is what it is. Then please make it quick and clean. I've heard that your accuracy with a weapon is almost unparalleled."

"Well, we're about to find out."

As she spoke, Regan Dia took a step forward and began to squeeze the trigger.

Chapter 43

LACHLAN BYRN

"Don't do it, Dia. At least not yet. You need to step back and think this through."

Byrn had followed Dia through the door, arriving just in time to see the muscles in her fingers tense on the pistol's trigger.

"Lachlan. You were surprisingly quick to reach this same conclusion."

Dia spoke but didn't take her eyes off Nazar.

"I'm not convinced it's a conclusion yet," replied Byrn. "There may be more information we should access."

Byrn noted that Dia still hadn't pulled the trigger. At least he had her attention.

"What more is there? This asshole murdered my husband, so now I'm going to end his life. It's a straightforward transaction."

Nazar sat at the table, immobile. He gazed at the two figures, wondering how the hell they had got past his men. He was all too aware that his weapon lay inches from his fingertips, but it appeared that to budge an inch would mean certain death, at least in the woman's eyes.

Byrn strolled toward Dia. He stopped three yards short and to her left.

"How about you give me five minutes with him? If no further information is forthcoming, then you shoot him."

"And if he tells us something we don't know?"

The assassin sighed. "That's up to you."

Dia nodded.

"Five minutes."

Byrn continued toward Nazar, sitting upright at the table, the assassin's Glock trained at the terrorist's heart. The man remained motionless, like a statue. Byrn reached the table, leaned down, and picked up the gun. He placed it gently on the floor, far from the man's reach. A spare chair was positioned across from Nazar; the assassin sat down.

"I know who she is," said Nazar, nodding toward Dia, "but who are you?"

Byrn gazed at the man, searching for any sign of fear. He found none.

"I'll be asking the questions today, Dominic."

The terrorist grunted.

Byrn sat back in the seat.

"Let's take it as a given that you murdered Bradley Byers. What I want to understand is why?"

Nazar stared at Byrn, his expression a mixture of amusement and contempt.

"If I answer truthfully, will I be permitted to live?"

Byrn smiled. "Pertinent question, so I'll allow it."

Nazar frowned. "You sound like a fucking court of law."

"In more ways than you know, Dominic, but in this particular case, the lady over there is the ultimate level of appeal."

They both looked at Dia. She shrugged her shoulders.

"Answer the question, asshole," said Byrn.

Nazar nodded. "It seems that I have nothing to lose. I killed the man for the hundred million dollars."

"But you already had the money."

"I did, and that fool Brill was my insurance policy. It turned out I didn't need insurance, so his services were terminated." Nazar smiled.

Byrn nodded.

"Okay. You reclaimed Brill's commission and had secured all the cash. Why not just release Bradley Byers as per the deal?"

Byrn didn't need to look around to appreciate that Dia's nerves would be on a knife's edge at this moment. For her, this was as personal as it gets.

Nazar raised his arms slowly, palm open.

"You are not understanding, my friend. That wasn't the deal."

Dia interrupted.

"You demanded the money, my father-in-law paid. You were meant to release my husband. That *was* the arrangement."

"There can be arrangements within arrangements," Nazar responded.

Byrn glanced at Dia. Her furrowed eyebrows suggested she was perplexed. Byrn didn't blame her. He wasn't certain where they were going with this himself, yet he had a fair idea.

"Was there an outside party involved in the arrangement?" he asked.

Nazar shook his head.

"None."

"This doesn't make sense," said Dia. "This man murdered my husband because he didn't want any further risk to himself or his men. I'm going to end this now."

Byrn raised his right hand without taking his eyes off the terrorist.

"You promised me five minutes, Dia. I have two left."

Dia's gun didn't fire, so Byrn continued.

"You clearly don't have long to get to the point and make your case. I suggest we cut straight to the end game. Who paid you to kill Bradley Byers?"

"It was a package deal. Kidnap the man and dispose of him. I was compensated generously for my services."

"How generously?"

The clock was ticking.

"As I said, one hundred million dollars," Nazar replied sarcastically, as though talking to a child.

"And the person who commissioned you?"

"From the tone of your questions, I suspect you already know the answer to that question," Nazar responded, before pausing.

The terrorist played the gap in the conversation for as long as he could. Byrn decided he was looking for a way out and probably slowly accepting he wouldn't find one.

Finally.

"The arrangements were made through intermediaries and encrypted communications."

Byrn waited.

"But I did my due diligence. The man manipulating events, the individual responsible for hiring, paying and instructing me was Randal Byers."

Byrn heard an intense gasp emanate from Dia.

A second later, the sound of a single shot resonated around the shed's metallic walls. Dominic Nazar's head smashed onto the table, spewing a stream of crimson blood.

Chapter 44

Almost immediately, there was another shot. The glass on the window near where Nazar had been sitting shattered.

"Get down," shouted Byrn.

Dia didn't need to be told. She knew she hadn't fired the second shot and was already on the floor.

"Who?" she shouted.

"Who do you think doesn't want the information we just learned to become public knowledge?"

Another gunshot echoed through the shed.

"Byers?" Dia yelled.

"We'll talk about it later. Let's get out of here."

Then the peppering began.

Bullets ricocheted off the walls and shattered the remaining windows. Lying flat on the floor, Byrn glanced back toward the only door. The floorboards in the entrance's immediate vicinity were being pulverized.

"I'll return some fire to keep them occupied," yelled Byrn. "Stay low and away from the doorway. Check out the floor for any points of egress."

"Got it," she shouted back over the din. "How many of them do you think there are?"

"Too many," Byrn responded. The assassin perched on one

knee, firing out the first broken window.

Byrn figured their attackers would continue their barrage for another few minutes. When the return fire stopped, they'd listen for an additional minute before making a coordinated assault through the doors and windows. If he and Dia were inside the shed at that moment, they were essentially dead.

The assassin fired three more rounds at no one in particular.

"Here," yelled Dia. She lay flat in the north-western corner of the building. The former ranger was using a knife to pry a couple of floorboards loose. "Two minutes."

Byrn fired again.

In response, the gunfire from outside doubled. As rounds bounced around the space and tore up the floorboards, Byrn wondered if he'd even make it over to Dia.

"Now," she yelled.

Byrn fired one more shot out the window before slithering across the floor toward her. All around him, bullets smashed into the floor, showering him with slivers of wood. The situation was a crap shoot.

"Don't wait for me," shouted the assassin. "Just get out."

"Roger that," Dia responded.

Byrn watched her exit the hole she'd created in the floor.

A second later, he felt a round tear into his upper right thigh like a burning arrow. Despite the pain, he struggled forward.

Chapter 45

REGAN DIA

Dia reached under the floor, her fingers finding a thick wooden joist as she pulled herself down. She noted Byrn's grunt of pain as she hit the dirt, but there was nothing she could do from her position.

Such was its intensity that the roar of the gunfire was almost as loud under the building as it had been inside. Dia knew she still wasn't out of the woods as several rounds penetrated the floorboards and thudded into the surrounding earth.

With less than three feet between the floor above her and the ground below, she struggled forward on her belly in the darkness.

A minute later, her hand touched the coarseness of the outer brick wall. She pivoted and tried to kick through the solid foundations. It was futile.

The former ranger scrutinized her environment, her desperation rising. She needed to get out and pave a trail for Byrn - if he made it.

Fifteen yards to her right, she noticed a small shard of light penetrating the underfloor area. Rolling back onto her belly, she slithered toward it. As she got closer, the source of light became clearer. A small grate of some kind for subfloor ventilation. She pushed herself along on the dirt as rapidly as the confined space would allow.

When she'd covered the distance, Dia stretched forward, clutching the grate with both hands. It didn't budge. She tried a second time with the same result. With mounting exasperation, she extended her arm in the dim light, searching for any tool that could assist her. Three seconds later, her knuckles collided against something solid. She peered down at three quarters of a brick. After wrapping her fingers around it, she heaved it forward toward the grate.

Nothing.

Keeping a tight grip on the brick, she tried again.

Was there the tiniest bit of movement in the concrete surrounding the grate?

She smashed it again and again; the noise lost in the cacophony of the gunfire. As she felt the sweat pour down her face, the former ranger beat the grill with furious intensity.

Suddenly, she saw a crack appear in the adjacent concrete. She pounded some more.

Frantically.

A couple of seconds later, another crack appeared, then abruptly, she was through. The bricks adjacent to the grate collapsed onto the dirt outside.

Almost the second they hit the ground, Dia was struck by a frightening silence.

The shooting had stopped.

She craned her neck to look into the darkness behind her. There was no sign of Byrn.

There was some yelling from outside the building and then

the shuffling of boots on the dirt.

They were going in.

Dia closed her eyes for a second. There was no doubt.

Lachlan Byrn was a dead man.

Chapter 46

LACHLAN BYRN

The onslaught of silence hit just as Byrn thudded down onto the dirt under the shed. The assassin glanced around, seeing no sign of Dia. Then, in the distance, he noted what seemed to be a leg and foot disappearing through a hole in the wall.

Byrn instinctively headed toward the light.

He'd made it halfway across when he heard boots scuffling on the wooden floorboards. It would only be seconds before their assailants discovered their makeshift escape route.

Byrn pushed himself harder. The leg hurt like all hell, but over the years, thanks to Zhen Zu's morbid training, he had become a master of compartmentalizing pain. All that mattered was the light.

The assassin glanced behind him. Suddenly, the distant glare didn't matter anymore.

The only other illumination under the shed came from their hole in the floor. Byrn saw one pair of boots hit the dirt directly underneath it. It was followed a second later by another.

Byrn immediately headed away from the light. What he needed now was darkness.

He watched the men crouch down and scrutinize the underfloor space.

"We need a fucking light," yelled the first man.

"We ain't got one," came the reply from above. "Spray the whole area, and for God's sake, keep your aim low. We don't need you hitting us."

Byrn noted a further commotion from above as he watched the second man join the first, crouching down under the floor beside his partner. The assassin could make out the shadows of the automatic rifles in each of their hands.

At that moment, Byrn decided not to die today.

Still laying on his gut, he brought the Glock to bear on the first operative just as the man raised his weapon. The assassin used the clearly outlined silhouette of the man's rifle as a sight to his victim's forehead.

He squeezed the trigger.

The man lunged back into the joist behind him and slid awkwardly to the ground. The second guy turned his head. Byrn fired again. The sickening click of an empty chamber filled the air.

The second man turned into the sound, lifted his weapon, and released a volley of automatic fire in Byrn's direction. The assassin pressed himself hard into the dirt. Shards of dirt and rubble saturated the space as bullets connected with whatever object they could find. Miraculously, Byrn wasn't one of them.

The attacker stopped, shifted position and then fired toward the eastern quadrant of the underfloor area. After spraying that, he turned and repeated the process to the north.

The shooter was firing in a logical sequence, covering

all areas to ensure his kill. Instead of trying to escape the barrage, Byrn slithered toward it, staying behind each quadrant that was under fire. When the shooter started moving counterclockwise, Byrn was only ten feet away.

The deafening volume of the onslaught had completely masked any sound of Byrn's approach.

As the shooter finished a second attack on the area where Byrn had been, he shifted to repeat the process on the eastern quadrant, exactly where Byrn was now positioned. An unexpected change of strategy.

Damn.

The shooter frantically brought his gun to bear at the looming shadow just as Byrn's fist connected with the man's jaw. His head snapped back, but the gun kept rising. Byrn reached out with his left hand and shoved the weapon's barrel down and away. A cannonade of bullets peppered the ground, inches away from Byrn's body. The assassin yanked on the rifle, bringing both it and the assailant's arms forward. He then thrust the rifle backwards, the heel of the stock smashing hard into the operative's face.

Desperate, the man pounded the side of Byrn's head. With pain exploding through his skull, the assassin repeated his previous move with the gun three times in rapid succession, until his victim grunted his way into unconsciousness.

Byrn figured he had no choice about what to do next.

He flipped the rifle around, poking it upward through the gap in the floor. He followed the weapon through the hole and then, without pausing to seek out a target, sprayed the inside of the shed with a fusillade of rapid fire.

But nobody was there.

Crap.

Byrn pulled himself up through the gap. As he stood, his right leg took his weight, but not without pain. Only a graze. Ignoring the stabbing sensation, Byrn sprinted toward the building's entrance. Three feet from the entrance, he slowed before peeking his head through the door frame.

The first thing he noted was a crumpled body laying splayed awkwardly on the ground next to the adjacent shed. He followed the sightline along the building's brick wall just in time to see a figure disappear around the furthest corner. A female figure.

Dia.

Byrn immediately assumed she was circling the shed to come in on the other side. Keep the enemy guessing. That's what he would have done. It didn't occur to the assassin for one second that Dia was abandoning him, although she had every justification to do so.

The immediate problem lay in what Byrn saw to his right. Three large men had obviously noticed their comrade sprawled on the ground and were heading around the other side of the shed to ambush the former ranger.

Byrn raised his weapon, clicked the switch onto manual to save ammunition and fired. He eliminated the last man, but the other two escaped.

The question now was how prepared was Dia to confront these men, and how quickly were they moving?

Byrn rushed across the space between the sheds. When he reached the building's edge, the two men had disappeared. The assassin sprinted forward just as a round hit the wall immediately above his head. He dived to the ground, bringing his weapon up as he landed.

Fifty yards away, in front of the chain fence that guarded

the perimeter of the property, stood an operative, his rifle aimed directly at Byrn. The assassin rolled to the right as another bullet impacted precisely where he'd been. This guy was a marksman.

Instead of continuing his roll, Byrn reversed direction reclaiming his original spot. As he tumbled, his mind whirred with calculations. When he came up, his rifle was in position, and he fired two rounds. The shooter arced back as the first bullet hit his chest before tumbling forward when the second round hit his gut.

Byrn was a better marksman.

The assassin leaped to his feet and ran forward. Vital time had been lost.

Again, he paused at the corner of the building, just long enough to crane his head around.

It wasn't good.

Dia stood with her arms raised, pressed against the shed wall, blood pouring from a wound on her head. One man stood six feet back from her, his rifle pointing directly at her back. The second man was frisking her, taking way too long to complete the task.

The longer that remained the status quo, the more control Dia's assailants would have.

Fuck it.

Byrn stepped forward directly into the open, his rifle pointed at the operative covering Dia.

"One of you is going to die within the next minute, the other will kill me. You decide," he yelled.

As the man frisking Dia reached for his weapon, the second guy pivoted, swinging round to aim his gun at Byrn.

The assassin shot him in the head.

By the time the frisker had his gun in his hand, Dia's boot had connected with his groin, sending him doubling forward. She spun around and kicked directly up under his chin. Byrn heard the bone crack from where he stood. As he hit the ground, Dia casually strolled over and stomped her heal firmly in his face.

Ignoring the pulsing in his thigh, the assassin limped up to her. She turned to look at him.

"You didn't mean a word of that, did you?" she asked.

"Not for a second."

"Either way," she continued, "appreciate you showing up."

Chapter 47

"We've got to go," said Byrn.

"Never a smarter man was born," Dia retorted.

"Now," instructed Byrn, his impatience showing. "You can't have a truckload of gunfire in an area like this without attracting attention. The police will be here within minutes."

The assassin walked off toward the gate.

"I'm right behind you," replied Dia.

Three quarters of the way down the road, heading in the direction of Byrn's car, the assassin raised a flattened palm indicating they should halt. He then stepped sharply to the left, behind a roadside tree.

"These guys are controlled and professional," he said.

"What do you mean?"

"Anyone listening for it would have heard the gunfire from here."

He pointed his forefinger around the tree in the direction of his vehicle.

"There. Near my car, the white Nissan."

"I don't see anything," Dia replied.

"Wait."

Sure enough, a few seconds later, Dia noticed movement on the wall of a laneway just beyond the car.

"The shadow?" she asked.

"Yup. Most people would come running if they heard their comrades struggling under fire. The person on point here didn't leave their post. Professional."

"What if it's coincidence? The person in the alley might have no connection to us or our recent skirmish."

Byrn offered a condescending half-smile.

"We've got to get out of the area, and we don't have time to swing around that guy."

"Or woman," corrected Dia.

"Point taken. So, let's test your theory. I want you to walk straight up to the car. Leave your gun in your pocket."

"That leaves me kind of vulnerable, doesn't it?"

"Not if that person has nothing to do with this. Besides, I've got your back."

Dia shrugged her shoulders, stepped out from the tree's cover, and strode confidently toward the vehicle. Her fingers had just touched the driver's side door handle when the deep male voice spoke.

"Stand perfectly still please, Ms. Dia, and raise your hands where I can see them."

As the man appeared, Dia glanced upwards.

"My advice to you would be to run like your life depended on it," she said.

The guy laughed.

It was the last thing he ever did.

A red dot appeared on his temple as the shot echoed down the street. He was dead before he hit the ground.

Byrn covered the remaining distance in a few seconds.

"I'll drive," he said, pushing past Dia.

"Why does the man always get to drive?" she responded,

already moving around the vehicle.

"Because I know where we're going and you don't," replied Byrn, "besides, you need to get your daughter's nanny on the phone. See if she's willing to get the child out."

Dia was already reaching for her cell. A minute later she shook her head.

"Straight to message."

Byrn nodded. "Money talks. Don't expect too much."

The assassin headed west, away from the railway yard and the bodies.

After five minutes of morbid silence, Dia stated, "We need to talk."

"No, not yet." Byrn reached over to the back seat and produced two baseball caps. "Put one of these on. When we get out, look down. Use your peripheral vision to guide you. Do not raise your head under any circumstances. Got it?"

Dia did as instructed.

A few minutes later, Byrn drove straight into the city center and turned left up Grand Avenue. When they reached a multi-level parking lot, he turned in, taking a ticket from the automatic vending machine as they entered.

"Remember, don't look up."

Byrn had his cap pulled low over his face. He guided the Nissan carefully, yet without hesitation, navigating half a dozen ramps before he found what he was looking for. He pulled into a vacant spot opposite a red Chevrolet Equinox. The vehicle's driver had just climbed out and was grabbing a briefcase from the rear seat.

"Wait here and watch for my signal," he instructed.

Dia nodded.

Byrn reached over and retrieved two small black boxes from his backpack on the rear seat. He waited until the owner of the Chev had walked away from the vehicle, allowing it to lock automatically with the keyless fob. When the man was about thirty yards away and about to enter the elevator down, Byrn grabbed his backpack, got out of the Nissan and strolled over to the Chev. He then pointed one black box at the departing driver while aiming the other at the Chev. The car's lights flashed. The assassin quickly looked back toward the driver, who was now disappearing behind the closing elevator door. He then waved Dia over and climbed into the driver's seat. As Dia joined him, Byrn pressed the start button on the dash and the engine sprung to life.

"Bet they didn't teach you that in Ranger school," said Byrn.

"How?" Dia asked.

"Pretty straight forward," Byrn responded. He held up one of the boxes. "This is the scanner that reads the code of the legitimate key fob." He placed the second box on the console between the seats. "That's the relay. It boosts the signal, making the vehicle think that the real fob is now inside the vehicle, so we're ready to roll."

"And by stealing a car from a parking lot, you're figuring the owner will be away for some time?"

"He had a briefcase, that most likely means business meeting. We'll probably be out of the state by the time he realizes the vehicle is gone."

Byrn pressed down on the gas pedal and guided the car carefully down the ramps, ensuring he allowed the owner plenty of time to clear the building. He used the card he acquired on the way in to exit.

A short while later, as they passed Norwoodville, Dia said, "I assume we're turning right onto the 80 to New York."

Byrn remained silent as they pressed through the interchange and headed north along Interstate 35.

"Or not," she added. "So, where are we going?"

Now that they were out of the area, Byrn began to relax a little.

"Civilian covert ops 101, Dia. The people chasing us are well resourced. They'll probably have all local airports, bus stations and train stations covered. Our only clear path out is by road."

"In the wrong direction?"

"Exactly," the assassin replied. "Despite their resources, these people can't cover every road, so they'll prioritize. We came from New York, so they will assume that we are making our way back in that direction. They'll focus whatever resources they have on roads leading that way, especially the 80. So, we track north. Minneapolis is a hub for Delta, so we can lose the guns and head wherever we must from there."

"Right," Dia responded.

"Speaking of Covert Ops 101, let's talk about our get together with Byers back at the beach house," said Byrn.

"Sure."

The assassin glanced at his passenger.

"When you came out from behind the door and got the drop on me, you were standing way too close, hence the reversal of fortune."

"I believe you mentioned it at the time," Dia replied.

"Yes, well, I was thinking about it. They would have covered that and several other close contact maneuvers in great detail at Ranger school."

Dia nodded, a fraction of a grin on her face.

"I do believe they did. Clearly, I wasn't paying attention to the teacher."

"Nobody passes Ranger training without having practiced those moves a hundred times, Dia. You knew exactly what you were doing. You wanted me to take control of the situation, but you didn't want Randal Byers to think you'd given him up."

"Perhaps."

"Go on," instructed Byrn.

Dia turned in her seat to face Byrn.

"The truth is that I was beginning to have doubts by then. I thought there may be more chance of an honest dialogue with you in charge."

Byrn stared ahead, straight out the windscreen, pondering the point.

"All right, Dia. Now, we need to talk about your in-laws."

Chapter 48

"What we really need to talk about is Clementine."

Byrn nodded. Darkness was closing in and the Chev's automatic headlights had just switched on. Even in the dim light, he noted the worried look on Regan Dia's face. She'd been placed in one hell of a position.

"I've got to assume that Randal wouldn't harm Clementine. Surely not his own granddaughter," she stated.

Byrn considered her words.

"No. Chances are he'd gain nothing by harming her. However, I don't like saying it, Dia, but if the man could arrange the killing of his own son, we're dealing with some kind of sociopath here."

Silence.

"Whatever happens, Lachlan, we've got to get her out."

"And we will. But now is all about strategy, not emotion."

"Easy for you to talk in such a cold-hearted manner. You're not invested in this situation the way I am," she said.

"No, I'm not. Which makes me best placed to make the right decisions here. You can process what you need to later, but for now, we have to plan," Byrn responded.

Dia glared at Byrn through the semidarkness.

"Do you even know what it's like to lose a loved one, let

alone discovering he was murdered by a member of his own family?"

"As a matter of fact, I do. I lost my father when I was quite young."

"I'm sorry, Lachlan. I was out of line. What happened?"

"I killed him."

More silence.

The quiet rumble of the tires on the highway lessened the tension as the miles wore down.

Byrn broke the impasse.

"Our initial question should be why. What reason would a man as successful as Randal Byers have for turning against every natural force within the human condition and murdering his own son?"

"I don't know, but he must have been desperate," Dia responded.

"And what makes such a formidable player that desperate?"

"I have no idea."

"It was a rhetorical question. I have some experience in these matters. The fear of losing power is often enough to drive even the strongest individuals to the point of imprudence. So, my question for you is, how did Bradley threaten Randal's position?"

Dia remained quiet. Byrn assumed she was processing.

"When Bradley first left Byer Corp, he was disillusioned. He was uncomfortable with how his father operated. He saw a lot of people, good people, he said, needlessly hurt. When he brought it up with Randal, the matter was repeatedly dismissed."

"That would have been difficult," Byrn responded.

"It was. Bradley grew up rich, but he also developed an

empathy for others. He craved success as much as the next person, but not at any price."

"Sadly, in this case, the next person was Randal Byers. His thirst for success banished compassion and, it appears, morality to the shadows. That makes it even more amazing that your husband was the type of man he was," Byrn responded.

The assassin waited for Dia to continue. This was not a conversation he needed to control.

Finally.

"When Bradley returned to take up a new position in the company, his father promised him a stronger profile in the organization, and an opportunity to make the changes he sought. He remarked on Randal's near desperation to have him back.

"So, what happened?"

"Despite the red-carpet treatment, Brad didn't trust the old man. Once bitten, etc. He decided to gather information, data, proof, whatever he could get his hands on. I guess something in him just snapped. He figured the only way to fight ruthlessness was with ruthlessness."

"Smart man," said Byrn. "The concept has worked well for me through the years."

Dia continued. "So, Brad kept trying to initiate changes. His negotiation strategy was to create an equitable outcome for all, a win-win approach. Then, at the last minute, the old man would intercede, stymy the process and re-negotiate the contracts overwhelmingly to Byer Corp's advantage."

"Business?"

"Beyond business. It became savage. The final straw came when the proprietor of a regional media network that Byer

Corp was planning to purchase approached Bradley. At that point, the deal was done, and the lawyers were simply tying up loose ends. Out of nowhere, the seller appeared in Brad's office. He told my husband that Randal had revised the terms of the sale, and the new arrangements would leave him with nothing. He would even lose his house."

"Then why go through with the deal?" asked Byrn.

"There's the crunch. Apparently, Randal had come across some rather unsavory images of the man's daughter doing a lot of things with several men. He told the network's proprietor that he would publish the photos if the contract wasn't signed."

"What happened?"

"Bradley confronted his father. Randal responded by criticizing him for being weak and overpaying for the business. He pushed Brad out of the negotiations and concluded the arrangements himself."

"And?"

"The seller lost everything. Somehow, the daughter found out about the photos. Seeing her family's state of grief, she immediately felt profoundly guilty and embarrassed. A week later, she committed suicide."

Dia turned to look at Byrn.

"Lachlan, she was eighteen years old."

"Fuck."

Byrn paused to assimilate the information.

"How did Brad take that?" he continued.

"Not well. He told me that he'd reached the end of his tether and was going to resign. But it turned out he hadn't seen the worst of it...yet."

"What do you mean?"

"When Brad told his father he was leaving, again, the tirade of abuse was overwhelming. The old man lost it completely. Brad was about to walk out when Randal came up with what he thought was his trump card. He told Bradley that he was so stupid that he hadn't even realized how the deal had gone down. He said that Randal had actually sent his people to a night club where the daughter was partying, quiet innocently, and instructed them to spike her drink. Then, they took her to a motel and had the photographs taken."

"Shit."

"Bradley said that the old man genuinely smiled as he told the story. When Brad raised the girl's death, Randal said it was simply an unintended consequence. He informed Brad that if he had any chance of success in business, he needed to play harder."

"What was Bradley's reaction?" Byrn inquired.

"He was gob smacked. He couldn't believe his father would actually sink that low. By the time he got home to me, he was full of scotch and fury."

"So, he quit the firm."

"No," Dia replied. "Brad said he had some sort of revelation, as his old man was in his face, losing it. He realized it wasn't enough to leave the company and seek a new career. He needed to stop Randal dead in his tracks… from the inside. And, probably foolishly, he told his father exactly that."

"What was Randal's response?"

"As you'd expect. He smiled and said to Brad, 'give it your best shot.'"

"He didn't know Brad had been building a case against him?"

"I don't think so, not then anyway."

"Okay, so how did Brad proceed from there?"

Dia sighed.

"We discussed it when he'd sobered up. My husband said that it was useless to take his father on alone."

"So."

"So, the next day Brad copied everything he had and went to the FBI."

"That would have done it," Byrn responded.

Chapter 49

They were a couple of hours into the drive to Minneapolis, and darkness had well and truly settled in. Byrn found night driving meditative. Dia dozed in the seat beside him, giving him a chance to process all he had learned from her.

There were no two ways about it. Randal Byers was about as low on the human totem pole as you could get. It never ceased to amaze Byrn that success was no indicator of humanity. He had dealt with some of the most powerful and successful men on the planet. The most common denominator appeared to be that many of them existed in a moral swamp, obsessed with their own position and influence.

That's why the assassin had truly 'dealt' with them.

Byrn would deal with Byers, but it would not be an easy task. The man was well protected, but as always, that was a surmountable issue. The real concern was the child. How would Byers force his daughter-in-law's hand? How low would he stoop?

Pretty damn low, Byrn figured.

For the assassin to develop a concise plan, he required more data, and the best source of data was sitting beside him.

"Dia, Dia, wake up. We need to talk."

The woman began to stir. Byrn gave her a minute as he gazed ahead into the oncoming lights.

Eventually.

"What?" she asked.

"I get that you're pressed for sleep, but I need more information to make this work."

"Shoot," she responded.

"I plan to, but not just yet," Byrn taunted. "So, tell me, did your husband take all his documentation to the FBI straightaway?"

The former ranger rubbed her eyes.

"No. Bradley's father's reach was broad, and Brad didn't know who to trust."

"Even in the FBI?"

"A person in Randal Byers' position has an amazing breadth of influence. That includes in the corporate world, governments and government agencies. A bit like Hoover, Byers knows where all the bodies are buried. Brad wanted to suss out the local office and make his way up the chain until he was comfortable with who he was talking to."

"Smart. Did he? Make his way up the chain, I mean," asked Byrn.

"In the end, yes, he did. He found an assistant director that he felt he could trust, but he had to give out dribs and drabs of detail along the way to get there. Remember, he was going in cold, without his father's contacts."

"Did he pass on all the information he had to the AD?"

"No. The relationship had only just developed to a point where Brad was ready to do that when he was kidnapped."

Byrn paused his questioning for a moment and considered the timing.

"Could Randal have somehow learned about Brad's activities? I mean, I get he that knew what your husband planned in principle, but leaking to the FBI is taking things to a whole new level."

"We didn't think so. Brad was extremely careful. In hindsight, I'd say we were wrong. Somehow the old man had worked it out."

As Byrn glanced over to Dia, an oncoming headlight lit her face. Eyes wide and jaw firm, she appeared focused and determined. The assassin knew she would require every ounce of determination and drive she could summon if they were to pull this off. The question that worried the assassin was Dia's ability to compartmentalize her concern for her daughter from the job at hand. It was a huge ask.

"I need you to think very carefully about your next answer, Dia," Byrn continued. "I'm assuming Brad didn't leave you with any of the information he gathered, or you would have said something. Do you have any idea at all where that data could be?"

Byrn heard her sharp intake of breath above the road noise.

"I've been racking my brain about that since I discovered that Randal had tracked the hundred million in cash. But I'm no closer now than when I began. The fact that terrorist, Nazar, so clearly named Randal as the man behind Bradley's killing has sent my emotional stability into a spin. To be honest, I'm worried sick about Clementine and want to get to her as soon as I can. I'm beyond furious that Randal orchestrated this, yet I'm still dealing with the fresh grief of losing my husband. In reality, I'm just attempting to figure out how the hell all this went down."

Byrn again glanced briefly at his passenger. Her face was

even more scrunched, with lines etching around her eyes, but there were no tears. She was one tough lady… for now.

"All right," he began. "Everything you're going through is enormous, but you should tackle this one step at a time. Deal with the situation issue by issue. And more than anything, you must separate your own feelings from the practicalities of this operation."

"Like you," Dia responded.

Byrn waited before replying.

"Yes, I suppose, like me. However, in my case, there is no choice to make. I am what I am, and nothing will change that."

"I don't know if I can be that clinical and separate myself from myself," said Dia, her voice as emotional as Byrn had heard it.

"If you don't, we fail. It's as simple as that."

Twenty minutes of driving time elapsed before Dia spoke again. Her tone was firmer, more assured.

"Brad once said to me that if anything happened to him, I'd know what to do to look after myself and Clementine. He didn't say much more except that I should think about what is special and important to me."

"Cryptic."

"Unfortunately, yes."

Dia stared ahead into the darkness.

"But I've been thinking," she continued. "Brad and I ran away to be married, not far, but we had a special place. A cabin we'd rent on the coast near Old Saybrook."

"Connecticut?"

"Yes. We rented the cottage directly from the owner. He worked nearby."

"Where are we going with this?" Byrn inquired, feeling himself growing testy at the trip down memory lane.

"Well, here's the thing, and it only just occurred to me. Of course, Brad wouldn't have trusted the documents to anyone that had any connection to Byer Corp, yet he would have sought out someone or somewhere reliable to hold such important information."

Byrn waited patiently for her to get to the point.

"Sorry, I'm just thinking out loud. As I said, the thing is, Brad became quite friendly with the old man we rented from, and I've just remembered what the old guy did for a living. He's a lawyer."

Byrn processed the information. It was a long shot leading, at best, to a paper-thin trail. Then again, they had nothing else.

"To have any chance of you and your daughter making it out of this in one piece, we need those documents, Dia. It's the hold you will have on Randal."

The assassin snuck a quick look at her now ashen face.

"Get out your phone and check flight times out of Minneapolis. We're going to Connecticut."

Chapter 50

"I want us on the same flight, but we need to travel separately," said Byrn.

"If we're being monitored, they may detect one or both of us, but even if they spot both, we divide their attention," Dia responded.

"Exactly. We'll make a covert operative out of you yet, Dia."

Dia tried to smile, but it wasn't in her.

The main terminal building at Minneapolis-Saint Paul International Airport towered above them. Bright lights and people filled the facility even at night.

"You have your ticket. Now go," Byrn ordered.

Dia appeared uncomfortable. She kicked at the ground like a troubled teenager before looking up at Byrn.

"Lachlan, you know I am capable of taking care of myself, but this has become too personal. I'm losing my perspective."

Byrn nodded. That was about as empathetic as he got.

"Can you promise me that we'll get Clementine back safely?" she asked.

Byrn stopped nodding.

"No, I can't. We're up against a powerful man with limitless resources. I can't guarantee you anything, Dia."

"Not very comforting."

"Not many people come to me for comfort," Byrn replied. "In this situation, one of my regular trump cards has been negated."

"What's that?"

"Ruthlessness. I don't seek nor adhere to limits that shackle others. The trouble is, that quality is matched by your father-in-law. He'll do anything to anyone to get his way. The man's track record speaks for itself."

Dia nodded. Byrn shrugged.

"We do have one small edge, though," said Byrn.

Dia waited.

"Without a doubt, Randal Byers values his own skin a lot more than I value mine."

Regan Dia looked up at the assassin and shuddered.

"I think you're wrong Lachlan," she said.

Byrn pressed his lips tight together.

"No," Dia continued. "Not about Randal valuing his own life more than you do yours. I mean about adhering to moral limits. I'm not so sure you know yourself as well as you think you do."

Byrn paused.

Then he nodded toward the terminal door.

"Get the fuck in there before we miss that plane."

Conversation closed.

It was almost midnight when the Delta Boeing 717's wheels touched the tarmac at Bradley International.

Throughout the three-and-a-half-hour flight, Byrn had scanned the aircraft's cabin from his seat at the rear. Dia was up front. The assassin hadn't spotted anyone paying Dia or himself any undue attention. It either meant no one was tracking them, or whoever was on the job was extremely capable.

Byrn had a second reason for traveling independently. Dia had no fake identification, so had to travel under her own name. That made the former ranger a liability. Byrn had almost limitless sources of false ID. It was a requirement of his profession. Someone who could gain access to flight manifests could track her movements. Byrn suspected Randal Byers had access to almost anything he wanted.

As the plane drew up to the terminal, the assassin waited. People got up from their seats before the seatbelt light dimmed and began claiming their onboard luggage from the lockers above them. Byrn paid close attention. No one seemed to be edging closer to Dia.

Byrn matched his movements with hers, moving forward to keep her in sight as they moved up the jet bridge toward the interior of the terminal.

So far, so good.

Dia had exited through the arrivals gate and was midway up the concourse when Byrn noticed the first indiscretion. A tall lanky man in jeans and a track suit top followed her progress a little too closely, his eyes tracking her every movement. Dia's attractiveness would surely attract attention from the opposite sex. But this guy's gaze never left her.

As Dia passed the point where the guy had positioned himself, the fool gave the game away. He glanced across the concourse toward a similarly dressed, but thicker set man in a similar position on the other side of the walkway. Almost in choreographed unison, they both stepped into the moving crowd in pursuit of their target.

Yet even fools can be dangerous.

Byrn had some decisions to make, and he needed to make them quickly.

Dia couldn't be allowed to leave the terminal with those two men behind her. Despite her astounding skill set, it would only take a second for them to usher her into a waiting vehicle and disappear into the night. It appeared that Dia was the sole target, not him. They were either ignorant of his presence or didn't care.

Byrn decided it was the former. Instinct.

The problem was the crowd. Even at this late hour, many people were milling around. The assassin would need to act with subtlety.

Byrn's final quandary was he wasn't aware if Dia knew she was being followed. That was an easy fix. Byrn had bought each of them a burner phone at Minneapolis-Saint Paul International. He reached into his jacket pocket, withdrawing the cell. Then he typed:

'Behind you. Two men. Next restroom.'

She would understand.

From where he was positioned twenty yards behind the men who were following Dia, Byrn couldn't figure out if she'd read the message. A couple of minutes later, the assassin noted a ladies' bathroom sign on the right about thirty yards ahead of her.

Dia's next movement would tell the story.

She had almost reached a point level with the sign without indicating any inclination toward it when Byrn decided she hadn't got the text.

Damn. Another strategy would be required.

Then suddenly, Dia stopped in her tracks, as though remembering something. She looked around before heading toward the restroom door.

Clever.

Byrn slowed down. The man on the left glanced at the man on the right. The second man nodded before changing direction toward the restroom entrance. The man on the left stopped parallel with the door, staring across the crowded walkway.

Sometimes opportunities just present themselves.

Typically, a male restroom was directly opposite the female facility. The man had halted less than two yards short of its entrance. Byrn veered left, heading straight toward him. The guy appeared totally focused on his target over the way. He stood scrutinizing Dia attentively as she entered the female restroom. He didn't even see Byrn coming.

Two feet shy of his prey, Byrn feigned a trip, shoving himself into the man's left side.

"Hey, watch yourself asshole," the man exploded.

"So sorry," Byrn responded, clamoring to stabilize himself.

As he straightened, the assassin pulled a pen from his own pocket, grabbed the man's right wrist and pressed the tip of the pen hard into his victim's radial artery.

"A fraction further and you'll begin to bleed out here and now. The blood loss won't kill you immediately, but I'll see that you're unconscious within seconds if you make a fuss."

As he spoke, Byrn twisted the man's arm behind his back without taking the pressure off the artery. He pressed his own torso up close to the guy's back to hide the move from prying eyes.

"Dead straight into the bathroom. Don't even think of

giving your mate across the way the eye."

Realizing his predicament, the man reluctantly shunted forward.

"No time to drag your feet now. We have business to conclude," Byrn whispered into his ear.

As they walked together down the short, stark white hallway, Byrn surveyed the area. When they reached the main bathroom, the assassin was relieved to see just one man finishing up.

"Last cubicle on the right. Now," Byrn instructed.

Byrn waited at the cubicle door until the guy left, then pushed his captor inside.

As he fell forward, the man almost hit the hard, tiled floor. Finding his equilibrium, the man swiftly turned around, a knife appearing suddenly in his hand.

"In honesty, I expected no less," said Byrn.

The man lunged at Byrn, the blade scraping the assassin's jacket as he stepped sideways. Byrn then slammed the man's wrist against the side of the cubicle. He tightened his hold before forcefully pounding the guy's forearm against the wall three more times. The weapon clattered to the ground.

Eyes glazed either in fear or anger, the man leaped forward, punching wildly as he drove toward the assassin. Byrn foiled most of the punches with his forearm before bringing his knee up, driving it hard into his opponent's gut. Winded, the man fell back onto the toilet seat. Aware of the urgency, the assassin swiftly retrieved the knife from the tiled floor.

"You know you can tell a lot about a person by who they work for. I'm sure the money was good, but in the end you chose poorly. And by the way, this is the end."

As his opponent attempted a desperate final lunge, Byrn

slashed the blade across the man's throat. His victim slumped to the floor.

Byrn stepped backward to avoid most of the blood, wiped the knife on his dead opponent's shoulder, pocketed it, and slid out of the cubicle. He shut the door firmly behind him and headed back to the concourse.

He scanned the doorway on the opposite wall. There was no sign of Dia, nor of her pursuer.

Two possibilities. She'd dealt with her man, or he'd taken her. It could go either way.

Byrn strode quickly across the width of the walkway toward the bathroom door. An awkward scenario, but he'd have to enter. Just as he reached the doorway, Dia appeared. Her hair was recently brushed, and she seemed calm and in control.

"How'd it go down?" Byrn asked.

"He came in after me but waited too long."

"He was probably trying to figure out what happened to his partner," Byrn responded.

Dia nodded.

"Either way, by the time he got in there, I'd explained to an extremely nice lady that I was being harassed and stalked. She was kind enough to lend me her pepper spray. That did the trick."

"Is he alive?" asked the assassin.

"Yes, but he's sleeping."

"Then he's the luckier one of the two. Let's get out of here before the cops or airport security descend upon us."

"Roger that," Dia replied as they headed toward the exit.

Chapter 51

RANDAL BYERS

"Are your men complete morons, Hemmings?"

The security man remained silent.

"You had over half a dozen armed operatives at the railway yard in Des Moines and two of what you call your best operators on the woman at Bradley International. What have you achieved? Zip."

"Not completely, Mr. Byers. Dominic Nazar and his associates are no more," Hemmings responded.

"And did your men kill them?"

Hemmings looked his boss in the eye, but his gut rolled within.

"No, sir."

"You've been utterly outmaneuvered by my daughter-in-law and that mercenary at every turn."

"In all fairness, Mr. Byers, the intelligence you provided suggested that only Ms. Dia was on that flight. My men weren't aware Byrn was still in play."

Randal Byers stared out the study window. The gray clouds and foaming white caps appeared brooding and angry, but it wasn't a patch on the way he felt. He turned back to

Hemmings.

"I can tell you one thing for certain, Hemmings. Until you are standing over Lachlan Byrn's lifeless body, you need to assume that man is always in play. Do I make myself clear?"

"Yes, of course, sir," Hemmings responded.

"Now, begin making arrangements. We're going to the farm," Byers instructed.

"That's good news, sir. We can better protect you there. And the child?"

Byers inhaled deeply, turning back to the ocean view.

"She comes with us. Thanks to your series of fuck ups, she is now our only layer of protection."

"I don't think this man, Byrn, will penetrate our security at the farm, Mr. Byers."

The tycoon pivoted sharply, his eyes narrowed and dark.

"Just like you didn't think he could escape your men in Des Moines. From now on, I will manage the situation. I have made plans for this eventuality. Simply do what I say and when I say it. Now, get out of here."

The security chief nodded, turned, and left.

Byers resumed his study of the stormy weather outside.

How had this all gone to hell so quickly? In spite of what he had said to Hemmings, this was one occasion when, despite his power and influence, Randal Byers couldn't be sure of the result. Byrn was a loose cannon. The worst type of opponent.

Notwithstanding that, the tycoon did hold one trump card, and she was happily asleep downstairs.

Regan Dia just needed to be reminded of what was at stake, and that losing now meant losing everything.

Chapter 52

The brazen golden hue of the rising sun seemed to calm the ocean. With every passing moment, fewer white caps dominated the horizon. Byrn gazed across the coastline where a series of small cottages sat dotted amongst the dunes. It was a far cry from Byers' affluent beach house in the Hamptons.

"Our cottage is the third one along. This place, Cornfield Point, was a haven for Brad and me, and then Clementine. No one knew we came here, and no one here knew where we came from. It was perfect."

Dia's tone was tinged with a quiet sincerity.

"I hope you're right, Dia. Your contact here is our single opportunity to get to the truth and the evidence that can disarm the beast," said Byrn.

"Brad trusted old Edward Celie completely. He once told me that if that man isn't a rock of integrity, then no such thing existed."

Byrn remained respectfully silent.

"You wanna take a walk?" Dia asked.

Byrn glanced at his watch. The lawyer's office wouldn't

open for another ninety minutes. They had the time.

"Why not?"

The hour-long drive from the airport had gone smoothly. The rental car was booked with a false name. The only diversion was a brief stop in Middletown to collect weapons arranged by Byrn's New York connection. The compact armory was locked in the rental's trunk. Better to be over prepared than caught short.

As the sand and pebbles kicked up under their feet, Dia and Byrn walked along the beach in silence. The sound of the now gently settling waves struck Byrn as meditative. Maybe he was growing soft.

Eventually.

"I've got to ask you, Lachlan, why?" asked Dia.

"Why what?"

"You know exactly what I mean. You've had several opportunities to cut and run. I'm sure your life would be a lot easier somewhere else."

Byrn paused to consider his response.

"My life is never easy. So, I may as well be here."

Dia paused briefly, gazing up at him.

"Good try, but not good enough."

Byrn shrugged his shoulders and proceeded with his walk.

"Your father-in-law paid me to eliminate whoever kidnapped and murdered his son. In my business, commitment is everything. If I'm going to do the job, I'll do it completely. This wouldn't be the first time that a commission has backfired on the person who tasked me."

"Better," said Dia, "But not quite there yet. Something tells me there is more."

They walked on in silence until Byrn chose to respond.

Before he spoke, the assassin stopped and turned directly toward Regan Dia.

"Don't try to understand me, Dia, and don't over think my actions. But, for your benefit, Randal Byers has pissed me off. He set me up with Zhen Su's team in China. I regard that as unforgivable. I've been used before and rewarded for the pleasure of it in the most inhumane ways imaginable."

The assassin gazed out over the waves.

"I've learned from that experience. I delayed closure of my relationship with Byers for the money and for your peace of mind. I owed you for helping me in China, and now I have repaid that debt."

"And yet, you're still here," Dia interrupted.

"I told you; I have a job to finish."

Dia stared up at him.

"I think you speak the partial truth, Lachlan. You don't do jack shit just for the money, so that's not it. Byers has sparked a fire within you and I've no doubt you'll claim retribution, but you could have done that already. Somewhere deep inside, you're looking out for me and my daughter."

Byrn sensed himself growing angry. He didn't need this.

"I'm no fucking Jack Reacher hero type, Dia. So don't make me into one inside that complex head of yours. We finish this job and I'm gone. Understand?"

Dia nodded, turned and walked on, appreciating that was as much as she was going to get.

Chapter 53

Edward Celie LLC held offices in an older brick and wood building on Elm Street in Old Saybrook, not far from Cornfield Point. The structure was tidy and well kept. A small lawn framed a stone path leading to the main door. A driveway ran up the side of the building. Byrn had ensured that it pointed to a parking lot at the rear.

Byrn and Dia sat in the rental car in front of the building.

"You ready for this?" asked Byrn. "Whatever we may find."

"What scares me the most is finding nothing," Dia responded. "If this trail runs cold, we have no other options. My daughter and my life will be at the mercy of that monster."

Byrn opened the vehicle's door.

"Well, it's time to find out, one way or another."

He climbed out. Dia followed.

"Are you certain that was old man Celie in the car?"

"No doubt," replied Dia.

She had pointed out Edward Celie at the wheel of the ageing Mercedes as it pulled into the driveway a few minutes earlier.

They traversed the path and pushed the large wooden door open. The reception area of the office was painted in an inoffensive cream color with polished floorboards, two comfortable looking chairs in a waiting area and a receptionist's desk opposite. Several doors led off the space. They were all closed.

Behind the desk sat a well-dressed, slender young woman with a slightly hawkish nose. Byrn calculated her to be in her early thirties. The woman looked up as the door opened.

"Good morning. May I help you?"

Dia spoke.

"We'd like to see Edward, please."

"Do you have an appointment?"

"I'm sorry, we don't," interrupted Byrn, stepping directly into the role. "But Ms. Dia is an old family friend. I'm sure if Mr. Celie has time, that he will meet with her."

The receptionist smiled again.

"Please take a seat. I'll check on Mr. Celie's availability."

Before she could move, the phone rang.

"Excuse me one moment."

She answered the call.

"The offices of Edward Celie, Attorney at Law. May I help you?… no, I'm sorry, Mr. Heathington isn't in today… yes, he's been called away on a family emergency… can we reschedule your appointment please… certainly, next Thursday at 10 a.m.…I'll send you a confirmation email, thank you."

She hung up, turning back to Dia and Byrn.

"I'm so sorry. Mr. Celie's paralegal, Mr. Heathington, has suddenly been summoned elsewhere. I'm afraid we're in a bit of a panic. I'll go and check with Mr. Celie right now."

She pivoted and strode through a doorway almost directly behind her desk.

Two minutes later, a voice boomed across the hallway.

"My goodness, Regan, it's so good to see you."

A short, somewhat rotund man, probably mid-sixties with thick gray hair, came barreling into the reception area. He held his arms out.

Dia stood up.

"Edward. It's wonderful to see you too." She walked toward the old man and embraced him.

"I was so sorry to hear about Bradley. Such a fine young fellow and a dear friend. I can't imagine what you've been going through. I sent you a letter."

Byrn noted that Dia seemed on the verge of tears. He offered his hand to the lawyer.

"Lachlan."

"Edward." The old man clasped Byrn's hand firmly, checking him out with a steely gaze. "Now, please, both of you, come into my office where we can talk."

The receptionist, who had followed the lawyer through the doorway, stepped aside.

Two minutes later, Byrn and Dia sat opposite Edward Celie, a large oak desk between them.

"Now, how may I be of service?" he asked.

Byrn was quick to judge people, and he was generally very good at it. At first glance, Celie appeared to be the genuine article.

"Thank you for your condolences, Edward, and the lovely letter you sent," Dia began. "It has been a difficult time, and to be honest, the circumstances of Brad's death have not helped."

Byrn was impressed by how quickly she'd pulled herself together.

"I can only imagine, Regan," Celie responded. "And given the complexities of Bradley's relationship with his father on top of that, I'm sure things haven't been easy for you."

Dia smiled.

"You and Brad spoke a lot, didn't you?"

"Yes, my dear. Sometimes when he was down here with you and could tear himself away from your arms, and occasionally when he'd venture down this way alone. I suppose I was some sort of confidential counselor for him, and one who shared his taste in fine scotch."

Celie smiled warmly.

Dia sat back a little in her chair.

"You look surprised, Regan. Brad didn't tell you of his little jaunts down to Old Saybrook?"

"No, Edward, he didn't, but I'm not surprised. I know he valued your friendship," Dia responded.

"As did I," replied the old man.

Dia leaned forward again.

"Edward, did Bradley…"

"Yes," came the lawyer's prompt response. "Bradley informed me that in the event of any incident, I should expect a visit from you. He clearly specified that you would know when the time was right, and I shouldn't come to you."

Byrn noted Dia's sharp intake of air. Now she was surprised. The assassin decided to inject himself into the conversation.

"Mr. Celie. I'm an old friend of Regans. She asked me to help her out and look out for her personal security. May I ask, do you have any idea why Bradley left such explicit instructions?"

"I'm sorry," Celie responded. "I'm afraid I didn't catch your surname."

"Because I didn't offer it, sir."

A stilted silence overtook the conversation as Celie and Byrn eyed each other off. The old man turned to Dia.

"I must ask you, Regan. Do you feel safe? And do you trust this gentleman?"

"I do, and implicitly," Dia responded.

Celie gazed at Dia. Byrn assumed he was searching for any physical mannerism that may signal alarm. Evidently satisfied, he continued.

"Forgive my rudeness," he said, turning to Byrn.

Byrn nodded.

The lawyer turned back toward Dia. "I must say he does look rather scary."

Dia laughed.

"In this situation, Edward, that's scary in a good way."

"Very well, my dear. Let's continue."

The lawyer reached down to his right and opened a drawer. A second later, he produced a crisp white envelope and placed it on the desk between himself and Dia.

"For you."

Dia leaned forward and picked the envelope up. Immediately, Byrn noted tears once again swelling in her eyes. He assumed she'd recognized Bradley's handwriting. Without speaking, she opened the package with her fingernail, retrieved the single piece of paper inside, unfolded it, and began to read.

A couple of quiet minutes slipped by before she passed the paper to Byrn. He read it.

My Love,

Of course, if you are reading this, I am dead. I know you will mourn, but please remember our beautiful Clementine will carry me and you inside her forever. In time, you must celebrate that.

Now down to business. I have left Edward with some valuable information. You will know what to do with it in order to ensure your own and our daughter's future. Please, do not rush, do not be impetuous, but use your ranger qualities to be strategic and wise.

I will love you for eternity.

Your Brad, forever.

Byrn and Celie watched on as the tears flowed mercilessly down Dia's cheeks. They both looked away.

"All right," Dia announced eventually. "I'll have plenty of time for that later. Let's keep moving forward. What exactly did Brad leave with you, Edward?"

Edward Celie suddenly became very business-like.

"You may not be aware that I keep several safe deposit boxes in a vault downstairs. They are completely secure, especially as I don't advertise this service to clients unless they ask. Regan, your husband, is one of those who asked."

"How do you access the boxes?" asked Byrn.

"Thumbprint recognition and a code."

Perhaps the old man didn't live in a bygone era after all.

"But I don't know the code, and I haven't recorded my thumbprint. How can I access the contents?" asked Dia.

"Don't worry, my dear. I have the code memorized and I believe that Bradley may have surreptitiously gained a copy of your thumbprint. It's not impossible to take a print from someone you live with," announced the lawyer. "Shall we go downstairs and put the system to the test?"

Celie led the way out of his office, through the reception area and across to a locked door on the far side. He produced a key and opened the door. After flicking on a light, he led Dia and Byrn down a steel stairway. The old man unlocked another door at the bottom of the stairs and entered a code.

The door swung open. As the automatic light came on, it revealed a large safe. By Byrn's calculations, it was at least ten-foot square.

"Impressive, Mr. Celie," said Byrn.

The old man smiled. He then entered another code, pressed his thumb against a scanner, and pulled the heavy metal door open.

Byrn and Dia peered through the small doorway.

A series of safe deposit boxes framed the center aisle. Each one had a thumb print scanner, and a keypad built in.

"Again, sir, impressive," said Byrn "Steel?"

"AR500 steel. No one will get through that unless I want them to," Celie responded.

The lawyer guided them to the vault, pausing by a deposit box at head level on the far wall. He reached his right hand up and tapped in a twelve-digit code before stepping back.

"Regan?" he said, inviting her forward with a wave of his hand.

Dia stepped up and pressed her right thumb against the scanner. Fifteen seconds of taut silence followed. Finally, the word 'accepted' glared in red from the small screen. Celie shuffled forward, opened the safe deposit box door and withdrew a long enclosed rectangular steel box.

"If you follow me to the outside room, there is a desk and chairs where you can examine the contents in privacy and comfort," invited the old man.

Dia and Byrn followed him out to a small table with a single chair on either side.

"I'll leave you to your task," he announced before disappearing up the stairs.

Dia sat down and ran her hands over the box.

"Well, this is it," she declared. "All or nothing."

Byrn remained standing, peering over her shoulder as she slid back the lid.

The assassin felt his gut tighten as Dia let out an anguished cry.

Staring up at them from the bottom of the box, time stamped twenty-four hours earlier, was a picture of Clementine.

Dia screamed again.

Chapter 54

"We're going," said Byrn as he took Dia's hand.

"Where?"

"Out of here,"

Byrn led her up the stairs, past an astonished-looking Edward Celie who had just stepped into the foyer and out the front door.

Celie began to speak, but Byrn raised a hand to silence him.

When they reached the car, Byrn pulled out his phone and checked the map.

"There's a turnoff up the road onto the Clark Memorial Field. The field leads down to the Oyster River. I need you to drive down there and wait for me. Lock the doors and don't move. I won't be long."

"What are you going to do?" Dia asked.

"Best you don't know."

"Then after that, what?"

Byrn looked her directly in the eye.

"I think you can figure out the answer to that, Dia. We no longer have any chance of reining Randal Byers in through legal means or blackmail. If you want to protect your daughter, you'll need to go to him and plead for mercy. There is no other choice."

She nodded vacantly.

"No other choice."

"Give me a minute," Byrn instructed.

He wrenched opened the driver's door, bent down and released the trunk catch. He then approached the rear of the car, lifted the trunk open, and retrieved a couple of items. After closing the trunk, he stepped back onto the sidewalk.

"Good to go," he proclaimed.

Dia climbed into the driver's seat, started the engine, and sped off down the road.

Byrn watched her go before turning and striding up the path toward Edward Celie LLB's front door. The lawyer stood in the doorway.

"Your office… now," commanded Byrn.

Celie followed him past the wide-eyed receptionist as Byrn led him into his own office.

"What happened? What was in that box?" asked Celie.

Byrn produced the photo of Dia's daughter from his pocket and passed it to the lawyer.

"My God. Time stamped yesterday. That's impossible," he said.

"That's reality," Byrn responded. "Who paid you? How much? And when?"

Edward Celie appeared to stagger backwards under the weight of Byrn's allegation. He sat down in his chair.

"I can assure you, and Regan, that I have not opened that safe deposit box since Bradley Byers entrusted me with the care of its contents. You have my word."

Byrn stared across the desk at the lawyer. This was the moment of judgement. The assassin would either believe him or not. For Dia and Celie, a great deal relied on Byrn's decision. Byrn remained silent and continued to stare, deep beyond the surface of Edward Celie's glistening eyes.

Eventually.

"No, I didn't think you did," the assassin stated.

"Then why…"

"I had to be sure. Now tell me about your paralegal, Heathington isn't it? How long has he worked here? How did you first come into contact with him?" Byrn asked.

"Pertinent questions," replied Celie. "Shane came to us around six months ago. I'd advertised for a paralegal. My last one resigned rather abruptly after fifteen years' service. Shane was given a glowing recommendation by one of the top New York law firms. At the time, I questioned why he wanted to come and work here, in a small town away from the large litigation work he was used to."

"And his response?"

"Sea change. He said he wanted out of the big city pressure."

"What was the name of the law firm that recommended him?"

"O'Donnel and Haggerty," Celie replied.

"I don't suppose O'Donnel and Haggerty do any work for Byer Corp, do they?" asked Byrn.

Celie leaned back in his chair.

"Not to my knowledge. But I do believe he mentioned being involved in some litigation against Byer Corp. But Shane was on the opposing side, not working for Randal Byers."

"Did Heathington's team win the case?"

"I understand they managed a small victory. From memory, it wasn't a large settlement."

"But it was enough for Byer Corps lawyers to recognize Shane Heathington's talent or perhaps even his moral flexibility. Either way, it doesn't matter. I need his address… now."

Celie leaned forward and tapped some commands on his keyboard. He then wrote something on the back of one of his business cards and handed it over to Byrn.

"He's in North Meadow Road. Walking distance from here."

Byrn took the card, glanced at it, stood up, and stepped toward the door.

"What do you intend to do?" asked Celie.

The assassin swung around.

"I suggest you keep practicing the law in the manner you see fit. In the meantime, I shall see to it that justice is delivered promptly and efficiently."

Celie's jaw dropped.

Byrn left the room.

Chapter 55

The house on North Meadow Road was small, but tidy. The front yard appeared well looked after, but there was little sign of activity coming from within. The blinds were drawn closed, indicating the occupant could be away or perhaps even inside and unwell… or hiding.

Byrn stood on the sidewalk at the eastern corner of the block. A driveway led to an older style garage beside the home. Two small windows on each garage door allowed viewing access inside. Byrn stole quietly up the drive and peered through one of the windows.

A late model Toyota sat inside the building.

Byrn marched across the front yard, stepped onto the porch, and rapped forcefully on the timber door.

No response.

The assassin knocked again. Listening carefully, he picked up a slight shuffling of feet from inside.

Byrn thumped on the door one final time.

"Shane. It's Jeremy from up the road. I just need to check if you know who belongs to this stray terrier."

More shuffling, and then the door opened.

Shane Heathington stood around five feet ten tall with broad shoulders and a slicked back businessman's haircut.

"Who are you? I don't know any Jeremy and where's the…."

Byrn responded by punching Heathington hard on the bridge of his nose. The man staggered backward, tripping over the two suitcases behind him and landing awkwardly on the floor.

Byrn stepped around the cases, raised a foot, and kicked the prone man forcefully in the ribs.

Heathington let out a muted cry of pain.

"What the fuck? Who the hell are you?" he stammered.

Byrn kicked him again.

"I'll be asking the questions today, Shane."

The assassin glanced down at the cases.

"Going somewhere, are we?"

"I… I… I have a sick relative in New York that I'm going to look after. Now get out of my…"

"We both know you don't have a sick relative, Shane." Byrn looked across the entrance hall to the lounge next door. "Now, stand up and go and sit on that couch. No sudden movements, please."

"I have money. I can pay you, or take what you want. There's no need to hurt me," Heathington pleaded.

Byrn didn't respond.

Heathington clambered to his feet before turning and heading into the lounge. Halfway across the room, he changed direction, pivoting to his right before sprinting toward what Byrn assumed was the back door. The assassin stepped forward with lightning speed, slipping his left foot in front of the fleeing man. As Heathington faltered, Byrn jabbed him hard on the side of the head. Again, the man fell to the ground.

"This is needless, Shane. On your feet and sit on the couch, please."

Heathington didn't budge.

"All right, then," Byrn said Byrn as he reached a hand under his jacket. He withdrew a SIG Saur P226 pistol from his jacket.

Heathington's skin paled.

"You can't shoot me. This is a quiet neighborhood. The cops will be on you in a flash."

Byrn smiled, tilting his head slightly before removing a MODX-9 segmented, titanium printed, 9mm suppressor from his other pocket. He screwed it into the SIG's barrel.

Heathington began to shake.

"Get up," said Byrn, pointing the pistol toward the couch. Heathington did what he was told.

Byrn reached over and grabbed a chair from the dining setting. He set it down opposite Heathington before perching on it. He crossed his knees, holding the SIG loosely in his right hand.

"Today I'd like to talk to you about inevitability, Shane," he began.

His captive didn't respond.

Byrn shrugged his shoulders.

"It's a funny word 'inevitability'. The notion suggests an eventuality, regardless of circumstances. From experience, I can share with you that this is not necessarily the case. In fact, to make the lesson relevant to your current predicament, I'll give you an example. When the person from Byer Corp contacted you with an invitation to perform seemingly harmless covert duties by taking employment with Mr. Celie, you could have said no. At that point, your fate was not inevitable. You had choices. Different paths you could follow.

Do you get my meaning, Shane?"

Heathington nodded.

"But when you accepted their offer," Byrn continued, "you chose a road that made it inevitable that you and I would end up here in this room. That's why it's a funny word. Inevitable. Your fate wasn't inevitable. You made a certain decision and now what happens to you is totally inevitable. I'm sure you appreciate what I'm saying here. Shane."

"Tell me what you want," demanded Heathington in a withered voice.

Byrn sighed.

"I want you to understand the consequences of your actions."

"You can't prove that I was paid by Byer Corp. You can't prove anything."

"Two points I'd like to make here, Shane. Number one, you haven't denied my charges. An innocent man would have gone to denial as a first course of action. Number two. I don't have to prove anything. I simply need to be satisfied with my own judgements."

Silence.

"Now, back to the consequences. Or perhaps we should begin with the chain of events that led to those consequences. And no, I'm not particularly concerned with how you did it. I do assume, however, that through an intermediary, Randal Byers supplied you with Regan Dia's thumbprint."

Heathington remained mute.

Byrn continued. "I do have one question I'd like answered. I'm not fully understanding why you didn't just break into the safe deposit box earlier in your employment. Randal Byers could have accessed the evidence that threatened his interests sooner if you'd done that."

More silence.

Byrn leaned forward.

"There seems to be a level of misunderstanding here, Shane. When I ask a question, I expect it to be answered."

"Go fuck yourself."

Byrn sighed again, raised his weapon, and shot his captive in the crook of his elbow. Within seconds, blood was gushing down the man's forearm.

"Holy shit, God Almighty, you should be certified," Heathington screamed.

"Now, now, Shane. Calm yourself. I appreciate that your wound hurts, and I'll get you a bandage shortly. Now please answer my question. Why didn't you act earlier?"

Heathington had doubled forward, his right palm clasping the wound on his left arm. His ashen white skin oozed beads of sweat.

"Shit. I wasn't even told why I was sent to Celie's office. I just know I was paid a shitload of money to take a relaxing job for a year. My only task, apart from daily work, was to find out if Celie kept documents securely on the premises for his clients. The old man took three months to admit it, and a few more weeks to show me the damn vault."

"And the code?"

Heathington struggled for breath.

"When I reported the information about the documents and the vault, my minder pressed me to find out the code. He said he could provide me with the thumbprint."

"And you didn't question why?"

"Hell no. The money was fantastic. I was being paid not to ask questions."

"Who was your contact, your minders, as you say?" asked Byrn.

"I can't say."

The assassin raised the SIG.

"All right, all right. It was a big guy, with reddish hair. I think I heard one of his people call him Hemmings."

"Good. Well done, Shane. We're making progress. Now, let's not dwell on the details. I assume you made a case to Edward Celie that you should be able to access his codes in the event anything untoward happened to him. I don't really care how you did it, but it does seem you gained the old man's trust, eventually."

Heathington nodded.

Byrn paused to process the timeline.

"When were you instructed to replace the box contents with the photo?"

"Yesterday morning, before work, the photo was delivered personally to my door, along with the instructions."

"By Hemmings?"

Heathington nodded.

"Was he alone?" asked Byrn.

Another nod.

Byrn stood up, walked casually over to the dining table, and wrenched its tablecloth from the surface.

"Wrap that around your arm," he instructed as he threw it across the room.

Heathington seemed relieved.

The truth was, he didn't want his captive bleeding out too early.

"Tell me, Shane, what did you do with the items that you removed from the safe deposit box?"

"Hemmings hung about in town. He collected them after I was done. It was only two thumb drives. He mentioned he was taking them back to New York for verification."

Byrn nodded slowly, absorbing it all.

"You didn't make a copy for yourself?" he asked.

"No," Heathington replied emphatically. "I'm not a fool."

The assassin considered the man's response, finally believing him. Although he would have preferred otherwise.

"Now, this next part of our conversation is important, Shane. I require your full attention."

Heathington nodded, despite still grimacing in pain.

Byrn continued. "When you saw the photo of the young child, the one you placed inside the box after you removed whatever data or papers were there, what did you think?"

Byrn scanned the man for his true reaction.

"I didn't think anything. I was paid to do a job and, like I said, not ask questions."

"Just following orders?"

"Yes."

"It didn't occur to you that someone may be using a child's life as leverage in a difficult situation?"

For a moment Shane Heathington hesitated. Byrn could see the lie forming behind his eyes.

"No, not at all."

"That's not the truth, Shane, and we both know it."

"I swear."

Byrn raised the pistol.

"Okay, okay. I figured something pretty bad was going down, but I didn't want to get involved."

"Even if a child's life was at risk?"

"What could I have done?"

"I'll answer that question for you, Shane, as concisely as I can. You could have called the cops. You could have informed Mr. Celie of your arrangement and instructions, or you might have simply refused to perform the task."

"I was scared."

"Did they pay you a bonus for this extra service?"

The younger man hesitated.

"Yes."

"How much?" Byrn fingered the SIG as he asked.

"One hundred thousand dollars."

Byrn whistled.

"I believe this moment, Shane Heathington, is when we need to address our final interpretation of the term 'inevitability.'"

Perspiration dripped down Heathington's face. His lower lip quivered.

Lachlan Byrn leaned forward until his face was only a few inches from his captive. He spoke in a low, intense drone.

"Consequence: a young child's life had been put in danger. Consequence: A friend of mine is in a great deal of emotional pain. Consequence: An extremely bad man looks like he's been enabled to continue to do extremely bad things."

Byrn suddenly leaned back, gazing hard into Shane Heathington's eyes.

"Inevitability, my friend, equals this."

The assassin raised his weapon and shot Shane Heathington through the temple.

Chapter 56

Lachlan Byrn walked briskly up the road. He felt good. Satisfied.

It took the assassin just over ten minutes to cover the distance to Clark Memorial Field. As he rounded the screen of trees sheltering the field from the road, he spotted the rental car in the parking lot on the other side of the field. It was the only vehicle in the lot. He strode quickly toward it.

Byrn had made it halfway across the space when he realized something was wrong. The car's driver's side door was ajar, and Byrn couldn't make out Dia's profile as he approached.

The assassin withdrew his SIG and bolted the remaining distance. He wrenched the door open. The vehicle was empty.

More to the point, a stream of bright red blood dripped from the top of the steering wheel.

This changed everything.

Chapter 57

RANDAL BYERS

"We've got her, Mr. Byers. Your daughter-in-law."

"Where is she?"

"In the back of a van with Mellion and Triller," Hemmings replied. "On the way here."

Byers stood up and paced the space behind the large desk. The study here, on the farm, was even grander than the beach house. Its dark paneled walls lent an air of formality. Byers appreciated that. Although he'd been reluctant to purchase the property originally, in the end, he was glad he let his ex-wife talk him into it. He was even more delighted when he paid off the judge to ensure she didn't get it in the divorce settlement.

"Where was she?" he asked, still pacing.

"At Old Saybrook."

"The lawyer?"

"Yes, sir."

"What about the data?"

Hemming reached into his pocket and produced the two thumb drives. He placed them on the desk.

"Have you checked them?" the tycoon asked.

"Only the provenance, just as you instructed. The files were created by Bradley Byers."

"Good. You can pull our people out of the other potential drop-off points as soon as I've confirmed the contents."

"Yes, sir."

"And the data source in Old Saybrook?"

"When you have verified the contents, Mr. Byers, we'll eliminate the trail."

"Fine."

Finally, he looked up at his security chief. The man's demeanor had grown in confidence with the arrival of good news. Byers would fix that.

"Do you think we are well placed for a positive result, Hemmings?" asked Byers.

The security guard seemed to hesitate, perhaps suspecting the question from his boss was loaded. He chose his words carefully.

"Much better placed than we were, sir."

Byers noted the man's fists tighten. The tycoon turned to stare him down.

"What about Byrn?"

Hemmings maintained his posture.

"My men didn't sight him. It seems he's disappeared, sir."

The old man felt the anger surge within, he decided to ride the sensation.

"Well, fuck you and the horse you rode in on, Hemmings. Holding Regan Dia in custody, and the return of those damn documents, means jack shit if I'm assassinated by this thug. Just find him and stop him."

Hemmings stared back at his boss.

"We'll find Byrn, sir. And I'll personally see that he won't be bothering you again."

The old man smiled.

"Do you have any idea where to start looking?"

"We'll find him, sir."

Byers shook his head.

"I didn't think so. You know Byrn has unique skills when it comes to disappearing… and reappearing."

"I'm aware of his background, sir."

Byers raised his voice purposefully.

"Well, make sure you do find him before he finds you, or worse still, me. Now go."

Chapter 58

REGAN DIA

Dia's fury encompassed herself, the men in the front of the van, and her father-in-law. Her head throbbed from the blow she hadn't even seen coming. Now with hands and feet bound while thudding from wall to wheel arch in the back of the vehicle, she knew she would ache for days. If she lived that long.

But none of that was significant.

Only Clementine mattered.

As soon as Dia saw the child's photo in the safe deposit box, she realized her fate was sealed. She'd have to go to Randal Byers and throw herself at his mercy. She laughed silently at the thought. Using the words mercy and Randal Byers in the same sentence was absurd.

But even that plan hadn't worked out. Now she was being dragged back to Byers as an escapee.

"My father-in-law will have a lot to say about the way you are treating me," she yelled to the open cab.

"We are simply following Mr. Hemmings' direct instructions," replied the guy in the passenger seat. The driver chuckled.

Hemmings. He'd been a pain from the start. The moment Byers employed Dia and involved her in the corporation's security, the man had disliked her. He made it very clear that he resented her ranger pedigree and regarded position as a 'family hire.'

Prick.

"Where are you taking me?"

The driver glanced at his passenger and nodded.

"The farm, Ms. Dia," announced the passenger.

Great, the freakin' farm. Dia wondered if Lachlan Byrn was even aware the place existed.

Chapter 59

CADE HEMMINGS

Every fiber of Hemming's being was alert. The old man was right. The boss was capable of dealing with the daughter-in-law alright, but Lachlan Byrn posed a more formidable challenge. Despite what he'd said to his employer, Hemmings appreciated that Byrn worked at a different level. Normal security measures would have little effect in bringing the wily assassin to his knees.

So, what would?

Hemmings had made all the regular arrangements. He'd doubled the personnel at every entry point to the property and instructed armed patrols to walk the fence lines consistently. No one was allowed a break unless someone else replaced them. He'd ensured his people were more than adequately equipped. They all carried automatic weapons with laser targeting, in addition to radios and grenades. Hemming's even employed a helicopter that constantly patrolled the skies above the estate. One bird didn't go down until its replacement had moved into position.

The child was guarded by a different squad, locked in the nursery with her nanny. Hemmings presumed the mother would be allowed to see her, but he had not received any instructions on that so far.

At this point, there was nothing more he could do.

And yet he felt like he'd missed something.

No reports indicated Byrn's presence in the area. There was no intelligence indicating that the assassin was even aware of the farm's existence.

Then Hemmings wondered how many of Byrn's victims received information of his presence just before they died.

In the unlikely possibility that the assassin made it into the main house, he'd be greeted by a dozen armed and highly trained operatives. Surely, there was no chance that any lone wolf could surpass those odds.

Surely.

Hemmings had overheard Dia telling Byers about the rumors that surrounded Byrn's reputation. The US secretary of defense. Even the damn Russian president. Absolutely not. Not one fucking man.

However, the security chief had played the game long enough to trust his own gut. And his gut was telling him to be very nervous. He returned to his small office next to the comms room, deciding to go over every element of the arrangements one more time.

An hour later, nothing had changed. Hemmings wondered about rotating the child and Byers himself through a series of different rooms within the house, enhancing the element of unpredictability. On the other hand, would they be more exposed in transit?

Damn it. Now he was even second guessing himself.

The security chief shoved his chair back, rose to his feet and marched through the doorway into the comms room.

Six split screens showed over twenty images of key locations around the property. He scrutinized each of them.

"Anything?" he asked the operative scanning the screens.

"Nothing untoward. Only the odd bit of wildlife." The man turned to look at his boss. "Is there any chance we are just jumping at shadows here, sir?"

Hemmings stared down at the operative. He knew from experience that remaining on full alert over the period of an extended operation was a difficult task, but he'd counter no restlessness.

"Unless you want a bullet in our heads or those we are guarding, I suggest you jump at every shadow you see. Am I clear?"

"Crystal, sir." The man leaned forward, refocusing on his assignment.

The women sitting at the adjacent wall behind two extra screens monitoring all communications had turned to hear the interaction, but quickly swung back.

"Anything Styles?"

She removed her headphones.

"Nothing, sir, but I'm remaining alert to all stations."

Hemmings nodded.

Was there any chance one man could really penetrate all this?

Chapter 60

RANDAL BYERS

"Regan, please sit down."

The tycoon gestured at the chair opposite the desk. He wanted a formality to this meeting.

He watched as Dia was escorted to her seat. Hemmings refrained from touching her, but his presence suggested it best she follow instructions, as did the bulge in his coat pocket.

Dia didn't speak.

"It seems we were at an impasse," announced Byers. "It's time for some honest conversation."

"I demand to see Clementine," replied Dia, her tone strained and urgent.

"Fair enough."

Byers tapped a couple of keys on his keyboard and flipped the desk top screen around to face his daughter-in-law.

"There you go. As you see, she's safe and sound."

Dia stared at the display for a moment before returning her gaze to Byers.

"I meant in person."

"I'm sure you did," said the tycoon. "Perhaps we can address your wish, depending on the outcome of this meeting."

Byers sensed Dia fighting to control her urge to get physical.

"It would not serve your daughter well to leave her motherless, my dear. Anyway, I'm a reasonable man. Let's talk."

"Reasonable men don't murder their own sons," Dia spat out the words.

"Is that what you think? Do you really believe I murdered Bradley? No, my dear, he made that choice. He wasn't smart enough to walk and stay away from this company when he had the opportunity. Instead, he did the exact opposite. He attempted to destroy an extraordinary lifetime of achievement. Like every good parent, I counseled him to take another road. He refused to listen."

"So you killed him." shouted Dia.

Byers shifted in his seat, restless but not uncomfortable. He felt no pressure.

"No, I consulted my people. They advised on an appropriate action as they would with any other major security leak threatening the corporation's interests. I simply approved their decision."

"You murdered your own boy," exclaimed Dia.

"I reacted to a threat. Bradley was too weak and too stupid to appreciate the ramifications of his actions. Accordingly, he paid the price."

"You are a monster."

"I am a businessman. Many people rely on me to make the correct decisions so they can continue to earn a good living. This was one of those decisions."

Byers leaned forward, resting his chin on his hands. He found the tears cascading down his daughter-in-law's face amusing.

Suddenly Dia leaped up, springing across the desk toward him. Just as suddenly, Hemmings' wide arm swept over her chest and planted her back in her seat.

Byers smiled.

"Pointless, Dia, and so numbingly predictable."

Like any experienced negotiator, Byers remained in control of the conversation. He paused, carefully awaiting the moment to press further.

Dia broke his enforced silence.

"What do you want from me?"

Byers grinned. The first sign of submission. The businessman was delighted, but wisely chose not to express his gratification aloud.

"Well, I'm glad you asked, Dia," he replied. The tycoon leaned back in his chair, entwining his fingers in front of him. "Listen closely and I will explain."

Chapter 61

LACHLAN BYRN

Byrn ignored all the texts. It was obvious from the first communication that Dia was messaging him under duress. It was enough that she'd clearly been forced out of the car back at Old Saybrook, but the situation was confirmed when she signed the initial text 'Regan.'

Thus far, Byrn had never addressed the former ranger as Regan. It was always 'Dia'. And she would know that. Message received.

The assassin waited until Dia's abductors had an opportunity to reach their destination, assuming it was in the New York greater area. He then turned on the tracking app that he'd downloaded onto Dia's burner without her knowing. He thought it most likely she'd be taken to the beach house in the Hamptons.

He was wrong.

Her location came up in North Salem in Westchester County, New York.

A quick internet search informed Byrn that Randal Byers owned a significant equestrian property nearby. Over two hundred acres in the heart of an area known as 'Billionaire's

Dirt Road'. Clearly Byers enjoyed being surrounded by wealthy neighbors along with the prestige that accompanied being a resident of such a salubrious enclave. The initial article that Byrn read featured one of Byers' former wives, a reputable equestrian, luxuriating in their vast estate. The second piece simply stated that Byers won the property in their divorce settlement, despite having no noted interest in horses.

What a guy.

An hour earlier, Byrn had received Dia's latest message.

Please read the attached. It will be published in 24 hours if we don't talk.
R.B.

The assassin broke his policy and opened the attachment. What he saw alarmed him.

Formatted as a two-page newspaper piece, the article was entitled:

IS THIS THE WORLD'S MOST DANGEROUS MAN?

It went on to speculate about the death of the former US secretary of state, Thomas Ireland, the assassination of Russian Federation president Vadim Aleyev and numerous other high-profile deaths covering a period of around five years. The two most worrying aspects were the publication of Byrn's name and several photographs, which appeared to be taken by security cameras in Byers' study at the Hampton's beach house when Byrn had met the man.

Less than two hours later, the assassin scratched his

stubbled chin as he read through the piece one more time. He then gazed out over the green manicured fields and meticulously maintained parcels of forest that lead down the hill from his current position toward Byers' property.

On second perusal, Byrn decided that the tycoon had misread the situation. Rather than a threatening media article, the proffered document was more akin to an invitation to a funeral.

Chapter 62

REGAN DIA

At least she'd been allowed to see Clementine. Dia's daughter bubbled with excitement when she laid eyes on her mother. There was something about motherhood that surprised the hell out of Dia. Each time she held her child in her arms, the world seemed right.

Dia regarded herself as independent, bordering on defiant. She loved her training in the military and managed to graduate at the top of her cohort. Of course, with that came a certain level of resentment, not only from her male contemporaries but also from the hierarchy above. The discomfort she felt combined with her rebellious attitude made short shift of her time in the armed forces. Working for Randal Byers gave her purpose... until it didn't. Falling in love with Bradley changed her outlook. The arrival of Clementine changed her world.

Now it was all crashing down. Brad had been murdered and Clementine's wellbeing was in danger from Randal Byers, Cade Hemmings' quasi-military goons, and even Lachlan Byrn's apparent inactivity.

Why the hell hadn't Byrn called? Dia anticipated some

response from him, acknowledging her unsettling message. Yet, a whole day had elapsed and there was no word.

The assassin knew her predicament. He'd appreciate that she and Clementine were at her father-in-law's mercy. Had Byrn just walked away? Maybe the man was right. She'd built him up to be some kind of warrior hero in her mind when he was really nothing more than a soulless mercenary.

So, she'd have to get Clementine out of this situation herself.

Dia scanned the room. The solid oak door was locked from the outside. Dia was certain an armed guard was permanently posted in the adjacent corridor. The French doors leading out onto the patio initially gave her hope, but the two men who swiftly arrived on the other side of the doors, equipped with automatic weapons, put paid to any chance of escape in that direction.

Then there was Clementine.

Byers had only allowed her brief contact with her daughter. To the best of Dia's knowledge, Clementine was still being held along the corridor under the supervision of her nanny. Dia wondered how much blood money her father-in-law paid the woman to continue working under the current circumstances.

Earlier, she'd left the nursery without making a scene, not wanting to upset her daughter. However, when that bastard Cade Hemmings, Randal's chief henchman, had put a hand firmly on her shoulder informing her that she wouldn't be permitted to see Clementine again until the situation was resolved, Dia's anger swelled. She wanted to tear the man apart limb by limb. She would have probably done it, if not for the heavy weaponry that Hemmings and his offsiders carried.

Heavy weaponry.

You didn't require Colt AR-15 assault rifles, Glock 22s and stun grenades to hold a woman and her daughter captive, even if she was a former ranger.

They were expecting more. They were expecting Byrn.

Dia plonked herself into the armchair beside the bed and stared out the French doors. The twilight outside was edging toward darkness. She wasn't keen on the idea of playing damsel in distress, yet she didn't want to do anything to place Clementine's life at further peril. The former ranger found herself tapping on the chair arms as the tension mounted in her body.

Three questions.

How long would Randal Byers wait before giving up on Byrn and pursuing a different strategy?

How much time could Dia afford to hesitate before throwing caution to the wind and attempting to bust herself and her daughter out of here?

When, if ever, would Lachlan Byrn come?

Chapter 63

RANDAL BYERS

"Enough. Get Dia."

"Yes, sir," responded Hemmings, before leaving the room.

Byers sat back in his study chair. He expected the assassin to have appeared by now, either surrendering through the front door or launching an assault through the back. But the mercenary had done neither. Byers supposed he shouldn't have been surprised. If there was one thing that he'd learned over the years, it was that people consistently failed to meet expectations. The manner in which Dia spoke of the man suggested there was more to him.

Or not.

Either way, Byers would now systematically proceed to destroy Lachlan Byrn. The media article was just the beginning.

The tycoon glanced at his watch. Two hours until the twenty-four-hour deadline that he'd set evaporated. There was no point in waiting. Wherever in the world Byrn had snuck off to, Byers' people would find him.

Chapter 64

The darkness had just settled in. Byrn went through his options one final time.

The twenty-four-hour deadline was almost due. Byers couldn't be certain that Byrn had seen the message, nor if he was planning a response, or simply fleeing the country. Judging from the activity below, Byers and Hemmings were planning for the worst-case scenario.

The assassin figured there were over fifty security operatives on the sprawling estate. He'd performed a sweep around the external perimeter of the property, noting guards posted at all entries in addition to numerous teams patrolling the grounds. Without doubt, there would be more inside the mansion.

Then there were the helicopters.

There was only ever a single aircraft in the air at a time unless there was a changing of the guard. Byrn had been in position for over fifteen hours. The choppers swapped over regularly every two hours. It was a smart move. Keep the sentries alert. Now that the daylight had disappeared, Byrn assumed they'd use a multi-sensor imaging system to scan the grounds below.

The assassin wondered how popular Byers would be with his reclusive neighbors. He likely didn't care, and they wouldn't complain. Randal Byers was not a man to offend. Even for the wealthy.

But the helicopters had given Byrn an idea. A one-man ground assault would be a suicide mission. Of course, Byrn didn't mind the idea of dying, it was the thought of not killing Byers before the assassin took his own last breath that really got him pissed. Then there was Dia and the child. For a second Byrn wondered which was the greater motivation, the young family or Byers' execution. Better not to dwell. It didn't really matter anyway.

The helicopters.

Byrn decided to launch his attack by air.

Chapter 65

RANDAL BYERS

"He's not coming. No knight in shining armor for you, my dear," said Byers, his smile broad.

"You filthy scum," spat Dia through her taut jaw. "Whether it's Lachlan Byrn, or some other form of retribution, I'll see to it that you pay for what you did to Bradley."

Byers grimaced with fake sincerity, his contempt for his daughter-in-law palatable.

"We've covered that subject, but yes, we do have to talk more about your ongoing attitude. If you decide to spend the rest of your life attempting to make me suffer for something you regard as unjust, I'm certain Hemmings and his men will have no difficulty in shortening your time with us. And I don't mean by sending you away somewhere."

Dia responded with a silent stare.

Byers continued.

"And of course, then we need to discuss the future of your daughter."

With some satisfaction, Byers watched the woman's muscles tense further. Pointless anger.

"Your granddaughter," Dia whispered under her breath.

"In business, I find everything is a matter of perspective."

Dia didn't respond.

"To continue. If you acquiesce to a peaceful coexistence, I can provide a comfortable lifestyle for you and the child. You'll remain here, only traveling with my approval. Your daughter will be educated at the best schools and her future will be assured."

"What's the other option?" asked Dia, finally finding her words.

"Exactly as I just described, only you won't be around to be part of the arrangement."

Right on cue, Byers noted Dia ball her fists in frustration. A warrior who'd been sanctioned. How satisfying.

"You don't leave me much choice. Allow my child to grow up directly under your influence or stick around to temper the evil," Dia replied.

Byers allowed himself a self-congratulatory grin.

"Very melodramatic, my dear. Perhaps you could write a book or a play to fill in your spare time. But perhaps I should reconsider my position. Your own sway over the child could be potentially damaging. Maybe I'm being too generous."

Dia looked up at Byers. His chair was higher than hers. Old school psychological advantage.

"What if Byrn turns up?" she asked.

Byers tilted his head and pressed his lips tightly.

"You better hope he doesn't. Lachlan Byrn's presence would certainly place your daughter's life in jeopardy."

"You wouldn't…."

"You have one hour to decide, Regan."

Chapter 66

LACHLAN BYRN

Byrn pulled his recently stolen hatchback off Wallingford Road into the car park at the Danbury Municipal Airport. A brief analysis of facilities in the area suggested that Danbury, although across the state border in Connecticut, was the closest airfield that could provide appropriate refuel facilities for the helicopters covering Byers' property. The airport was a fifteen-minute drive from Byers' estate. It would take less time in a chopper.

The small facility was not busy when the assassin arrived. It didn't take long for Byrn to scan the small array of buildings and identify lights and activity beyond a large hangar adjacent to the parking lot.

Byrn climbed out of the car and heaved himself over the fence. The nearby looming building provided shadow as he stalked his way down its southern side. Sure enough, the lights on the western side of the building lit a large area of the tarmac in front. In the middle of the space sat a Bell 407GX patrol helicopter. Painted a metallic dark gray, the bird had no other makings. It was, however, identical to the choppers Byrn had spotted over the Byers' estate.

The assassin glanced at his watch. If the chopper crews remained on their two hourly rotation, this aircraft's crew would be taking off sometime in the next twenty minutes to relieve their colleagues.

Byrn didn't have long to act.

The assassin headed down the side of the building and proceeded to make his way south, disappearing in the relative darkness. Careful to remain beyond the glare of the hangar lights, he then changed direction to the west. Finally, he stood sheltered in shadow at the center of the field. The assassin jogged silently toward the gray chopper. With all the activity on the other side of the helo, it was probable that nobody would see him coming.

Byrn ducked down as he reached the machine. Stooping down to get a look underneath the chassis, he saw two pairs of boots around thirty yards away, heading toward him.

No time like the present.

Reaching up and forward, Byrn grabbed the rear cabin door handle and yanked it downward. The assassin wrenched open the heavy door just wide enough to slide inside. He then lay flattened on the floor. Hidden in the shadows while the crew's energies were focused elsewhere, Byrn figured he had a chance. That was as good as it was going to get.

Three minutes later, both front doors opened and Byrn heard the sound of the two crewmen climbing in. He pressed himself harder to the floor.

"Do you reckon we're going to be at this all night?" asked a low, gravelly voice.

"Probably. I don't particularly like this sort of work, but the double-time for working nights helps me suffer in silence." A second voice.

"Yup."

"I know we're just following the flight boss's orders, but this Byers guy must be worried as all hell about something. I hope it doesn't come back to bite us on the butt."

The conversation stopped as the pilot went through his preflight check. Two minutes later, the four-bladed main rotor began to swirl. Shortly after, Byrn felt the aircraft ascend.

So far, so good.

The assassin pondered the situation. These men seemed like hired hands, not necessarily Byers' or Hemmings' thugs. Byrn had long ago decided he believed in 'purposeful killing.' He would kill these men to achieve his goal if he had to, but if another option appeared, he would take it. Their deaths would serve no immediate purpose. However, if there was no choice…

"Graystone two to Graystone One. We're crossing the eastern perimeter. Consider yourselves relieved," said the gravelly voice.

"Roger that. Graystone One exiting the search area to the west. Have a good one, guys."

The voice over the radio was female.

Byrn decided to allow the crew time to relax into their routine before he acted. If he got this wrong, everyone on board the chopper was about to have an extremely bad night.

Chapter 67

CADE HEMMINGS

Hemmings felt himself on edge. The old man was kidding himself if he thought Byrn had scampered. Based on what the security chief had heard about the assassin, it seemed that retreating from a fight wasn't part of his DNA.

After depositing Dia back to her quarters and ensuring the guards posted on both potential exits were fully alert, he did the same for the detail around the child's nursery. Finally, he returned to the comms room.

"Nothing to report, sir," offered Styles, removing her headphones.

"Likewise, Mr. Hemmings," reported the operative behind the multi-screens.

Hemmings hadn't even asked. His people were clearly on task.

"I'm going to walk the immediate grounds again. You can get me by radio or phone."

"Roger that, sir."

Hemmings checked that both his cell and his radio transmitter/receiver were charged and active before stepping outside.

"Hemmings to all personnel. I'm out and about," he

announced into the radio.

The security chief strode along the well-lit paths. Accidentally surprising his team, thereby provoking an unnecessary incident, was the last thing he needed.

As he walked, the security chief scanned his eyes around the huge mansion, the equally impressive stable complex, and numerous outbuildings. The absurdity of the old man's wealth frequently left him agape. Randal Byers could have whatever the hell he wanted in this world. However, Hemmings forfeited the right to pass judgement when he accepted his first paycheck from the tycoon. In the course of his duties for Byer Corp, Hemmings had performed many tasks that his former police buddies would not admire. They did, however, admire his large lakefront home, and the prestige cars in his garage.

We choose the roads we choose.

Hemmings shrugged his shoulders and marched on.

But would the old man really harm his own granddaughter?

Chapter 68

RANDAL BYERS

Byers sat in his study, brooding.

Right from the beginning, none of this unfolded in the manner he'd expected.

If Bradley had just kept his nose away from the corporation's buried skeletons, he'd be alive today. But he chose otherwise.

If Byrn had simply performed the job Byers requested of him and eliminated Dominic Nazar and his team without asking questions, the situation would have been resolved.

And if Regan Dia, his damn daughter-in-law, would stop being so freakin' obstinate and simply toe the line, they could all move forward.

Well, screw them all. Randal Byers hadn't spent a lifetime building an empire that was so successful, so powerful and so influential that it could rival many small and medium-sized nations just to have it torn down by a bunch of misguided miscreants, no matter who the hell they were.

The tycoon reached across his desk and wrapped his fingers around the crystal tumbler containing one of his finest single malts. He put the glass to his lips and took a long sip before setting it down.

Yes. He would do what was required.

Chapter 69

LACHLAN BYRN

"Are you picking up anything?"

Byrn assumed him to be the pilot. They were currently thirty minutes into their shift.

"Nada. Maybe we're all jumping at shadows here," the gravelly voice said, probably the spotter who would be the one monitoring the imaging system.

"But being paid damn well for our trouble, so jump away, I say."

"Probably a bad choice of words, gentlemen," announced Byrn.

"Holy mother... who the fuck are you?" shouted the monitor guy, turning around in his seat.

"Shit, where did you come from?" asked the pilot.

"Allow me to introduce myself," Byrn responded. "I'm the shadow."

Byrn sat up in the rear seat, his pistol pointed in front of him.

"Just to confirm, I'm the one in control of this situation. Any attempt to use your radio to communicate with the ground won't end well for you."

"Shit. The dickhead has a gun," exclaimed the monitor guy.

"Yes," Byrn confirmed. "The dickhead does have a gun, and he's extremely proficient at using it, so for all our sakes, please do as I instruct."

"What do you want?" The pilot was the first to regain composure.

"Well," began Byrn. "A change of flight plan. We're going to have an accident and I've got our crash-landing site all picked out. If you do your job correctly, there's a good chance we'll all walk away from this."

"A good chance?" exclaimed monitor guy.

"It's not a perfect world," Byrn responded.

Byrn noted the pilot's jaw set squarely under his helmet. Purposely crash-landing an aircraft contradicted every part of his training.

The pilot shouted, "If you think I'm going to intentionally destroy this helo, you're insane!"

"If you don't, you'll die in that seat," the assassin responded flatly.

Byrn allowed the pilot a few moments to process the situation.

"Now let's get started," he ordered. "I'll be honest. I'm not a pilot, but I know enough. I need you to take us down to three thousand feet and around eighty knots of airspeed. Then turn off the engine. Don't just reduce the revs like you do in training. I require the sudden silence of the aircraft to be noticed. Once the needle is adequately split and you're satisfied the rotor is pinwheeling, you can bring her down dead-stick."

"Where'd you learn the terminology?" asked the pilot.

"I'm ex-military."

No immediate response from either man.

"We'll probably be okay," said the pilot to his comrade. "I'm trained for this."

Byrn didn't think the second man appeared reassured. His demeanor seemed jittery, his hands trembling slightly. Byrn presumed he'd never served.

"There's one more thing," Byrn continued. "When you go to take her in, do not, I repeat, do not, raise the collective. Am I clear?"

"Listen buddy, if I don't pull up on the collective and lift the nose, we'll dig in and most likely nosedive into the ground. I'll have no control."

"Exactly," replied Byrn.

"You're certifiable," said monitor guy, his shaking increasing by the second.

"Ain't going to do it," the pilot shouted over his shoulder.

"Fair enough," Byrn responded. "Then your pal here gets a round in the back of the neck, and you get one more opportunity to follow my instructions. If you still refuse, you and I die together."

"I reckon you should do it," said monitor man, his voice clearly quaking.

"Asshole," the pilot stated, "you know there's a strong chance none of us will make it out of this." One last plea for rationality.

"And as I said, if you don't do it, you'll both be dead before we hit the ground and I'll die on impact. Worst-case scenario, that may offer a distraction for my friend inside that house and provide her with an opportunity to get out. For me it's win-win."

"You sure have a strange way of defining 'win,'" the pilot

responded.

"Now," said Byrn.

Reluctantly, the pilot pushed the chopper's nose down as they descended to the required altitude.

When Byrn observed the altimeter read three thousand, he yelled, "Engine off."

As the words left his mouth, he pressed the muzzle of his pistol into monitor guy's neck.

The pilot glanced around, noted the gun, and then reached down to turn off the engine.

Within seconds, the mechanical clatter of the motor had ceased. Only the rushing wind and swirling rotors could be heard.

The aircraft descended rapidly.

"Between those two rows of trees on the left, please," instructed Byrn.

The ground came hurtling towards them. Without the roar of the engine, it seemed surreal.

"We're going in too hard," yelled monitor guy.

The pilot remained focused on his task.

A moment later, the whole view through the windscreen was dominated by the looming grass and shrubbery.

Twenty feet from the ground, with the bird still in forward motion, Byrn slipped back in his seat and buckled his belt. It was too late for the pilot to try anything now.

As the skids touched the dirt, the aircraft, shuddering and screeching at the abrupt contact, lurched to the left. Wordlessly, the pilot reached his left hand down toward the collective.

"Touch it and I'll shoot your hand off," Byrn shouted.

A second later, the left skid dug in, followed quickly by the right. The chopper began to tilt forward before picking up momentum and somersaulting hard into the ground with a ferocious thud.

Byrn heard the crashing of the front windscreen before everything went dark.

Chapter 70

Byers reached for his phone.

"Hemmings, what the hell was that?"

"We think the chopper went down to the west of the house. I've got men on their way. I'll verify and get right back to you, sir."

"Be damn quick about it, and without any delay, go back and check on Dia and the kid," ordered Byers.

"Yes, sir."

"And Hemmings, was this Byrn?"

"Doubtful, sir, but I'll seek clarification."

Byers disconnected.

'Doubtful.' Then why were the hairs on the back of his neck standing taut as piano wires?

Chapter 71

LACHLAN BYRN

Byrn snapped awake. Apart from the bird's crew, nobody appeared close-by, so he must have only been out for a few seconds. The assassin undid his seatbelt and leaned forward. He touched two fingers on each man's neck. They were both unconscious, but still breathing.

Byrn's head throbbed, yet he had no time to waste. Using his shoulder, he heaved the back door of the aircraft open, climbed down, and listened. He heard distant voices but couldn't pinpoint the source. Despite being unsteady on his feet, the assassin sprinted toward the nearest strand of trees, away from the main house.

Seconds later, beams of light appeared across the lawn. Almost instantaneously, the shadowed figures of darkly clad security operatives swarmed the stricken helicopter.

Perfect.

It was time to initiate some action.

Chapter 72

Dia knew it was Byrn. There were a hundred reasons why the thumping noise could have been something else, but Dia just knew.

She peered through the French doors. Both guards were still there, but they appeared distracted. The man on the left spoke into his radio. Dia waited a minute to let the confusion set in before tapping on the glass. The guard on the right turned around and motioned with his palm for Dia to stop.

She continued.

Eventually, the guard walked up to the door, unlocked it, and opened it a few inches.

"What's going on?" she asked. "That noise, what's happened?"

"We don't know Ms. Dia. We think that maybe one of the choppers came down." He nodded toward his partner on the radio. "We're finding out more now. With respect, miss, you'll need to stay in your room."

The guard began to close the door. Unobserved, Dia had stuck her boot in the gap.

"Not going to happen," she said before forcefully slamming

the wooden door hard into the guard's shoulder.

As he shunted sideways with the blow, Dia stepped out. Raising her right hand with lightning speed, she chopped into the man's neck, hitting his brachial nerve. The guard crumpled.

The second operative lowered his radio and swung around. Dia kneed him in the groin with such force that he doubled over in pain. She then kicked him in the side of his head, sending him into temporary oblivion with his partner.

Fully alert, the former ranger turned and scanned the immediate area for further threats.

Nothing.

She sprinted along the length of the house. No matter what Byrn was planning, she had to find Clementine.

Chapter 73

CADE HEMMINGS

Hemmings surveyed the wreckage. It looked like the machine had hit the ground with a fair force. The pilots were lucky to be alive. Both were still unconscious.

"The team medic is on his way, Mr. Hemmings. Should we get them out?"

Hemmings could smell aviation fuel in the air.

"Yup, pull them clear. The medic can approve them to be moved into the house."

"Yes, sir."

Hemmings knew he'd have to call his boss. He wasn't looking forward to the experience. He grabbed his cell out of his jacket pocket.

"Mr. Byers. It was the helicopter. It looks like they've lost power and come down hard. There's been no fire, but the crew are unconscious."

"And Byrn?" came the angry voice.

"No sign, sir. But I'll instruct the team to be vigilant, just in case. Do you want me to call in the second chopper?"

A pause.

"No, that will just alert the authorities. I don't need a bunch of bureaucrats climbing all over the place at the moment. We'll do without aerial coverage."

"Yes, sir. What about the flight guys? We should get them off to a hospital, at least to be checked out."

"No," came the quick reaction. "Have your medic assess them and wait."

"Yes, sir."

"And Hemmings, get your ass over to Dia's room and check on her… now."

"On my way, sir."

Hemmings clicked off the phone.

It was always business with the old man. He really didn't give a shit about anyone. The security chief strode off across the garden, knowing that he would never fully understand the motivations of the obscenely rich.

Chapter 74

LACHLAN BYRN

Byrn watched the security chief, Hemmings, head toward the main house. No doubt he'd be checking on the prisoners before reporting back to Byers. Routine procedure after an invasive incident.

Also, an opportunity.

The assassin didn't take his eyes off the man as he crossed the lawn and stepped onto the rear patio. Byrn maneuvered himself along a row of trees about ten yards out, following Hemming's progress. When he came to the corner of the western and southern walls, the security man paused and turned, scrutinizing the vast lawn before proceeding. Byrn ducked behind a tree just in time to counter the surprise move. Apparently satisfied, Hemmings continued around the building.

Byrn scurried along the tree line and rounded the same corner, maintaining his distance ten yards out. To his astonishment, Byrn saw Hemmings sprinting down the length of the patio. He passed the main rear entrance and headed directly to a pair of open French doors. An instant later, the assassin understood why.

One man sat leaning against the wall, massaging his throat. Another lay unconscious on the ground.

Dia.

Byrn grinned to himself. You couldn't keep a good soldier down. This did, however, complicate things.

Chapter 75

RANDAL BYERS

"What do you mean, she's gone?"

Hemmings had to lift his cell away from his ear, such was the volume of the old man's rage.

"She exploited the chopper crash to manipulate a guard into opening the patio door. She then overpowered both men."

"A single woman against two highly experienced security operatives. Are you kidding me, Hemmings?"

"No, sir. But with all due respect, she is a trained ranger. They operate on a different level."

"Clearly," Byers replied. The tycoon was going to end the call when a thought struck him. "Fetch the child and bring her here."

"You're sure about that, sir?"

Byers was incensed. Being challenged by an employee at any rank wasn't in his playbook.

"Now!" he shouted before disconnecting.

Chapter 76

Dia clutched Clementine close to her chest. Her daughter had been asleep when the former ranger burst into the child's room. By the time the guards outside realized that Dia had arrived at the nursery door unaccompanied, it was too late. They didn't even have a chance to raise a weapon.

No rage like a mother scorned. Especially when that mother was a trained killer.

Dia's most satisfying moment had been punching her formerly faithful nanny hard on the jaw, sending her sprawling unconscious to the ground. Services no longer required.

The nursery lacked direct access to the patio outside, so Dia would need to make her way out through the labyrinth of corridors. She knew the route. It was simply a question of who blocked her way.

She pulled her daughter in tight.

"It's all right, my darling. We'll be out of here soon. Then it will just be you and me, forever."

Tears streamed down the young girl's cheeks, the violence too much for her to comprehend. But she tucked herself into her mother's chest.

Regan Dia stepped over one of the prone guards, turned left, and strode briskly down the corridor.

Chapter 77

LACHLAN BYRN

Byrn took a calculated risk by approaching the French doors. Hemmings and his stunned colleague had passed out of view. The third man remained comatose on the ground.

The assassin paused at the entrance as the two men exited through the door on the opposite side. With his SIG Sauer leading the way, Byrn crossed the space. Hearing no immediate sound, he craned his head around the doorway. The corridor was broad and ornate, the plush carpet soft underfoot. Ten yards distant, Hemmings led three men at a brisk pace. Byrn assumed the number now included the two operatives who had been posted on the room's internal entrance. As they rounded a sharp right-hand corner, Byrn jogged silently after them.

Once again, peering around the sharp bend, Byrn saw a familiar panorama. Two more men lay semi-conscious on the thick carpet several yards ahead.

Dia had been hard at work.

The assassin jerked his head back out of sight just as Hemmings reached for his radio.

Chapter 78

CADE HEMMINGS

"This is Hemmings to all stations. Both our guests are out in the wild, repeat both parties. All off-duty personnel are to report to your next rostered duty station. No one gets any downtime until the absentees have been retrieved."

The security chief paused for a moment. He disliked being on the back foot, and he certainly abhorred giving bad news to Randal Byers. He'd give the situation a few minutes. There was a better than strong chance the circumstances could be reversed quickly.

He then decided to make one extra call.

Chapter 79

LACHLAN BYRN

Byrn followed Hemming's entourage. There was a decent chance they'd lead him to Dia, whom Byrn assumed at this point was accompanied by her daughter. In the event of Dia being found by Hemmings' associates, Byrn would provide assistance. If they didn't, the assassin would turn his attention to Randal Byers.

After waiting until Hemmings rounded the next corner, Byrn pressed ahead.

Chapter 80

REGAN DIA

Why was this house so damn big? It was taking forever for Dia and Clementine to wind their way out of the place. The former ranger wouldn't dare risk her daughter's life, so careful evaluation before entering any new space became a necessity.

Fortunately, Clementine seemed comfortable, secured in her mother's arms. The young girl had calmed and was now remaining blissfully silent. Perhaps this was all an adventure for her.

Dia had reached the approach to the rear foyer, which led out to the mansion's back door. The area wasn't lit, so she remained poised at the farthest point of the corridor, listening for any untoward sounds.

She heard nothing.

Until.

"It was a fine attempt, Ms. Dia, but in the end, a wasted effort. Despite your impressive close combat skills, did you truly believe you had the capability to outmaneuver sixty operatives on their home soil? Now please drop your borrowed weapon on the floor and turn around."

Dia froze at the sound of Hemmings' voice. She momentarily closed her eyes as fear ripped through her heart. Not for herself, but for her child.

She could spin and fire. In normal circumstances, she might stand a chance, but not with Clementine in her arms.

No, it would all end here. It was time to give up.

Chapter 81

RANDAL BYERS

"Mr. Byers, sir. It's Styles in the comms room. We can't get hold of Mr. Hemmings, but we thought you should know. The helicopter pilot has just regained consciousness."

"And?" replied Byers impatiently.

"The medic says he's quite groggy, but the pilot is saying that the chopper was hijacked and forced to crash."

Silence.

Byers flicked the phone off, stood up, and walked to the window. He looked out into the darkness.

"Fucking Byrn," he said to no one in particular.

Chapter 82

LACHLAN BYRN

Byrn watched the scenario unfold.

He saw Dia drop her pistol silently on the carpet as she swung around. Despair lingered on her face, as though a gloomy dusk had overtaken her soul. Her jaw hung loosely in defeat.

But then Byrn witnessed it tighten.

Because Dia had seen him.

It was time.

Byrn shot the man closest to him before turning his weapon on Hemming's other sycophant. The child screamed at the noise, but Byrn ignored her. As the second operative went down, Hemmings turned, reaching into his coat pocket. Byrn couldn't shoot him because Dia and the child stood directly behind him, dominating the assassin's line of fire. Byrn stepped to the right, changing his angle.

"Don't go for it, Hemmings, in the chest from me or the back from Dia. Either way, the result is the same.

"Fair enough," Hemming responded, relaxed and willing.

Too relaxed.

At that precise moment, the lights flicked on in the space

beyond Dia. Six men armed with assault rifles stepped forward. From the horrified expression on Dia's face, the assassin figured a similar scenario was playing out behind him.

"Ditto, to what you said, Byrn. Now, if you both would carefully dispose of your weapons onto the floor, we can proceed up to Mr. Byers' study."

Despite his rising bile, Byrn complied.

Chapter 83

"Quiet the child," Byers ordered.

Clementine was crying her heart out. Her anguish filling the air.

"Unsurprisingly, she's upset," Dia responded.

"I don't give a damn. Shut her up."

Byrn gazed across the impressive room. The rich hardwood panels and the green velvet wingback chairs suggested a level of comfort that Byrn wasn't feeling at this moment.

Randal Byers positioned himself behind his desk. Dia and Byrn each sat in a chair opposite. Clementine was perched, inconsolable, in Dia's arms. Hemmings stood directly at their back, and there were four other security operatives in the room. Byrn knew there were more outside.

The child screamed even louder.

"Mellion, take Ms. Dia's daughter back to the nursery and double the guard," Byers instructed.

"No," cried Dia. "I want her with me."

"I'm afraid we're way past what you want, Dia," responded the old man.

The guard yanked the child from her mother's arms and left the room. The girl's cry slowly faded into the distance.

Byrn was stuck on Byers' words. 'Take Ms. Dia's daughter,' not 'take my granddaughter'. Conscious uncoupling.

Byers turned his attention to the assassin.

"Well, I've got to hand it to you, Byrn. You did give us a run for our money, or should I say my money? The helicopter crash was quite ingenious. I suppose, given your nature, the event was calculated to within an inch of its life."

Byrn remained mute.

Byers smiled before continuing.

"Yet, sadly, to no avail. You have failed miserably."

Byrn returned the tycoon's smile.

"Yes and no, Byers. We almost succeeded in getting Dia and her daughter away safely. If it wasn't for the oaf behind me actually thinking one step ahead of the game, we would have probably got away with it."

Byrn sensed Hemmings' glare without looking.

"Also," Byrn continued, "I now have the opportunity to discuss matters directly with you. Had I attempted a regular one-man incursion, I suggest I would not have made it this far alive. So really, not a miserable failure at all."

Byers leaned forward.

"Matters, what matters?"

The assassin matched the older man's stance.

"First, allow me to explain why you won't harm me and will let Dia, young Clementine, and me leave without any obstacles."

"And second?" enquired the tycoon.

"And second," repeated Byrn. "I feel a growing need to share with you exactly why I am going to kill you. It's a personal thing, really."

Byers began to laugh, not a belly laugh, but certainly one of genuine amusement. None of his men dared join in, although Byrn caught two of them smiling.

"You've got balls, Byrn, I'll grant you that. Now, always being a person to hear the opposition's final offer before closing a deal, you may as well put your proposal on the table."

Byrn knew he had nothing. There wasn't a single, solitary, solid reason for Byers to let them walk. But the assassin also appreciated that he'd now managed to cast a tiny seed of uncertainty in the man's mind.

Byrn straightened himself in his chair and began his pitch. "Shane Heathington."

"Who?" Byers asked.

"Shane Heathington," repeated Byrn. "Your man in the lawyer, Edward Celie's office in Old Saybrook. I'm surprised you've forgotten his name, considering he's the one that returned your son Bradley's corporate dossier to you."

Byers looked up at Hemmings. Byrn presumed the security chief at his back had nodded.

"To continue, I had a long chat with Heathington," said Byrn. "He confessed what he'd done for you and told me all about returning the two thumb drives to Hemmings here." Byrn jerked his thumb behind him as he spoke. "But I'm assuming that he didn't mention to Hemmings that he'd made a copy of both drives before he handed the originals over."

Byers raised his eyebrows toward Hemmings, who presumably shook his head.

"Where are those copies now?" asked the old man.

"In a safe place," Byrn replied. "I shall be happy to send them to you or destroy them if you prefer once we are well clear of here."

"It's a wild tale, Byrn. But I suppose it's one we'll have to attempt to verify." The tycoon looked over Byrn's shoulder. "Hemmings, can you get someone down to Old Saybrook to confirm the existence of the copies?"

Byrn waited for the response.

Hemmings cleared his throat before speaking.

"I'm afraid that would be futile, Mr. Byers. I sent an operative down there later the same day I'd collected the drives. After you'd verified the contents, of course. We intended to erase the trail and ensure no duplicates existed."

"But?" said Byers.

"But I'm afraid Shane Heathington was already dead."

"Because I killed him," announced Byrn.

Byers shook his head.

"It's a tangled web we weave, isn't it, Byrn? What evidence can you provide of the existence of those copies?" asked Byers.

"I would have thought Heathington's corpse would have sufficed. I can furnish the details of his manner of death if you like. To be honest, he wasn't keen to hand the copies over," Byrn responded darkly.

"An indication perhaps, but not positive proof," Byers replied.

The conversation stalled as Randal Byers appeared lost in thought.

"I'll need to consider the situation further," the tycoon eventually responded. "Hemmings, please return Ms. Dia to her quarters. Put Byrn in a separate room and for God's sake, don't screw up again. Post people in each room with them."

"Yes, sir." The four agents in each corner of the study moved forward, two behind Dia, two behind Byrn.

"What about the second matter I wished to discuss?" asked Byrn.

"I provide lectures on individual's inadequacies, Byrn," responded a scowling Byers. "I don't receive them. Now, get out."

Chapter 84

The procession had reached the ground floor corridor and was almost at Dia's room when she whispered to him.

"Where are the copies? Are you sure they're safe?"

Byrn grinned.

"Absolutely safe. Byers will never find them because they don't exist. They never did," he responded.

Dia's gasp of breath was audible.

"Fucking great. So, you've just bet the farm on a complete lie."

Byrn nodded as they walked.

"Yes, but quite a good one, I think."

Chapter 85

Yet again, Randal Byers stood by the study window, gazing out into the blackness. Much of the property below remained hidden in shadow, but the tycoon knew what was there.

His domain.

The old man noted the occasional security patrol stepping randomly into the glare of the pathway lighting before receding into the darkness of the grounds beyond. He held no doubt that Lachlan Byrn and Regan Dia would soon be retreating into their own permanent darkness. He just needed to ensure they left no surprises in their wake.

Byrn had presented him with a problem. The greatest likelihood was that the assassin was lying through his teeth. Yet a small element of hesitation lingered in the businessman's mind. Could he really afford to ignore it? If Byrn spoke the truth about the existence of the extra thumb drives, Byers lay exposed to enough credible information to have a detrimental impact, if not completely undermine everything he'd worked for.

No, the risk was unacceptable.

On the other hand, letting Byrn and Dia go was equally off

the table. To do so would leave him in a position of perennial vulnerability.

Byers had spent his entire life on the front foot. His aggression in business had been well documented and often underestimated. Over the years, he had been called many things. A dictator, a tyrant, even an amoral monster.

Water off a duck's back.

Randal Byers had a clear understanding of what he was. *Who* he was. An accomplished businessman whose astute and sometimes brutal tactics allowed him to achieve more in his life than most people ever dreamed about. So much more. He'd done it through commitment, focus and, above all, perspective. Byers never lost perspective. The entrepreneur was grudgingly aware of the addictive nature of power and influence. Fortunately, he had the intellect to wield his perpetual dominance for the greater good... of Byer Corp.

The tycoon sensed a smile crease his lips as a strategy formed in his mind. It was almost divine inspiration, the idea's boldness astonishing even himself. Of course. This was no time to yield to convention. Aggression must be met with overwhelming force. The ultimate truth was, Byers still held the trump card, the one remaining ace in the deck. If he played it shrewdly, he would control both the stakes and the players in Lachlan Byrn's dangerous game. It simply required a formidable stance, and a willingness to follow through, no matter the cost... to anyone.

A familiar formula.

Decision made. The cards would fall his way, as they always did, and always would.

Chapter 86

LACHLAN BYRN

Byrn glowered at Randal Byers, who sat opposite him at the desk. They'd been summoned back to the study, everyone assuming their previous positions. Clementine was still relegated to her nursery. Byrn was uneasy. The man across from him didn't look like someone about to cave in to external pressure. The wry smirk on his lips suggested that Byers had concluded that he'd already won the war. Byrn wondered if Dia noticed Byers' change in demeanor as well. If she did, she wasn't showing it.

"Your proposal does not hold sufficient merit," Byers began. "Though it's highly probable you're lying, Byrn, as you may well have hoped, a small doubt remains. That hesitation needs to be negated."

As he spoke, the tycoon stared directly into Byrn's eyes. The assassin presumed he'd pursued the same strategy a thousand times before. Byrn responded with stony silence.

"Accordingly, I must be sure you speak the truth, regardless of what it is. Are you following me here, man?"

The assassin nodded before being drawn into the conversation.

"You can threaten me all you like, Byers. To be honest, I don't really care that much if I survive this situation or not. So whatever ungodly plan you're cooking up, either just do it or shut up."

"Admirable words," Byers responded, "but, in effect, useless. I have no intention of threatening your life, at least not immediately."

Byrn knew what was coming. He and Dia had spoken briefly about this eventuality. She had insisted Byrn stand firm. It was quite clear to her that her father-in-law intended to kill her, so she may as well die for a purpose. The freedom of her daughter.

"We figured where you'd go with this Randal," interjected Dia. "If you're going to threaten my life, you might as easily straight out kill me now. You're not getting those drives until Clementine is safe."

Byrn stared at the old man. Worryingly, he didn't appear the least bit perturbed.

"Once more, you two have misunderstood my intentions."

Byers leaned forward and reached out with both hands. He pivoted the screen on his desk around and slid it sideways, placing it where Byrn, Dia, and he could all see it. He pressed a couple of keys and a live image appeared. Clementine lay asleep in her bed. The nanny, adorned by several sticking plasters on her face, sat in a chair nearby.

Dia gasped.

Byers shifted his gaze to Hemmings, who once again stood perched directly behind Byrn.

"Hemmings. I assume you're armed."

"Yes, Mr. Byers."

"I want you to go downstairs. I'll leave a live audio feed

between the nursery and this room. Once you are in position, I will ask Mr. Byrn to tell me the truth. If I'm not satisfied with his response, I require you to shoot Ms. Dia's daughter. Make it quick and painless. I am not a monster. Are my instructions clear?"

Momentarily, Hemmings didn't respond. He couldn't. The silence was filled with Dia's piercing scream. Eventually, she found her words.

"You may be the greatest asshole of all time, Randal, but surely even you wouldn't shoot your own granddaughter." Even as the utterance left her mouth, Byrn sensed its hollowness.

"He killed his own son, Dia. But no, in this case, it's just a distressed old man feigning a final act of desperation. He won't do it," announced Byrn.

The assassin hadn't taken his eyes off Byers while he talked. The old man's eyes showed no hint of defeat. That was concerning.

"Mr. Byers, sir. May I have a confidential word, please?" Hemmings words broke the impasse.

Byers nodded and the security man walked around behind the desk, leaned down and whispered something into tycoon's ear. Byrn couldn't make out either Hemmings' words or the old man's response. Thirty seconds later, Hemmings stood upright and marched out of the room. Byrn struggled to interpret the man's expression.

They sat in silence for several minutes. Dia silent in worried anticipation, Byrn glowering at Byers, trying to get a read of the man. The tycoon showed no sign that he was bluffing.

Eventually, Hemmings appeared on the screen. He directed

the nanny to the door before positioning himself next to the cot where Clementine Byers slept peacefully, totally oblivious to the circumstances.

Byrn stared closely at the image. It wasn't obvious, but the assassin was certain he noted a slight quiver in Hemmings hands as he held his pistol aimed at the sleeping child.

Not a good omen.

Byers sat back in his chair once more, glaring at Byrn before speaking.

"It's a shame that you've led us to this point, Byrn. But the situation is what it is."

Regan Dia quivered in the chair next to him.

"Make no mistake, Byers. This is your doing, not mine."

The tycoon shrugged his shoulders. "Semantics. Now I'm going to ask you one final time, and you clearly understand what is at stake here. I urge you not to underestimate my intent."

The old man leaned forward.

"Where are the additional drives?"

Byrn searched the man's eyes, hoping for a sign of his intention. The assassin had faced evil before, but this was different. There was nothing there for him to find.

Seconds ticked by.

Byrn remained silent. Surely Byers wouldn't do this.

"I require an answer, Byrn."

If the assassin told the truth, Dia was as good as dead. If he lied and Byers saw through it, there was a chance the child would die. But only a chance.

Silently, Byrn stared back at the old man.

"Very well then, proceed as instructed, Hemmings."

Byrn swung his attention to the screen. Hemmings lifted

his pistol and pointed it toward the little girl. He didn't look happy, but he didn't step back.

Byers glanced at Byrn one last time.

"Do it now, Hemmings," the strain now evident in his voice.

Byrn opened his mouth to speak.

"The…"

Suddenly, the screen went blank as the sound of a single gunshot resonated through the house.

Dia screamed.

It was too late.

Chapter 87

Hemmings hand trembled.

That was new.

He stood over the child's cot, her body perfectly still, apart from the gentle swell of her small chest as she claimed each breath. Surely the boss wasn't serious about this. Without doubt, it was a desperate ruse to shock the truth out of Lachlan Byrn.

Before he departed Byers' study, Hemmings had privately confirmed with the old man that he did not expect Hemmings to actually carry out the threat. The old man appeared immovable. Hemming's appreciated that in all the years he'd worked for Randal Byers, he'd never seen the man back down or retreat from anything. But surely, murdering his own granddaughter was different. Surely.

The security chief stood there in silence, awaiting a command instructing him to return to the study upstairs to resonate through his earpiece.

Throughout the years, Hemmings had engaged in various actions he did not feel particularly proud of in the name of Byer Corp. There'd been threats against opposing businesses.

A few beatings. Some cases of blackmail, mostly warranted, usually against people who would have done the same to Byers if they'd been in a position to. But the old man had never allowed himself to be put in that position until now.

Hemmings considered the worst of it the suicide of the young girl, the daughter of an opposing businessman Byers had ordered blackmailed into submission. The result was not what Hemmings intended. Who could have seen it coming? The guilt didn't rest on his shoulders.

But this was different.

Clearly, this was a last-ditch bluff played by a man under great pressure.

Come on Byrn. Just tell the old man what he needs to hear, you fucking idiot. If you don't, and this kid dies, it will be on you.

Who was he kidding? He was the one standing here with the gun.

Talk, you idiot, talk.

The earpiece stayed quiet.

Maybe Byrn was talking after all. That could take time.

Of course, if he didn't, Hemmings would follow through with his boss' instruction. He had never failed the old man before, and he wasn't going to start failing him now.

But was the old man slipping? Over the last couple of years, Hemmings had witnessed Byers make some strange decisions. The man used to be a creative, dominating force in business, wielding his influence as he saw fit. But recently things had changed. Byers seemed obsessed with maintaining his powerbase and etching his place in history.

His second born, Bradley, had threatened that. Hemmings was certain the old man wouldn't follow through with his son's death.

He'd been wrong.

Still, the earpiece remained silent.

Until.

"Proceed as instructed, Hemmings," Byers' voice resonated in his earpiece.

Shit.

Screw Byrn, screw Dia. Hemmings detested them both. Sanctimonious pricks.

He stared down at the kid and raised the gun. The tremor increased.

"Do it now, Hemmings,"

It was too late to go back. Hemmings closed his eyes and began to squeeze the trigger.

Chapter 88

LACHLAN BYRN

Byrn sat motionless, cocooned in a sullen, internal silence.

Next to him, Regan Dia wailed violently in a deep, tormented sea of anguish.

The assassin regarded himself as having no conscience. Guilt never played on his mind. It just didn't happen.

Death was part of life, and he was part of death.

But this was different.

A kid.

A pure life lived in innocence. Until now.

For the first time in his own tortured existence, Byrn felt regret. He should have spoken sooner. Mitigated the risk. It was a miscalculation.

Also, for the first time in his life, Lachlan Byrn realized that he would never forgive himself.

Chapter 89

Hemmings leaned down and swept the kid up from the cot.

She was screaming after the loud gunshot.

He hoped that Byers hadn't noticed him draw the spare weapon from his belt. He'd positioned his body between the camera and the second gun. He held the pistol just under the crook of his elbow, hidden by his sleeve, and fired. The result was a direct hit on the camera lens.

The security chief had only a limited time to act.

Clutching the child to his chest with his left arm, Hemmings secured both his weapons. His team outside wouldn't yet realize what had gone down. Their ignorance was his one chance.

He stepped into the passageway. Both guards stood tense, ready for action. They'd obviously heard the gunshot.

"Byers wants me to get the kid out of here immediately," he said.

Without pausing to explain further, he strode confidently down the corridor.

The security chief repeated the story two minutes later as he exited the building.

After securing the still crying child in the front seat, Hemmings climbed behind the wheel of his car and headed down the driveway. This would be the real test.

Two guards were standing on either side of the main gate, just as Hemmings had ordered.

"The old man wants the kid out of here now. I don't know what's going down, but he doesn't want her around."

The guard, Mallory, peered down at him. Hemmings picked up the brief flash of hesitation that crossed the man's face. The eyes briefly narrowed.

"Sure Mr. Hemmings. You're the boss."

"Yes, I am," the security chief replied before pressing his foot down on the gas pedal.

He turned left and drove off into the night, wondering how much time he'd bought himself.

Chapter 90

LACHLAN BYRN

"What? Are you sure?… Hell, yes. Go after him, you fools… dead or alive, I don't care."

Byers was on the phone, his crinkled brow and sharp tone exposing his agitation.

Still gutted, yet acutely aware of his surroundings, Byrn looked on, the sudden change in Byers' manner having piqued his interest.

The tycoon clicked off his cell and drew a deep breath. He then turned to Dia, who continued to sob uncontrollably in her chair. A moment earlier, she'd attempted to throw herself at Byers, but was stopped by the two guards at her side. She now wore the bruises from the violent interaction.

Byers stared across the desk, watching his daughter-in-law's face gradually transform from tearful grief to a slow-burning hatred. The darkness in her glare cast a visceral shadow across the room.

The old man waited silently, exploiting the intensity of the moment.

Then he shrugged.

"Dia, I regret to inform you that your daughter is still alive."

Dia's eyes widened as she sat bolt upright.

"What? How?"

"My man, Hemmings failed me." Byers sighed. "He'll pay a price for his treachery."

"Where is Clementine now?" Byrn asked, sobering up from his misguided self-pity.

"It appears Hemmings had taken her and fled into the night. My people will catch up with him."

Byrn gazed at the tycoon.

"We both know that they won't. Hemmings is the smartest of the lot of them. If he wants to disappear, he'll be gone."

"Perhaps," the old man nodded.

Byrn smiled, quickly finding his feet.

"So, the impasse continues and thanks to one man's conscience, you've lost your ace in the hole, Byers."

The tycoon appeared crestfallen, but Byrn figured he wouldn't remain in that state for long. It was time to sort this, so he pressed on.

"We each possess the ability to destroy the other. You have the media article about me and my activities and the means to publish it. I hold in my possession files that could bring down your empire. I'm not happy about the situation, but it is what it is."

"What do you want?"

Byrn wondered how infrequently Byers must have asked that question in a negotiation.

Dia looked on silently, observing both men. Byrn knew she'd leave this up to him.

"Dia and I walk out of here unimpeded. I'm confident that we'll successfully reunite her with Clementine. We would both expect no further contact from you or your people. You are out of Dia's life; you are out of Clementine's life. Is that clear?"

Byers didn't respond. He gazed back in Byrn's direction, but the assassin figured it wasn't Byrn he was seeing. For perhaps the first time in his entire existence, Randal Byers was staring at the prospect of defeat.

Eventually.

"I could have you both killed now," he stated.

"And the plans I've arranged for the release of those documents through a multitude of intermediaries would be automatically enacted. Do you really want to take that risk?"

More silence. The brooding kind.

Byers got up from behind the desk before striding over to his beloved window. Byrn could see the man's confidence growing by the second. Each step more assured than the one before.

The assassin would wait, but only for a minute. After that, Dia and he would fight their way out. But negotiation was a better long-term solution.

Abruptly, the old man turned around, his pale skin drawing tight over the squarely set jaw.

"I'm left with no option. We have an agreement."

Chapter 91

"He can't get away with this. He can't be allowed to live," announced Dia.

She and Byrn sat in the lounge room of her mother's house in Montville. The old lady was in the kitchen with Clementine. Grandma was doing the dishes and Dia's daughter was watching a kids' show on the computer.

Hemmings had made contact and arranged the child's return to her mother several days earlier. After that, he disappeared. Who would have figured that Cade Hemmings turned out to be an okay guy?

Dia's feature were set hard in grim determination.

"I'm going back to kill him."

"No, you're not, Dia, and I'm going to tell you why," Byrn responded.

"You can't stop me," she replied defiantly. "That man has to pay for what he did."

"All I ask is that you listen to me. Dia. Then you can do whatever the hell you want."

Byrn eased himself up from his chair and strolled over to the fireplace. Dia remained seated on the couch.

"Go ahead," she said, her simmering anger evident.

Byrn nodded, not taking his eyes off her.

"Once you take out Randal Byers, you'll be entering a different world. Now, before you say anything, I know that you've killed people before. If you recall, I've witnessed you do it. The street thugs in Xi'an. Dominic Nazar and his crew at the rail yard in Des Moines. Those situations were not the same as this."

"How?"

"The care factor. Street gangs and terrorists. Nobody in authority is going to go out of their way to track down the killers of scum. There'll be perfunctory scrutiny, but quietly, those investigating the deaths will believe those responsible did the world a favor. That will be the end of it."

"But?" Dia questioned.

"But Randal Byers' murder would be something different altogether. The man is successful, and however misplaced, respected. Being a global figure, authorities will strive to not only appear to pursue his killer but also to actually apprehend them. To the winner goes the biggest prize in law enforcement and politics. Promotion and power."

"So, what do I do? Let it go? The man murdered my husband and tried to murder my daughter."

"That's exactly what you do, Dia. You let it pass. You've got a chance now, with Clementine. A short time ago, that appeared stolen from you on a variety of levels. We fought; you got your life back. You take out Byers and all that goes down the drain. They'll figure it out. Motives and opportunity would be leaping out of the walls at them. You'll become a hunted fugitive and, worse still, an absent mother. Your daughter will grow up alone. Is that what you want? Is it worth it?"

Dia slunk back onto the couch. Byrn could tell from the

pout on her lips that he'd prosecuted his case efficiently. She had the means and the skills to carry through on her threat, but as he watched, the former ranger's resolve withered as she confronted reality.

"So, he gets away with it?"

Frustration.

Byrn nodded.

"We had a deal. We honor it."

"Screw you Byrn. And screw your damn logic."

Dia paused, her eyes slowly moistening. Byrn assumed she was considering her daughter's future.

Eventually, she continued. "But dammit, you're right, I'd lose too much."

The assassin gazed down at her, sulkily accepting the inevitable. He felt bad. Not for what he said, but because he'd just blatantly lied to one of the few people in the world that he trusted.

Chapter 92

RANDAL BYERS

Byer's pupils snapped open. He didn't know why. He wiped his eyes and checked the clock.

3.17 a.m.

Something had woken him. He gazed around the darkened room.

"Chasing shadows again, Byers?"

He saw the human outline leaning against the wall by the curtain.

"You."

"Yes, Randal. Me."

Chapter 93

LACHLAN BYRN

"It's time to wake up and die, Randal."

Byers pulled himself up in his bed. His eyes darting around the room.

"I've disabled all the alarms. Nobody is coming to help you. In the event that any of your security team heard you scream, they wouldn't come."

"What have you done?" asked the tycoon.

"Let's just say that they're all currently indisposed," replied the assassin.

Even in the shadows, Byrn noted the whiteness of Byers' skin.

Fear.

Good.

"It's time for us to settle up, Randal."

"But we had a deal," Byers responded.

Byrn shook his head.

"To succeed, a deal requires two parties with integrity willing to move forward."

The tycoon remained silent, so Byrn continued.

"My own level of integrity is questionable, Randal. Yours

is non-existent, so the agreement is canceled."

"I can pay you. I have the means to make you a very rich man, Byrn."

Byrn tilted his head.

"A predictable response, but it's been tried before. You could give me every dime you had, and it wouldn't be enough."

Byers' bottom lip quivered as he spoke.

"You're not really going to kill me?"

"As a matter of fact, yes, I am," the assassin responded.

The older man's sharp intake of breath cut through the silence.

"You know, I've been doing some thinking," Byrn spoke from the shadows. "This is usually a crucial time for me, the few minutes before I take someone's life. Obviously, it's an important moment for them as well. You won't ever have the opportunity to experience this again, Randal."

"You're insane."

"Possibly, possibly not. Either way, my mental health will make no difference to your current predicament. The dilemma I'm facing is how to approach these next few moments. I want them to be impactful and significant to you. For your own personal growth."

Byrn could see Byers begin to shake. The inevitable sinking in, slowly.

"The thing is, Randal, this is the moment I set aside for explanation, education. I typically feel a responsibility to clarify to someone the wrong path they took. I like to aid them in understanding the cause of their premature passing. But in your case, I can't help but think any clarification would be pointless. A waste of my time."

"In God's name, what are you talking about, man?" The

tycoon croaked out the words, his attempt to hold his voice steady unsuccessful.

"Perspective, Randal. Perspective. You've lost all sense of where your priorities stand. To put it more simply, old man, you've lost any semblance of your own humanity."

Byrn watched as Byers' body went rigid and his nostrils flared.

"How dare you come in here and lecture me about perspective? You're just a mercenary for hire, a paid killer. You have no right…"

Involuntarily, Byrn burst into laughter. He knew the reaction was unprofessional, but he didn't really care.

"Thank you, Randal. Thank you so much."

"For what?" Byers' voice bristled with contempt.

"For confirming my thoughts, you fool."

"What the hell?"

"Any sane man would have been angry that I questioned his humanity. You reacted because I challenged your perspective, your decision making. I don't believe I need to explain more."

The tycoon sat forward in the bed, raising his finger angrily at the assassin.

"You are like so many others, Byrn. Trapped in your tiny black and white world. But that's not reality. That's not the environment we live in. It's all gray, a thousand different shades of gray, you imbecile. And it takes a man of my perception, a creator, manipulating the cesspit of humanity like colors on a canvas, to have the perspective and the balls to forge the world I've built."

Byrn uncrossed his legs.

"God complex, eh, Randal? So, I'll put this in basic terms to help you out. Most people would sacrifice anything to save their family. In the end, in that place where the hard decisions are made, that forfeiture is the best of the human condition. You threw your family under the bus for your fucking business. Perspective, negligible. Human qualities, totally absent."

"You arrogant…"

"Anyway, nice speech, but I'm bored now," the assassin interrupted.

That wasn't entirely true. Byrn found Randal Byers' unique mixture of terror and outrage quite stimulating, but enough was enough. Control was control.

Byrn sensed his own mouth tightening in anticipation.

The assassin reached to the table beside his chair, his finger wrapping around the handle of the Fairburn-Sykes fighting knife he'd placed there. The weapon felt balanced under his grip. His muscles tensed, his body wired and alert.

Without warning, Byrn sprang out of his seat, catapulting himself toward Randal Byers.

In the darkness, the whites of Byers' eyes widened in surprised alarm.

As Byrn reached the tycoon's bedside, he extended his arm, shoving Byers firmly back onto his pillow. Raising the knife above his victim's heart in reverse grip with his left hand, the assassin briskly swept his right hand around the weapon's pommel.

Randal Byers had a millisecond to note the briefest flash of a grin on his killer's face before Byrn thrust the weapon downward.

The tycoon cried out as the blade entered his chest between his fourth and fifth ribs. Once satisfied with the blade's depth, the assassin swiftly sliced the knife from side to side, targeting the left ventricle and maximizing the wound.

Byers gasped.

Byrn leaned forward, his eyes an inch away from his Byers.

"Usually, this is when I would celebrate witnessing my victim's life fade away, but in your case, any sign of life vanished long ago. For God's sake, you tried to kill your own baby granddaughter, you evil fuck."

Byrn guided the knife back and forth twice more before withdrawing it.

As the assassin withdrew, a jet stream of dark blood splattered both his face and the surrounding walls.

A few seconds after that, Randal Byers lay motionless amongst the crimson-soaked sheets.

The moment.

Gratification.

Lachlan Byrn raised a hand to wipe the fresh, warm blood from his eyes before turning toward the door.

Some days were better than others.

THE END

About the Author

Mark Mannock was born in Melbourne, Australia. He has had an extensive career in the music industry including supporting, recording with or writing for Tina Turner, Joni Mitchell, The Eurythmics, Irene Cara and David Hudson. His recorded work with Lia Scallon has twice been long-listed for Grammy Awards. As a composer/songwriter Mark's music has been used across the world in countless television and theatre contexts, including the 'American Survivor' TV series and 'Sleuth' playwright Anthony Shaffer's later productions.

Mark is presently writing the successful 'Nicholas Sharp' thriller series about a disillusioned former US sniper whose past plagues him as he makes his way in the contemporary music industry. Sharp is a man whose insatiable curiosity and embedded moral compass lead him to places he ought not go. The series is currently read in over 50 countries.

Mark also writes the exciting new Lachlan Byrn Thrillers. Assassin, vigilante or serial killer? Byrn has a passion for his work that transcends the rules of engagement. He gets up close and personal with his victims... very close, very personal and he's exceptionally deadly.

Mark lives in Kettering, Tasmania with his family. His travels around the globe act as inspirations for his writing.

Reviews are life's blood to an author. If you've enjoyed DEATH COMES EASY please consider leaving a review on the book's Amazon page or on GOODREADS.

You can connect with me on:
- https://markmannock.com
- https://www.facebook.com/markmannockbooks

Subscribe to my newsletter:
- https://markmannock.com

Also by Mark Mannock

ONE TWO THREE... DIE
A Lachlan Byrn Novella

Only a killer knows...

Driven by a deadly skill set and a wavering moral compass, Lachan Byrn barely straddles the thin line between assassin, vigilante, and serial killer. Tasked with stopping a murderous psychopath terrorizing a tranquil island community, Byrn becomes the dark remedy to a seemingly unsolvable problem.

Set a serial killer to catch a serial killer.

As the tension escalates and the body count rises, Byrn navigates a murky patchwork of deception, uncovering layers of mistruths and unexpected twists. However, amidst the chaos, doubts begin to gnaw at his conscience, hinting that not everything is as straightforward as it appears.

With boundaries blurred, Lachlan Byrn must first confront his own shadows to ensure that his lethal skills are brought to bear on the guilty target.

The trouble is... finding someone who is innocent.

If you sign up to Mark's mailing list at *https://markmannock. com* you'll receive this book for free, or you can purchase it on Amazon.

Available on Amazon:
https://storyoriginapp.com/universalbooklinks/90aa075 a-a866-11ee-aaa4-bb43891dc6c4

DIE AS YOU KILL
Lachlan Byrn Thriller #1

Assassin, vigilante or serial killer?

Vadim Aleyev, President of the Russian Federation is out of control. He's pushing his country, his people and the world to the brink of a catastrophic war.

Around the globe, world leaders are worried, yet no one seems prepared to act. Then one nation unleashes its most fearsome weapon: Lachlan Byrn.

Assassin, vigilante or serial killer? Byrn has a passion for his work that transcends the rules of engagement. He gets up close and personal with his victims... very close, very personal and he's exceptionally deadly.

As the clock ticks, can one man with a tenuous grip on his own sanity, achieve the unachievable?

Available on Amazon:

https://storyoriginapp.com/universalbooklinks/878d78da-5ff2-11ee-abdd-4beccef3e055

HE WITHOUT SIN
Lachlan Byrn Thriller #3

Lachlan Byrn just couldn't unsee it.

It began as a routine paid kill, but then the assignment became a crusade.

Over the years Lachlan Byrn has evolved the act of turning his back on problems that don't concern him into an artform. But what's different this time?

And why now, when the shear magnitude and power of the forces he faces are impossibly overwhelming?

It appears you can't keep a good man down… or a bad one.

Available on Amazon:

https://storyoriginapp.com/universalbooklinks/5e7f127a-4596-11ef-ad67-670ab8ec1aaa

PLAY OUT
A Nicholas Sharp Origin Novella

Sign up to Mark's mailing list and receive this book for free!

Set five years before **KILLSONG**

A Terrorist attack on the London Underground. Nicholas Sharp doesn't think so.

While on leave from Iraq, the U.S. Marine Sniper finds himself intervening when innocent lives are threatened. He walks away, but for Sharp it's never that easy. Something doesn't feel right. Twenty-four hours later everything is wrong.

The brief solace he finds in his beloved piano is shattered when Sharp becomes the attacker's next target. Step up or step away. Nicholas Sharp doesn't like to kill, but he sure as hell knows how to.

Somewhere between Clancy's *Jack Ryan* and Ludlum's *Jason Bourne*, Nicholas Sharp may be a flawed and reluctant hero, but you certainly want him on your side.

"I've read hundreds of books throughout the years and the pandemic has provided me with extra time to discover more reading treasures. Play Out is one of the best." **Goodreads Reviewer-5 STARS**

The Nicholas Sharp origins novella PLAY OUT is sent to you FREE when you join my mailing list at
https://markmannock.com

KILLSONG
Nicholas Sharp Thriller #1

Reluctant, determined, lethal. Nicholas Sharp is a killer musician… literally!

Nicholas Sharp knew there would be blood on his hands. It was just a question of how much.

The death of a child and her mother, or the loss of countless thousands. Sharp is ordered to choose, but the former Marine Sniper gave up following orders long ago.

Sharp's newfound refuge as a musician is suddenly blasted apart. While he is preparing to back well-known singer Robbie West on a USO tour of Iraq, a close friend and her daughter disappear.

Trapped in a deadly maze of colliding worlds and dark agendas as competing forces race to locate discarded biological weapons, Sharp is compelled to act.

One wrong decision, one misstep… and the consequences could be disastrous.

"I had to keep reading to the end, could not put it away until I had finished." **Amazon Reader- 5 STARS**

Available on Amazon:
https://storyoriginapp.com/universalbooklinks/1819a2 6e-94e1-11eb-a3f5-27192b353466

LETHAL SCORE

Nicholas Sharp Thriller #2

"Ethan Hunt has nothing on Nicholas Sharp... the pages flew by... " **Amazon Reviewer 5 STARS**

You can't stop someone with nothing to lose...

Nicholas Sharp is on a tour through Europe, the concerts are sold out and the former Marine sniper turned musician is living in luxury thanks to promoter Antonio Ascardi.

Suddenly it all goes wrong. People are dying along the way and Sharp is blamed. Now a hunted man, accused of terrorist crimes across the continent, Nicholas Sharp must fight for his life and freedom.

Available on Amazon:
https://storyoriginapp.com/universalbooklinks/88fb9910-94e1-11eb-9d39-fbf80ab2fc76

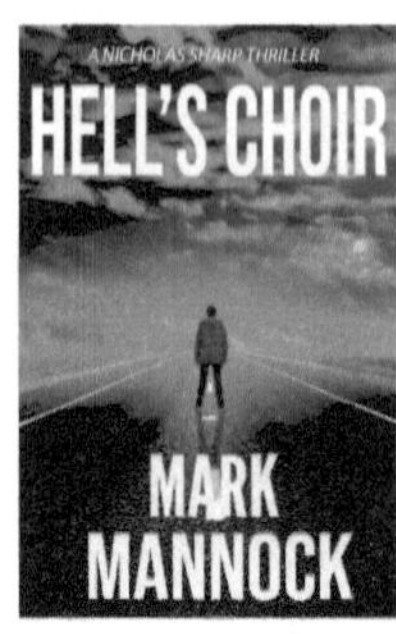

HELL'S CHOIR

Nicholas Sharp Thriller #3

A goodwill visit to Sudan, what could possibly go wrong?

Nicholas Sharp is performing as part of a political and cultural group representing the US. Suddenly caught up in the middle of a political coup, the leader of the American contingent goes missing and his security staff murdered.

Communication with the outside world is cut off. It falls to Sharp and Greatrex to track their missing leader down.

But then things get really complicated…

"The story then keeps at you in leaps and bounds! Full of action all the way. Just brilliant!" **Amazon Reader-5 STARS**

"Great read and a fun ride." **Amazon Reader-5 STARS**

Available on Amazon:
https://storyoriginapp.com/universalbooklinks/e479ecb0-94e1-11eb-a764-cf5a78d6bf2e

SILENT VOICE

Nicholas Sharp Thriller #4

It's dangerous to be right when the government is wrong...

Hunted down by their government's secret service, the members of protest band Kha Cring flee to Los Angeles to begin a new life. After an unexpected attack, the musicians' safe exile in LA is jeopardized. The desire to fight for their country's freedom undiminished, the band find their soaring popularity and politically messaged music no longer enough to protect them from the evil they escaped.

A deadlier weapon is needed. Nicholas Sharp.

In an instant things go terribly wrong as Sharp finds himself the focus of a network of international conspirators intent on wiping both he and the members of Kha Cring from the face of the planet.

Available on Amazon:

https://storyoriginapp.com/universalbooklinks/bcab78b0-94e2-11eb-ae88-033dd51c8bfd

COUNTERPOINT

Nicholas Sharp Thriller #5

Looking in the mirror, he saw only death...

Pursued by one of the world's most efficient and ruthless assassins, Nicholas Sharp almost admires the deadly operator's meticulous talents, until the assassin starts coming after Sharp through his friends. Sharp's investigations reveal that the killer also has another target in sight: the US Secretary of Defense. Is there a dark connection?

Face to face with a past he'd considered banished from his memory, Nicholas Sharp questions not only his own moral compass but also his slim chance of survival.

Available on Amazon:

https://storyoriginapp.com/universalbooklinks/634998b2-c7b0-11ed-b05d-6b92922aeb88

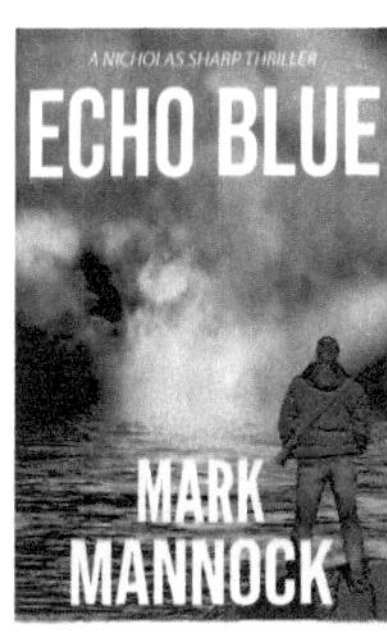

ECHO BLUE

Nicholas Sharp Thriller #6

Are you safe?...

Nicholas Sharp receives a mysterious phone call from Jack Greatrex... then Greatrex disappears.

In a hunt that takes him through South America, Texas, the mountains of Northern Spain and eventually the Middle East, Sharp encounters world renowned environmental activist Dr Deagan Jones from the notorious Crimson Wave. As Sharp uncovers a chain of complex deceptions, Jones' teenage son is kidnapped. The stakes never higher, the ex-Marine sniper turned musician fights to prevent an environmental and humanitarian catastrophe with unimaginable consequences.

Available on Amazon:

https://storyoriginapp.com/universalbooklinks/5117e352-1bd3-11ee-8179-9f645d9c6cf6

CURTAIL CALL

Nicholas Sharp Thriller #7

It's the Fourth of July and America is celebrating.

Former marine sniper turned musician, Nicholas Sharp, is performing with some of the greats at an Independence Day concert at the Forum in LA. The atmosphere is electric, and the 18,000 strong crowd is hungry for a good time.

The manic frenzy of blues legend Mickey Elvira's blinding solo has the audience on their feet crying for more. Suddenly the frenzied staccato of the guitar is overshadowed by the deadly mechanical clatter of rapid-fire weapons.

This couldn't be happening in America.

Rating his chances as zero, and the terrorists more formidable than anything he's ever faced, Nicholas Sharp knows the smart move would be to do nothing.

With the fate of thousands hanging in the balance can Sharp defy the odds? Can he confront a threat that strikes at the heart of the nation he once served while staying alive long enough to become the reluctant hero America desperately needs? And why, deep in his gut, does Sharp sense that all is not as it seems?

Available on Amazon:

https://storyoriginapp.com/universalbooklinks/0653fc0e-ca27-11ee-ab72-9f7790c72c31

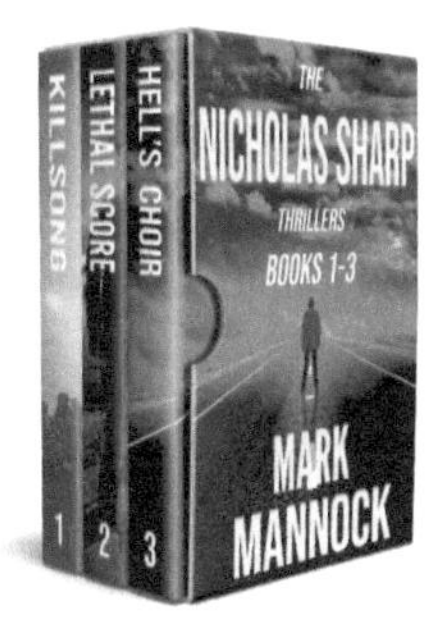

THE NICHOLAS SHARP THRILLERS BOX SET BOOKS 1-3

Nicholas Sharp is a killer musician... literally!

Nicholas Sharp is a disillusioned former US sniper fighting a troubled past and an uncertain future. Seeking solace in his work as a professional musician, Sharp is a man whose insatiable curiosity and embedded moral compass lead him into situations fraught with danger. Nicholas Sharp doesn't like to kill, but he sure as hell knows how to.

Somewhere between Tom Clancy's Jack Ryan and Robert Crais' Elvis Cole, Nicholas Sharp may be a flawed hero, but you definitely want him on your side.

Book 1: KILLSONG
  Book 2: LETHAL SCORE
  BOOK 3: HELL'S CHOIR

Available on Amazon:
  https://storyoriginapp.com/universalbooklinks/76a17f4c-94e0-11eb-a236-7fc041e6f217

THE NICHOLAS SHARP THRILLERS BOX SET BOOKS 4-6
The only thing necessary for the triumph of evil is that good people do nothing... for Nicholas Sharp, doing nothing is not an option.

Nicholas Sharp is back in the second omnibus edition of the Amazon best selling series.

This digital box set contains the fourth, fifth and sixth action thrillers:
Book 4: SILENT VOICE
Book 5: COUNTERPOINT
BOOK 6: ECHO BLUE

Available on Amazon:
https://storyoriginapp.com/universalbooklinks/e2e22e5 8-aad2-11ee-bf20-7f011f40b05a